Nightmares

Through a Dark Window

Brian S. Monroe

Nightmares through a Dark Window

Visions from the World beyond the Veil

BRIAN S MONROE

NIGHTMARES THROUGH A DARK WINDOW

CONTENT WARNINGS:

The opinions expressed by the characters in this book are not necessarily the views of the author.
Strong Language: 'Boirac's Coil' contains frequent use of strong language. Strong language occurs to some degree in all the stories in this book. Anyone offended by this language should avoid reading this material.
Graphic Violence: 'Boirac's Coil' contains graphic descriptions of violence including bodily harm, challenges to authority and destruction of property. Anyone offended by this imagery should avoid reading this section.

DISCLAIMER:

Although real locations are used and referred to, none of the events or people in these stories are based on or are intended to resemble any person, living, dead, or imaginary. These stories are not based on any event that has occurred or will occur. Any resemblance to any person or event is an unfortunate coincidence.

books.bass-x.net
Shelton Washington

ISBN: 0983885923
ISBN-13: 9780983885924
LCCN: 2012921520
Version 1.1

Table of Contents

DEDICATION

"Szkul" "Melissa" "Amanda" and "Pudding"
And above all "Sox"
"Qui de tenebris liberatus sum"
„Azok számára, akik megmentett a sötétségtől"
"Ne Plus Ultra!"

Elegy for a Dryad

"Do not call up that which you cannot put down"
H.P. Lovecraft, *'The Case of Charles Dexter Ward'*

I—Invocation I

It was a few minutes to noon on a hot sunny day. The sky was a deep blue with no clouds to mar its surface. The wind slowly faded into silence as the hour approached.

He lurked silently in the dim, green light within the laurel hedge, trying desperately not to make any sounds that would betray his presence. The heat and height of the hedge combined with the thickness of its intertwined branches made this extremely difficult. Forced to assume a contorted position with his legs and arms entwining the wood, it was painful and grew worse the longer he had to uphold it. Yet, there was a pleasant feeling of anticipation that somehow made it bearable.

Two minutes to noon.

As quietly as possible, he disentangled himself from the branches and crept forward, his knees aching as they scraped against the hard soil. He unexpectedly emerged from the hedge, blinking, dazzled by the blazing sunlight around him. He did not feel equal to standing up and continued crawling forward. The blinding light did not slow his progress: he already knew what he would see once his eyes cleared. There would be the glowing ring of the laurel hedge around an emerald-green lawn, the round, raised brick pedestal in the middle and the tall, ancient oak tree at the center. As a vision of that oak flashed in his mind, he shivered.

One minute to noon.

His head slammed unexpectedly into the brickwork and he reeled for a moment with the shock. The pain flowing through his nerves cleared his eyes. He found himself looking upward, following the path of the high trunk of the ancient oak with its curiously long branches. He shivered again with awe and fear.

Noon on the dot.

Noon on the dot on a significant day—a day not governed by artificially devised calendars or fraudulent digital timepieces. The equinox—the Fall Equinox—the day and night of equal length before the annual plunge into the darkness of Winter. The moment fixed by a particular point reached during the eternal dance of the Earth with the Sun.

A moment fixed by forces more powerful than the Earth itself.

A momentary flash of fear shook him—he did not have any time to wonder what caused it. He scrambled onto the brick coping and quickly made his way to the tree. He wrapped his arms tightly around it, looked straight up the trunk to the sun, closed his eyes and softly recited the invocation:

Ο Θεός των Δασών
Ο Προστάτης του δρύες
Ο φύλακας των Νυμφών
Δώσε μου την επιθυμία μου
Και εγώ θα σε ακολουθεί για πάντα
Στην πίστη και αφοσίωση

There was a faint tremor in his ears, which he associated with the sound of distant thunder, despite the cloudless sky above. He also thought of an earthquake but there was no corresponding rocking feeling beneath him. He shook despite himself and clung tightly to the tree.

All at once, he was roughly pulled from the trunk by the back of the neck, the bark cruelly scraping his arms. Dragged over the edge of the brickwork and brutally flung on the grass, his mind screaming in a raw panic, his emotions went instantly cold sober at the sound of the voice.

"What in the fuck are you doing?"

He looked up into the face of the landowner whose eyes blazed angrily, his dark brows tightly drawn together and teeth bared in a snarl. He could see the rivulets of sweat pouring across the dry parchment of his sallow, darkened, skin; the stubble on his face shot with grey, the muscles of his jaw working furiously. He scented the foul reek of his breath with a shudder.

Scrambling to his feet, he jumped as someone grabbed him from behind and instantly gripped him in a control hold, forcing him to remain still.

"Don't make it harder for yourself," growled a voice.

The landowner's expression relaxed and he stepped back a pace. The person behind the intruder patted him down, carefully searching his pockets. Forcibly turned around, he saw the person holding him wore a security guard uniform. His face was grim and unresponsive.

The guard gave a grunt as he reached into a pocket. His fingers closed on a piece of paper and swiftly pulled it out. He glanced at it briefly, shrugged his shoulders and handed it to the landowner who slowly read it over. The expression on the landowner's face passed from anger to puzzlement. He looked up from the paper, looked at the oak and then back to the man saying, mockingly, "What's *this* supposed to be?"

He said nothing. The landowner snorted in contempt.

"Where the hell did you pick *this* up from?"

The guard broke in, "What does it mean?"

"Oh," said the landowner dismissively, "It's Greek."

"Well, what does it say?" the guard persisted. The landowner glared at him.

"Something like:

'O God of Forests
O Protector of oak
O Guardian of the Nymphs
Give me my wish
And I will follow you forever
In the faith and devotion.'"

The landowner shook his head with a smile of contempt.

"Where did you get this translated? On the *Internet? 'O Protector of Oak,'"* he read out sarcastically. "Of *Oak?* You mean a *Dryad,* don't you? Or perhaps I should say *Dryads?"* and he handed the paper back. The man carefully replaced it in his pocket.

The landowner regarded him with a mixture of scorn and disbelief.

"Do you even know how to *say* this in Greek? I can tell you right now, if you tried saying this in Athens, they'd laugh you off the street."

The man said nothing and stared at the ground.

The landowner looked again at the tree and the sun; a curious expression came over his face. He turned to the guard.

"I can handle this. You can go," he said abruptly.

The guard gave a brief glance at the man and turned away without a word, the sound of his passage through the hedge muffled by the wind, which was blowing again. The man watched his departure, then turned back to find the landowner staring at him with that same expression of curiosity. As their eyes met, the landowner shook his head as though clearing it and spoke in a quiet voice.

"I've already told you there is *nothing* significant about this tree. All that bullshit about this being some remnant of a *'sacred grove'* is just that. Some stupid story they keep repeating," and the landowner indicated the rest of the estate with a sweeping gesture.

"Look, guy, there is nothing weird here, okay? It's just my house, my garden, the pasture and the orchards," but he had trouble meeting the man's eyes and stared at the ground as he said this. He looked up and saw the man gazing at him mysteriously. He waved his hand and looked away as though the scrutiny made him uneasy.

"Okay, okay, I *know* it looks strange having this tree surrounded by the hedge with no way through it. I can understand how these stupid stories start. But," he groped for his words, "I have it set up this way because my grandfather ordered it in his will."

He looked at the man hopefully but there was no change in his expression.

"You see?" he continued eagerly, "The will said this hedge and the tree had to remain undisturbed—just like he had it set up while he was alive. I mean, I know he's been dead a long time and it looks funny but, well, I still have respect for his memory. I could cut this tree and the hedge down if I wanted to…" but his voice faded away.

"But you haven't," said the man quietly.

The landowner flushed angrily.

"It doesn't matter!" he barked. "This is still *my* property and *you* are trespassing. I've told you before to stay away from here—this is the *last* time I'm warning you. Next time I'll shoot first! *Get out of here!*" and he made a menacing step toward the man.

The man did not move an inch.

The landowner stopped, breathing hard, his face ashen.

"Listen," he said, in a tense, urgent half-whisper, "You think you know everything. You don't know *shit*. If you knew everything, you wouldn't be *here*—you would be as far away from here as you could run. Whoever gave you that—that *paper* didn't do you any favors. *I can't believe you did it…*" and his voice sunk lower.

"You are messing with something you don't understand—it's too big for you to fuck with. You might call it murder if I shoot you the next time you come back, but if you knew the truth, you'd call it a mercy killing. Saving you from—" and then he stopped, seeing the resolution in the man's face.

He smiled sadly.

"Well, whatever happens, remember I tried to help you. Now, get out of here before I have the guard set the dog on you. *Now!*" he shouted, moving quickly toward him.

Without hurrying, the man turned, carefully made his way through the hedge and walked with a deliberate pace across the lawn to the driveway. Despite his flinch at the landowner's shout, he did not appear cowed in the least. He calmly walked up to the gate; the security guard held it open for him until he passed through. The guard slammed the gate shut and shot the bolts home with a loud clanking of metal. The man continued down the roadway without looking back and eventually vanished from sight.

The landowner slowly let out his breath; a great weariness came over him and his shoulders slumped as he made his way through the hedge toward the gate. The guard was gazing after the departing man, his expression unreadable through his mirrored sunglasses. He turned away just as the landowner came up.

"It's already too late," muttered the landowner.

The guard swiftly looked toward the landowner at this strange remark. The landowner paled, as though he had said something aloud he shouldn't have. He turned red, opened his mouth to speak, then abruptly shut it, turned on his heel and stalked back toward the house, the guard staring after him.

II—Interview

"M'am?"

The woman on the bed slowly turned her head toward him. It took her a moment to focus. It took a little longer for her to realize what he was. Then she reacted, her eyes hardening and her body tensing. The sedatives continuously running into her bloodstream intervened and her reaction metamorphosed into a long, drawn out sigh, her fists unclenching as her eyes drifted shut.

The man sitting in the chair stirred as though about to stand up but her eyes flew open at the sound and he remained where he was. The deadening of her emotions could not keep the glare from her eyes or the harshness from her voice.

"What is it?"

The man in the chair rose.

"My name is detective Tokasti," said the man, bringing his badge into view. She glanced at it and laid her head back, closing her eyes.

After a few minutes, she spoke again.

"What do you want?"

"Are you up to answering some questions?"

She clenched her jaws and shuddered but again her energy failed and she merely exhaled, opening her eyes and staring at the ceiling.

"What questions?"

Tokasti cleared his throat.

"About the incident last Friday."

This time her hostility did not fade away as she turned her head toward the detective.

"Just go away. I don't know what day it is, I don't even know where the fuck I am and I don't have a clue what you're talking about."

Tokasti blinked but remained impassive.

"You don't know where you are?"

"No," she mouthed and closed her eyes again.

"Do you know *who* you are?"

"Get the fuck out of here," she muttered, with her eyes closed. "Just go away," and she made a brushing motion with her hand as though warding off a mosquito. The tubes and lines plugged into her arm cut her movement short but the meaning was clear. She inhaled deeply and drifted back into sleep, breathing heavily.

"I will be back another time," said Tokasti as he stood up.

There was no response from the woman.

He turned and walked out of the room, shutting the door behind him. Approaching the nurses' station, he waved to a white-suited man with a stethoscope hung around his neck. He detached himself from the station and walked over to meet the officer.

"Well?" asked the man.

"When do you think she'll be able to talk, doctor?"

The doctor shook his head.

"She wasn't conscious?"

"She was but she went back under after only a few minutes. The only thing I got out of her, aside from *get the fuck out of here*,' was she doesn't know what day it is or where she is."

The doctor nodded his head.

"I'm not surprised. With the dose of sedatives she's taking it's amazing she could talk to you at all."

"How much longer will she be like that?"

"I'm not sure," answered the doctor, with a frown. "I've been gradually pulling her off the meds but it's going to take a while. At least another two days."

"Any idea what happened to her?"

The doctor shrugged.

"Can't tell you anything official—you know the rules. Off the record, I'd say some kind of shock, mental and physical trauma plus exposure. They got her here just in time."

"Physical trauma? What kind of physical trauma?"

"Bruises, scratches, the sort of thing you would expect to find if someone ran naked through the woods in a blind panic. She must have tripped and fallen several times."

"Ah," remarked Tokasti with disappointment, "no signs of assault?"

"No," said the doctor positively, "absolutely not. And, yes, we did check for sexual assault as well: nothing there."

Tokasti seemed unsure what to do next. He remained silent for a few minutes.

"How bad is this mental trauma? Will she remember what happened?" he finally asked.

"I don't know," said the doctor. "If it *was* a seriously traumatic experience her mind would do its best to block it from her memory. Sometimes it works, sometimes it doesn't. She has a strong spirit, so it may well be she will remember *something.*"

"Any sign of amnesia?"

The doctor laughed.

"Not remembering the date or where you are doesn't mean it's classic amnesia. It's a standard shock response. The brain is trying to get all systems stable and the mind is usually the last thing it restores. Survival instinct and all that."

Tokasti nodded and put on his hat.

"Don't let anyone else talk to her; not until I come back."

"Including her parents?"

"No—I got no problem with them."

Tokasti walked down the hallway toward the elevator as the doctor turned around and went back to the nurses' station.

III—Whistling in the Dark

"I understand he trespassed on your property several times in the last month," said the detective, his pen flying across the paper.

"Yes," the landowner confirmed, reluctantly. "We've had a lot of trouble with him. But this place is not easy to get into and we usually caught him before he got too far from the fence."

"Did he always head for the same spot?" the detective interrupted.

The landowner, thrown off his stride, wiped his mouth with the back of his arm and answered, "Yes. Always," and he looked away.

"Did he ever give any *reason* for what he was doing?"

"No," said the landowner with obvious relief. "No, he never said anything. He always left when told to—but it was for sure he would be back. He was like—*obsessed* with this place."

"Despite the incentive to stay away," remarked the detective.

"Oh yeah," the landowner agreed emphatically. "He got treated rough. The guards aren't trained to be polite. They have a way of making you feel seriously unwelcome—they don't want return visitors."

"And yet he did," the detective noted.

"Yeah," the landowner reluctantly agreed.

"How was it he got in the last time? I mean, this system you have—"

The landowner took this line up quickly.

"Most of the people who are stupid about this place try to get in after dark. That's what he did the first few times. I guess he figured it was safer at night—never mind about night-vision goggles," and he laughed shortly. The detective did not respond.

"But the last time, he fooled us and came in broad daylight. I still can't figure out how he got through unseen. There isn't a piece of cover between the fence and the—the hedge," finished the landowner.

"When did you discover him?"

"He just popped out of the hedge and crawled up to the tree. Didn't even try to hide himself—me and the guards saw him at the same time. We hustled down there and routed him out—"

"And that was the last you heard from him," finished the detective as he completed his writing.

"Yes," said the landowner.

"Did you know who he was?" asked the detective.

"No—I mean, I'd seen him around town—" but he stopped as the detective raised his hand and spoke:

"Because, if you knew who he was and you were having trouble with him, I'm surprised you didn't file a complaint or a no-contact order."

The landowner licked his lips and swallowed before he answered.

"Yeah—I suppose I should have done that. It's just that," and he made a frustrated movement with his hands, "I get so tired of dealing with that damned tree. The *last* thing I need is attention focused on this place in the newspapers—it's bad enough as it is."

The detective looked at him steadily.

"You know," he said, "You have quite a system here. Perimeter guards, motion detectors, cameras, night-vision goggles. That seems pretty heavy just to protect a *tree*," but the landowner interrupted him irritably:

"It isn't just for the—for a *tree*. I've got the orchard and the livestock as well as the house to look after. There's a lot of seriously valuable stuff in the house—"

"Yes," agreed the detective, nodding, "Although anyone stupid enough to try for the house would deserve what they got. I'm not sure what's so special about the orchard and the livestock."

"You must be new around here," remarked the landowner sourly. "I have several prize animals including two bulls worth several thousand dollars. There have been incidents before where people have stolen animals—it isn't *that* hard to pull off. I'm not the only one around here with security, you know. As far as the orchard goes, have you seen the price of—?"

"Yes, yes," said the detective, impatiently. "I admit all that stuff is certainly valuable. But I don't see the reason for such an expensive setup—it's overkill as far as I'm concerned. And anyway," and here the detective looked right at him, "it's obvious your main concern is protecting the tree."

The landowner stirred but the detective held out his hand.

"You can't deny it without lying. Otherwise you wouldn't have been so careful to correct yourself when you referred to it as '*the*' tree rather than '*a*' tree," and the detective smiled grimly.

The landowner looked at the ground sullenly.

"I don't like talking about it," he finally blurted out.

"Why?"

"Well—it's embarrassing, for one," he continued, a red flush rising in his neck, "and I don't see why I need to tell *you*. Everyone around here knows the story."

The detective blandly interposed, "You forget I '*must be new around here*,' as you pointed out. I haven't heard anything about your property or the tree."

"It has nothing to do with your business," said the landowner coldly.

"How do I know without knowing what's going on? It might."

The landowner remained silent for a few minutes longer.

"Well," he began, with obvious distaste, "let me tell you the *facts* as opposed to that shit they have on the Internet. Then, if you're interested, I'll tell you the tall-tales.

"This place has been in my family for a long time. My great-great-grandfather came out here when this place was still a territory and we've been here since then.

"We call ourselves Greek, but—yes, yes, I know," he added irritably as the detective started to say something, "I know. My last name isn't even *close* to Greek. But great-great-grandfather came through Ellis Island when they forced everyone to take an Americanized name if the immigration officer thought it was too outlandish. The name we use is not our real family name," and here the landowner hesitated for a moment.

"My father did a lot of research and saw a copy of the papers from Ellis Island. Great-great-grandfather wrote his name in four places and spelled it differently each time—sometimes *very* differently. We've shown the paper to several people but none of them can figure out what his original name might have been. And great-great-grandfather never told anyone what it was.

"The only evidence we have we are Greek, apart from our looks," the landowner added with a trace of irony, "is what great-great-grandfather put down on those papers. His birth certificate stated he was from Athens but it went missing during the entry process. There's no way to verify it—it could have been a forgery for all we know. He had a Greek first name, as all the children have, including me and my sons. All of us are fluent in it. But there isn't any hard, written proof we *are*."

He paused for a moment, shaking his head.

"Anyway, this estate has been in the family as long as anyone can remember. If great-great-grandfather *bought* this estate, the documents are lost. We haven't found any papers giving a description of this place or who owned it before he took possession. We don't know if that tree was here when he arrived or whether he brought it in from somewhere else. The only thing we know for certain is the tree and hedge have been there since great-great-grandfather's time onward."

The landowner took a deep breath and continued.

"Every member of the family who comes into possession of this property is given a copy of a paper great-grandfather wrote out—it isn't clear whether he did this himself or at the behest of great-great-grandfather. The paper simply states anyone who formally becomes owner of this estate must ensure the tree, the hedge and the brick pedestal remain unchanged and *inviolate*."

The detective looked interested at his emphasis of the last word.

"The way that has been interpreted is: no one under any circumstances is to pass through that hedge and approach the tree. Obviously, it also means nothing should happen to the tree either."

He smiled faintly.

"Several people have asked how many opportunities we've missed to sell the property because of that paper. We can't sell it without forcing the buyer to keep protecting the tree—and if they didn't follow through, I think we'd be responsible for the consequences. I know the world has changed since my great-great-grandfather's day and this whole thing is just a meaningless piece of drivel, but none of us want to take a chance…"

He turned and looked full at the detective with such an intense gaze the detective started.

"None of us have the courage to break that compact. I know," and at this he turned deep red, "I know—it's a lot of superstitious bullshit. I feel really stupid about it. But I don't want to put it to the test— neither do the others in the family. As long as one of us is alive, the property will never be sold."

He sat back with a sigh, the detective staring at him curiously.

"Those facts are interesting. So what else is there?"

The landowner flushed again and clenched his jaw although he still spoke calmly.

"Well—the short version is there is a—a—" and he cleared his throat and hesitated for a moment, unable to conquer his reluctance toward the subject.

"A curse?" prompted the detective.

"No!" snapped the landowner sharply, shaken free of his silence.

"No—nothing like *that* at all." The tone in which he said this permanently closed that line of questioning.

"The—the stories say this tree was brought over from Greece. That it is a *sacred* tree," and his face flushed as he said it. He turned to the detective.

"Do you know what a Dryad is?"

"Not really," responded the detective.

"Well, a Dryad is a spirit of the trees. It's an old legend that goes back before the Romans. Each tree has a Dryad assigned to it who is bound to the tree as long as the tree is alive. When it dies, the Dryad dies with it. That oak is supposed to be—" and he sighed in resignation.

"There is supposed to be a Dryad in that oak. And that is why it has to be guarded and watched."

The detective looked at the landowner with mingled surprise and suspicion.

"Well—" he began but the landowner continued:

"I don't know how that story started—it's been around for a long time—but it got on the Internet and since then we've had nothing but problems with people who want to come and see this tree."

"Well you could make that into a tourist attraction," suggested the detective but the landowner vehemently shook his head.

"No—no. They'd try to take pieces away with them—" and he hesitated before continuing.

"The real problem is these escapists, these new-age hippies and the like, think just because they took a mythology class in high school they know all there is to know about Dryads. They're even trying to revive the old religion, bringing back Zeus and all that," and the landowner frowned in disgust.

"Stupid. Especially because no one has a clue exactly what was involved in that religion. No one knows what the rituals were, the—" and he stopped again, trying to rise above his feelings.

"They don't take it *seriously*," he said at last. "They act all pious and respectful—but they don't have a clue. They ignore the fact every tradition had its dark side—I mean, the way these people think, the Dryads are just these harmless spirits that live with the tree and the only danger you run into is if you hurt the tree.

"That isn't necessarily right. We laugh at Leprechauns today—make fun of them and all—but in the older days, the ancient Celts were terrified of the '*little people*.' They did their best to avoid pissing them off. There's no reason it should be any different for other traditions just because the tradition is from a different country."

The detective looked curiously at the landowner for a moment.

"Do you believe this yourself?" he asked.

The landowner fell silent.

"I don't want to talk about this anymore," he said finally, rising from his chair. The detective rose likewise.

"You have anything else you want to ask?"

"No," the detective replied. "And I'm very sorry if I have offended you in any way, Mr.—" but the landowner waved him away, his eyes closed and his face averted.

"I know—don't mention it, just go, please."

The detective nodded, turned and walked out of the room. The waiting guard accompanied him to his car and rode with him to the gatehouse.

IV—Poisoned Dreams

"How in the hell did they meet if they live on two sides of the country?"

"On line," said Tokasti, checking his notes.

"One of those *chat* rooms I suppose?"

"No—this was more of a *social* site. People would put up artwork and stuff. It was like an artistic group."

"So they met at that site?"

"Yeah," affirmed Tokasti. "She posted some pictures she drew; he asked her about them; and everything took off from there."

"Was he an artist too?"

"Yeah. I can understand why they liked each other—they both thought along the same lines."

"So how did they communicate? Email?"

Tokasti nodded.

"At first. Then it went to texting. And finally phone calls. They both spent a fortune on their cell phone bills."

"How long were they corresponding?"

"At least six months. Maybe longer."

"Did she invite him out?"

"No—it was a surprise visit."

"Are you *serious?*"

"Yeah."

"Good grief! Was he crazy? He could have blown a fortune for nothing. What if he'd flown out here and she wasn't home?"

"I have no idea."

"Well—what was the deal? They in love?"

"*He* was. He was obsessed with her—he dropped everything in his life to make time for her. Quit his job and all that."

The Chief looked even more incredulous at this news.

"How did she feel about him?"

"I'm waiting to ask her. Just looking at the emails it seems she was attracted to him too."

"No doubt. You think maybe he flew all the way out here for a piece of ass and got turned down?"

Tokasti rolled his eyes.

"No, Chief. No. As a matter of fact, neither of them counted on getting physical."

The Chief laughed cynically.

"Really."

"No, seriously," said Tokasti, his face flushing. "She was hung up on her virginity and didn't want to lose it. He respected that."

"How old is she?"

"Let's see—twenty-four."

"A virgin at twenty-four? That's hard to believe."

"It happens," Tokasti remarked. "Anyway, they already checked her out for sexual assault: nothing. She still *is* a virgin, according to the doctor."

"What was the big deal over it?"

"It's hard to say," Tokasti mused. "It had a great significance for her—deep. Lots of mysticism in it."

The Chief snorted derisively.

"Sounds like a typical artist. Did Washington State have anything to say about him?"

"Just a trespassing complaint. I guess he and this farmer had a run-in. They're getting the details on it for me. Other than that, nothing. No family. No friends."

"Figures," said the Chief. "What did her parents think of all this?"

Tokasti laughed sarcastically.

"She lives with them, but they didn't even know she was missing until we showed up at their door."

"How the hell did she pull *that* off?"

"Looks like she went out the window. She probably counted on getting back in that way. I got the impression it wasn't the first time she'd done it. They didn't even know about her meeting at the restaurant," Tokasti shrugged, still dumbfounded at this unusual twist.

"So much for that angle," sighed the Chief. "You going to try talking to her again?"

"Not until the day after tomorrow. She's in no shape to talk right now."

V—Conflicting Interpretations

The key tag had the number G142. He looked across the lot and noticed signs identifying the row and stall numbers. He found row G, then stall 140 and walked out to that location. 142 was only two slots away. He carefully checked the key tag against the car: the license plate matched and the description agreed—a red Ford Fusion. He keyed open the door, slid into the front seat and quickly examined the controls. Having found the lights, signals and mirrors, he started the car and adjusted the ventilation.

He glanced through his paperwork and pulled out a map. He looked it over carefully and began plotting his course. After a few minutes, he seemed satisfied and put the map down on the seat. He shifted into reverse, carefully backed the car out and drove toward the exit.

At the exit, the attendant checked his paperwork and performed a quick inspection. The attendant signed off on the papers and, as he handed them back, asked him, "You know where you're going to from here?"

He nodded.

The gate opened, the attendant waved him through and he drove into the streets.

The distance to his destination was not great, probably twenty miles in a straight line. However, taking this on at seven in the morning during the commute was an act of insanity. He managed to get on the freeway without any problems but from then on, it was a struggle: endless stops and starts and the added pressure of trying to find an unfamiliar location. Once when he glanced at the map he nearly slammed into the car in front of him—after that he made sure he had at least one eye on the road.

At last, he reached the outlying township. The traffic eased. Even so, it was a different driving environment than he was used to—there were more people, the houses were closer together, the roads were rough and ill maintained. He drove aimlessly through the streets for a while, then pulled over at a safe location and took out his cell phone. He checked—no text messages—and then typed:

I am here. Where are you?

He pressed the send button and waited.

For a long time he heard nothing besides the pounding of his heart. As the minutes passed, a feeling of despair came over him and a sense of failure. *What was he thinking of? Making an unannounced trip over two thousand miles away? To meet with a total stranger whose feelings he couldn't be sure of?* As he brooded, the cell phone vibrated and he glanced at the screen with some anxiety as the words appeared:

OMG—are you really here??

He smiled and typed:

Yes.

The phone vibrated again, this time with a call coming in. The ID was hers and he picked up the call with a smile on his face.

"Hello my Dryad," he said.

Her voice, her delicious voice came across the connection and he could feel warmth flowing from his heart to the rest of his body.

"Oh my Gawd," she said. "Are you really, *really* here?"

"Yes," he replied with a chuckle.

"I can't believe this," she said softly. "When did you get here?"

"Landed about seven o'clock."

She was silent a moment.

"You came all the way out here to see me?"

His smiled broadened.

"Yes—to see you."

"Where are you?"

He looked out the window, noticed a street sign and read off the name. It didn't register with her. It wasn't until after a few minutes he realized he was mispronouncing it. She figured it out at the same time he did and laughed.

She gave him directions to a restaurant a few minutes away and said she would be there within half an hour. He confirmed the directions with her and told her he was heading over.

"I love you," he added.

"I love you too," she replied sweetly and the connection closed.

* * *

"Did you talk to her today?"

Tokasti grimaced.

"I *tried* to talk to her but she's still pretty hostile. At least she didn't tell me to fuck off this time. Not that it made any difference—she's just as baffled about this as we are."

"What *did* she say about it?"

"He called her from the airport. She had no idea he was on his way to see her and it caught her completely off guard—"

"Wasn't expecting him at all?"

"No."

"How did she feel about that?"

"I'm not sure," Tokasti said after a long pause. "She didn't say she had a problem with it but even talking about it made her upset. She wouldn't clarify."

"Upset how?"

"Shaky voice, tears, couldn't look at me when I asked, the usual."

"I still can't believe he did that."

"I don't know—" Tokasti replied slowly. "She didn't know he was coming but he felt confident everything would work out okay. It didn't sound like she had a problem with it either. The possible result didn't worry him; he was certain he would reach the fulfillment of his destiny one way or the other—something like that."

"*Fulfillment of his destiny?*" the Chief repeated.

"That's what he wrote in one of his emails. I couldn't figure out what that meant."

"What about that business at the—?"

"You mean at that farm in Washington State? I don't think that has anything to do with this. He was always surfing the Internet and looking up unusual items and one day he started doing research on Dryads for some reason—searching for legends, incantations and the like. He found some stuff but nothing to do with what happened later."

"And that led him to the farm? What does a farm have to do with a—a—what did you call it?"

Tokasti smirked.

"Dryad."

"What the hell is a Dryad?"

"You ever read any Greek myths? They're supposed to be some kind of protector of the trees. At least that's what all the stuff on the Internet says."

"I still don't get how that connects with that farm."

"Ah," said Tokasti, leaning back in the chair. "It isn't clear exactly where he picked this up—he went to several websites—but somewhere along the line he got some info that steered him there."

"Like what?"

"I think he expected to find one."

"One what?"

"A Dryad."

"At a *farm?*" the Chief asked incredulously.

"Our contact in Washington State talked to the landowner and *he* said there are rumors all over the Internet there is a Dryad at his farm," Tokasti laughed shortly. "Our guy wasn't the first person thrown out of there. Several people have tried to get in because of that story."

"They've got to be kidding."

Tokasti shrugged.

"You'd be amazed what people believe."

The Chief shook his head slowly.

"I don't get it," he said, finally.

"I don't either," admitted Tokasti. "But our guy definitely was starting to lose touch with reality. Some of his last emails are way out there. When that plane landed, he was pretty much in his own world. It was like he'd forgotten everything except the present."

VI—Meeting

With a sigh of relief, he closed up the phone and reentered traffic. The restaurant was a little further off than he thought; despite his best efforts it was nearly twenty minutes before he arrived. He found a parking spot, shut down the car, locked it, and, with a shiver of anticipation, tried to casually stroll down the sidewalk and enter the building. His hands were shaking as he opened the door and stepped into the foyer. The smell of breakfast—coffee, bacon, pancakes—came rolling out to meet him and the familiar scent did much to comfort his nervousness.

The hostess looked at him inquiringly and he said, "I'm meeting someone here in a few minutes." She nodded and went about her other tasks. He found a bench along the wall and sat down, his palms moist as he placed them on his trouser legs.

The door opened a few times and he looked up with his heart pounding but she did not appear. He glanced at his watch—it was nearly forty minutes since he had talked to her—a cold feeling sprouted in his stomach, spreading its numbing influence throughout his body. He was so far gone he almost forgot to glance up when the door opened again—and then he was on his feet, his face glowing.

Hers was too. She was even more beautiful than she looked in her pictures—and her eyes had the same powerful attraction. He stepped toward her, hesitated; she did the same—both of them reaching out and then shyly pulling their arms back. At last, he smiled, reached out his hand and she gripped it tightly in hers.

"It's me," he said.

"It's really you," she said with a smile.

On impulse, he raised her hand to his lips and kissed it gently. She turned red but looked pleased and squeezed his hand briefly. Then they turned to find the hostess staring at them with an odd expression on her face. He reluctantly let go her hand and gave his attention to the hostess.

"Two?" asked the hostess.

"Two," he confirmed.

She grabbed two menus and swiftly led them to a table by the window. He slid in on one side, she on the other. They were silent as the hostess arranged the table and cutlery—answering reluctantly when asked if they wanted anything hot to drink. The hostess poured out some coffee, some tea and then walked back to her station. They had not stopped looking at each other the entire time.

He reached out his hands to her and she gripped both of them in hers.

"Oh," she said softly and pulled his hands to her lips. She kissed them and then, blushing, let them drop back to the table. He was blushing too and there was just a touch of wetness in his eyes. He flexed his fingers and gently stroked hers.

The voice of the server broke in and they both started at the sound. Smiling, they placed their order and the server left them alone again.

They were still holding hands across the table. Something told him he should release them but he couldn't help himself and held on. She made no move to break free on her part.

After a few minutes of this she laughed.

"It's—it's—it's—I can't think of anything to say," she finally said.

"I know what you mean," he agreed, "It's like I'm all tongue-tied for some reason."

She smiled.

"Well," he said at last, "What are you up to today?"

She sighed and loosened her grip. He released his hold and they placed their hands on the table.

"It's a really busy day for me," she said, apologetically. "I had no idea you were coming out here and I have some stuff to do—"

"And it would be awkward if I came along," he added. She nodded.

"But I'm free tonight."

He smiled.

"That would work out fine as far as I'm concerned," he said. "I could take a nap and adjust to the time change."

She nodded again.

"How long will you be here?"

He looked at her and tried to answer her question but he could not speak.

"Is something wrong?" she asked.

He finally recovered his voice.

"I—I—I don't know when I'm leaving," he blundered out. She looked at him curiously.

"What do you mean *you don't know*?" she asked, laughing nervously.

He blushed and looked down at the table in silence for a few minutes.

"I don't want to think about it right now," he said finally, looking back up at her.

Her eyebrows rose at this but she did not pursue the subject.

"What time tonight?" he asked after a few minutes.

"Let's see," she said, "How about you pick me up near my house tonight about nine o'clock or so?"

"That's fine," he said. "What did you want to do?"

She hesitated.

"You know what I'd love to do," she said at last, "I want to take you to the forest."

An unexpected pang of terror swept through him.

Seeing his hesitation, she misunderstood it and continued, "It wouldn't work out until really really late. So maybe we could go to your room first and then go to the forest later in the evening?"

He nodded and she smiled at him.

She excused herself to use the restroom and he watched her as though following a dancer swaying in an ancient ritual, finding pleasure in every movement. As she left his field of vision, his thoughts returned to her question and he frowned: exactly when *was* he leaving? He couldn't remember.

He fumbled in his pockets and finally pulled out his ticket. He flipped through the first page and turned to the second—then stared at it in disbelief.

The ticket was blank.

Sweat broke out on his face and he felt faint. He knew he had bought a return ticket—*there was no reason he wouldn't have.* He had no friends in that part of the country. He brought the paper close to his face and looked at it intently but there was nothing on the second page. An odd idea crept into his head the ticket was *not* blank—his eyes couldn't see it.

These thoughts raced through his mind as he fought down a feeling of panic. He was frightened. He didn't understand what was happening—he felt unsure of everything around him and the sensation grew worse the more he thought about it.

Is this really happening?

He jumped when he heard the scrape of her chair and he looked up to find her eyes gazing at him with concern. Then she smiled, the colour returned to his vision and all was warm once more. He was about to reach out for her hands again when the food arrived.

For a few minutes, they both occupied themselves with eating and conversation was minimal. At last, they both sat back with sighs of satisfaction and looked at each other peacefully. After a few minutes, they realized they were both staring silently and laughed at the same time. She reached out as did he and they squeezed hands warmly.

The check arrived. He stood up and she followed suit. He paid the tab despite her protests and they walked out of the restaurant together. They were arm and arm almost at once and he savored the sensation of the warmth of her body so close to his. They both blushed and hardly said anything as they walked toward the car. They reached it and she instantly spun around, pulled him close to her and held him tightly. After recovering from his surprise, he pulled her close as well and they held each other for a long time, their heartbeats echoing in their ears, their breathing slow and in unison. Finally, they released themselves and leaned against the car, catching their breath.

"I'm sorry," she said at last, "I just couldn't resist. I—I had to know what you felt like."

He was glowing with happiness.

"It felt wonderful."

She blushed furiously and nodded her head.

"Do you want me to drop you off somewhere?" he asked.

She recovered herself quickly.

"Yes—you can drop me off near my house. That way you'll know where to find me when you come back."

He keyed open her door and held it for her until she was seated. Then he got in on his side and fired up the engine.

"Which way?" he asked.

She led him through the township until they were driving down a quiet street with few houses. She told him to pull over and he quickly brought the car to a halt at the curb. She was nervous and appeared a little flustered.

"That's my house there," she said, pointing to it.

He stared at it—wanting to remember every detail.

"Shall I pick you up right here?" he asked.

She nodded quickly. "Yes—that would be just fine."

She turned in her seat just as he did in his; their lips met and they gently kissed—lightly, softly.

Then she quickly gathered herself and left the car before he had a chance to open the door for her. She shut the door and walked swiftly down the street toward her house without looking back.

He watched her until she went in the door. Then, with a sigh, he turned the car around and headed back toward the main road. Something told him not to drive past her house and he did not try to do so. He beamed; everything around him seemed faintly luminous with its own inner light. He was still in this euphoric state when the cell phone buzzed again.

He looked at the message and smiled.

It was wonderful.

"It *is* wonderful," he said out loud and then, re-focusing on the traffic, began making his way to his hotel. He reached it quickly, checked in, parked the car, managed to stumble up to his room, lock the door and throw himself on the bed before falling into a deep, exhausted sleep.

VII—Investigation

"What's going on?"

Tokasti looked up from his desk with a discontented expression.

"I still don't know," he replied, sourly.

The Chief beckoned him and Tokasti rose from his desk, following the Chief into his office. The Chief whipped off his overcoat and threw himself in his desk chair, leaning back with his eyes closed. Tokasti remained standing at the desk. After a few minutes, the Chief opened his eyes and looked at Tokasti with some surprise.

"I'm sorry, go ahead and sit down. I'm kind of flustered about this myself," he said.

The detective pulled an armchair up to the desk and sat in it heavily.

"So, what's going on?" asked the Chief again. Tokasti frowned and pulled out a notebook. He flipped through the pages for a moment and then began speaking.

"The short version is someone reported the sounds of an assault in progress in the forest around midnight over there by—"

"Yes, yes," said the Chief rapidly, waving him on.

"Said they heard screaming and sounds of a struggle," and Tokasti stopped as though puzzled.

"What's wrong?" asked the Chief.

"I just thought of something…well, it can keep for now. Anyway, a unit was in the area and they responded within ten minutes. They didn't find anything suggesting an assault had taken place and they didn't see anyone. Not surprising considering it was pitch-dark in the woods."

"What time was this?"

Tokasti looked at his notebook. "A little after midnight."

The Chief nodded.

"About three-thirty or four, *another* call came in from that same area. The caller said they'd seen someone 'skulking' through their backyard. Unit responded. As they were en route, a second call came in: homeowner down the road from the first house said there was a body in her backyard. So the unit diverted to *that* location. Found a young woman collapsed on the grass, naked. She was alive but nonresponsive. They started the protocols, got the medics and rushed her off to the hospital."

Tokasti turned over a page in his notebook, cleared his throat and continued.

"The next morning, the forensics team sent out to the location of the original call found evidence something *had* been going on the night before. They think only two people were involved—and *one* of them left the scene in a hurry.

"They also found an abandoned rental car from the airport parked close by. That led them to the male—or rather it fixed his identity: they still haven't found him."

"So he's the one who fled the scene?" asked the Chief.

"No—*that* was the woman who turned up in the back yard on that second call."

"She make any statement when they found her that night?"

The detective glanced at his notes.

"Nothing at the time—she was naked and freezing to death. She was out of it for about three days. The doc said she showed signs she had been through some traumatic experience—"

"A sexual assault?" inquired the Chief wryly.

"No," said Tokasti firmly. "They ran all those tests on her and came up with nothing. Just lots of bruises, scratches, shock, exposure—no surprises there. But the doc decided to keep her in the hospital under sedation for a few days—he was more concerned about her mental state than her physical."

"Why was that?"

Tokasti looked at the Chief morosely.

"You know how the patient confidentiality thing works. He wouldn't tell me anything specific—all he said was she was in a state of emotional shock. That isn't official of course. He seemed to feel she was the edge of some kind of breakdown."

"Which means—?"

"That something happened to her that seriously upset her—but whatever it was, it *wasn't* assault."

The Chief drummed his fingers on the arms of his chair.

"What did the forensics team find?"

A strange expression crossed the detective's face.

"They found clothes. *His* clothes," he added by way of clarification.

The Chief raised his eyebrows at this.

NIGHTMARES THROUGH A DARK WINDOW

"*His* clothes?"

"I know—it starts to *sound* like sexual assault—but the forensics team didn't think so. For one thing, the clothes were in a neat pile—folded and put on a rock with his shoes and socks. As though he intended to come back for them. They weren't torn off or removed forcibly," he sighed, as though disappointed, then continued, "no DNA residue, no blood. No sign of a struggle. Just her footsteps when she left. Running like a jackrabbit."

"Oh?"

"That's what they gathered from the depth of her prints and how far apart they were," and he looked up at the Chief.

"The funny thing is," he said, slowly, "she was naked when she fled. And there was no sign of *her* clothes anywhere—trust me, they looked."

"How do they know she was naked when she ran away?"

"The prints were barefoot. She was naked when they found her in that backyard. They traced her movements all the way back to the woods. No clothes anywhere."

The Chief snorted.

"Yeah," said Tokasti, "I think it's kind of flaky myself. They did examine the area where all the business took place. They couldn't see any evidence of a conflict or struggle—although they did say the ground looked as if someone roto-tilled it. There were other prints too."

"Footprints?" asked the Chief, immediately alert.

Tokasti wearily waved his hand.

"No, no. Animal prints. Maybe several animals—they weren't sure."

"Deer, no doubt?"

"No—definitely not that."

The Chief frowned.

"I didn't think there would be *that* much wildlife in that forest this time of year."

"I didn't either—but they're convinced that's what it was. Pretty heavy animals too, whatever they were. The prints were sunk deep into the ground."

The Chief sighed irritably.

"Well, do we have a time-line?" he queried.

"As near as I can figure it runs like this:

"He bought the ticket four weeks ago. He got in on the fifth—no, actually the sixth. It was the red-eye flight."

"Where from?"

"Seattle."

Tokasti turned a page and kept reading.

"Boarded the flight with no problem. No trouble during the flight. He landed, went straight to the rental car counter, got his car and drove to the township."

"Straight there?"

"Yes," affirmed Tokasti.

"You sound very sure about it," remarked the Chief.

"There is no room for doubt. The car had a GPS tracking device installed—I guess they do that for rental cars, helps out with theft recovery and all—recording every move he made.

"He drove out. Parked, then continued to the, you know, that restaurant down on—"

"I know which one, yes," the Chief said impatiently.

"The woman met him there. They had breakfast. He dropped her off at her house—"

"Where is her house, by the way?"

"Not too far from the forest actually," admitted Tokasti. "It's within walking distance for sure. Anyway," he continued, "he drove to his hotel and stayed there until about nine pm. Drove back out and picked up the woman. Drove back to his hotel. They stayed there for about three hours—no—no—they've already checked. Nothing sexual took place there.

"They left the hotel and drove to the location forensics found the car. They walked into the woods together from there," and Tokasti leaned back in his chair.

"Now," he said, staring at the ceiling, "Forensics figures two scenarios. One, they walked into the woods; got naked for some reason; something disturbed them and they both ran off. Only flaw in that is, if he ran off, why did he leave his clothes behind? Why didn't he come back for them? Where are his footprints? They only found hers leaving the scene—not his.

"The second theory is they were ambushed by a person or persons unknown who forced them to strip. She escaped. He didn't. They took him from the scene and that's that."

"Sounds like that last one makes the most sense," ventured the Chief.

"Sort of," Tokasti reluctantly agreed. "Only, if they *were* attacked you'd think the perpetrators would have taken his wallet with them. It was still in his pants pocket. He had about two hundred dollars in there, some credit cards and his return ticket to Seattle. If there *was* a third party present with bad intentions, it doesn't figure they'd leave *that* stuff behind. Besides," Tokasti scowled, "there are no signs of anyone else arriving or leaving that could have been the unknown third party."

The Chief thought for a moment.

"Did she say what they were doing there?"

"Taking pictures. And, no, forensics did not find a camera at the scene."

"When was he supposed to leave?"

"The tenth.

"We got into her computer account and looked over her emails. They appeared to be very good friends. All of their exchanges were amiable."

"Were they meeting for sex?" asked the Chief with a cynical grimace.

Tokasti paused, annoyed at the Chief's persistence on that topic.

"Well—no. I'm pretty sure they weren't. I mean, they were very affectionate toward each other in their correspondence but they did not discuss anything intimate or sexual. Usually if a person is coming to visit for *that,* they engage in several '*hot'* emails ahead of time. We didn't find any.

"In fact," he continued, "she made it very clear she was *not* interested in casual sex. He agreed and never tried to persuade her otherwise," and he looked at the Chief again.

"I think he just came out to see her—and nothing else."

The Chief nodded his head but did not seem completely convinced.

"I had our Washington State contact do some finding out. Nothing there. He didn't have any friends or family; he was known at work as a loner—quiet, not really noticeable. Except for those trips he made to that farm there wasn't anything unusual leading up to this."

"Those trips, do they have anything to do with this case?" the Chief asked.

"I don't think so. It's just a weird aberration in his usual habits, which is the only reason I checked them out in the first place. But so was this impulse trip here."

"Sounds like the beginning of some kind of mental thing," remarked the Chief.

"Perhaps—however, all the witnesses who saw them together said they appeared to be perfectly happy with each other. He didn't strike anyone as *'mental.'*"

The Chief nodded, agreeing.

"The only other odd thing was *this,*" and Tokasti handed over a piece of paper.

"Where did they find this?"

"In her purse."

"I thought you said they didn't find her clothes—"

"She left it in the car under the seat."

The Chief looked at the paper; a puzzled expression came across his face.

"What the hell is *this* supposed to be? A secret alphabet?"

Tokasti laughed.

"No—although it might as well be. Dmitri caught a glimpse of it on my desk—he says it's Greek."

"Greek?"

"Yeah—although he also said it isn't very good Greek."

"Meaning?"

"He said it looked like someone had taken something in English and tried to translate it word for word with one of those Internet translators. That rarely works. He knew the words but they didn't make any sense the way they were laid out."

"Could he get anything out of it?"

"Something about Artemis, a word he thinks might be intended to mean *'virgin'* and something about safety. That's about as close as he could get to it. He says whoever wrote it does not know the language."

There was a pause.

"They still haven't found him?"

"No," replied Tokasti, clearly annoyed by that development. "He hasn't surfaced anywhere—alive *or* dead."

"I guess there really isn't anything else we can do unless his body shows up."

"They always show up eventually."

VIII—To the Altar

He woke up, strangled in the bedding he'd wrapped around him. It was hard to breathe and he panicked, fearing he was suffocating. He writhed, thrashed and finally managed to dislodge himself from the linen. He sat up, panting hard.

The sheet was soaked.

He absently ran his hand across his face. It was soaked too.

It was the dreams—those terrible nightmares shattering the peace of his slumber. Their horror lingered in his mind like a faint trace of perfume. He put his head in his hands, trying to calm his thoughts— disturbed at the intensity of the visions that forced him awake.

He had expected dreams, of course, but only dreams about *her*. The euphoria of their first meeting, the anticipation of their next, he couldn't think of anything else. It was all he had on his mind when he drifted off.

She never appeared. The world he found himself in had nothing to do with love and laughter—it was a world of darkness, pain and grief. Shadowy pictures, reeking of death, flitted across the curtain of his eyelids. There was blood spattering and oozing all over. There were screams of pain; pleadings for mercy; tormented, echoing howls shattering the silence; frequent flashes of lightning and deep-throated thunder shaking the ground.

There were other things but they were harder to remember. Running; frantic gasping breaths and pumping muscles; the sound of pursuit—a hideous soft pattering as of enormous paws galloping. Teeth—many jaws lined with cruelly sharp teeth. And a strange flute-like sound, a hypnotic melody that triggered unexpected responses in his brain at certain pitches.

Where did these visions come from if she was all he had in his thoughts? He tried to dismiss these ominous forebodings as irrelevant, but even as he thought this, his spirit collapsed as though accepting the inevitable. He bowed his head and lay crouched on the bed for a while.

He glanced at the clock: it was six.

He had three hours.

The light was fading outside the curtains as he dizzily got to his feet and made his way to the bathroom. The hot water revived him and he was almost his usual self when he toweled off and dressed. There was still a faint shadow of jet lag in his body but it wasn't weighing him down any longer.

He looked at his cell phone and smiled: there was a text message—no, two text messages waiting for him. He did not need to see who sent them. He activated the phone and read the messages:

I miss you.

I can't wait until tonight.

That last one caused a strange reaction—one he wasn't expecting. He smiled at first—then a cloud of darkness shrouded his eyes leaving him disoriented and frightened. His rational mind frantically searched for a logical cause for this sudden change of mood to no avail. Was he feeling *unsure* about something? His visions of their meeting that would shortly take place were *all wrong*. Instead of feeling happy and peaceful he felt—frustrated. Tense. Irritable. He kept seeing her naked body— her tantalizing naked body—drifting across his consciousness, into his arms, their skin burning, pulling her to him urgently, their mouths— and he could not think past that moment without the darkness falling yet again.

He snapped his head as though shaking the visions out, muttering, "No," repeatedly like an incantation. He trembled, struggling against a raw, animal passion boiling his blood hot enough to burst his veins. His head throbbed; he grew lightheaded...

...and, all at once, the episode passed and he sat on the bed, exhausted, shaking his head, bewildered.

"No," he said again.

Tears came into his eyes.

He rose from the bed and put his clothes on. The room felt too dark, too small, too stifling. He needed to get outside to clear his head. He went through the motions of locking the door, walking down the stairs, through the lobby and the exit. But all the time it felt as though he were outside of his body, a disinterested observer, watching himself walk through the corridors and down the street. A cold wind blew, gusting hard enough to bend back the shrubs and bushes—but he felt nothing, as if he'd wrapped himself in a thick, tight blanket.

He fused back together after a few minutes; life and feeling returned to his bloodstream. The dream hangover faded away and he was hungry, starving. There was a restaurant attached to the hotel, exuding a savory odor. Realizing he hadn't eaten for hours, his stomach growling, he made his way inside.

Perhaps, he thought later, as he was leaving, perhaps all he had needed was something to eat. He walked down the street, his thoughts at peace. He was calm and took an interest in everything—his dark dreams forgotten. He stopped and looked at the display windows of the different shops, most of them closed for the night, examining everything laid out for sale. He studied the patterns in the sidewalk paving, the cars parked along the side of the road.

A man being marched to the firing squad misses nothing with his eyes, for it will be his last vision before death.

He stopped short as this thought hit him. For a moment he stood, silent. Then he continued onward.

Dostoyevsky. Crime and Punishment. He smiled. Of course. He was paraphrasing the thoughts of Raskolnikov as he walked down the street leading to his doom. It wasn't a direct quote from the novel but the sense was the same.

Momentarily comforted, he continued. But deep down, he knew he was only whistling in the dark—avoiding confronting the underlying cause of his feelings. He felt a little ashamed at this, then resentful—angry at his mind for playing these tricks.

I refuse to spoil this.

He was almost convinced he wouldn't.

He returned to his room under a twilit sky—the first stars beginning to show. He walked in a little nervously, but once inside, he breathed easier. The dark feelings did not return and the walls did not feel like they were closing in. It was no longer stifling. He glanced at the clock.

Eight-twenty.

He quickly put himself to rights and walked out to his car. There was a faint chill in the air; he was glad he had brought his coat with him. He started the car, carefully backed out and eased into traffic.

She was on the lookout for him where he had dropped her off earlier. She seemed a little flustered, pacing the sidewalk and looking back over her shoulder toward her house. It occurred to him she wanted to avoid compromising herself so he obligingly doused the headlights as he approached. He slowed; she slipped inside and was seated before he had come to a stop.

"Let's go," she whispered.

He did not turn the lights back on until they had completely rounded the corner.

They drove in silence. A tense silence. He glanced at her every so often and she always smiled, but seemed distracted as well. Her fingers were drumming and she glanced around her as though expecting danger.

"Nervous?" he finally asked.

He instantly wished he hadn't said it.

She looked up, startled, saw his blush and laughed, breaking the tension.

"A little," she admitted and slipped her silken fingers into his hand.

Happy and glowing, they drove out to the hotel and parked the car. She vaulted out of her seat, clutching her camera and purse. They entered the lobby arm in arm. The clerk was not at the desk and no one was in the lobby. A little of her nervous manner returned as they walked down the corridor from the elevator. He let go her arm to open the door and she passed in behind him, shutting it behind her.

He turned on the lights—all the lights—and she looked around for something to sit on. There was only the desk chair and the bed. She settled into the chair like a butterfly coming to rest and he sat across from her on the bed. She looked at him and smiled.

After an awkward silence he finally said, "Read any good books lately?"

She giggled, blushed and they both collapsed with laughter. It was a gentle cathartic and when they both finally recovered, wiping the tears from their eyes, the tension between them had faded away.

She leaned back in the chair, her face glowing and her eyes intense. He returned her gaze.

"Gawd, I love your eyes," he said at last.

"Yours are pretty too," she whispered.

Without being aware of it, he reached out and took her hand in his. She slipped her fingers into his and impulsively grabbed his other hand, raised them both to her lips and kissed them. She held them there for a while, then slowly lowered them to her lap.

Her eyes gleamed wetly.

"I can't believe I finally got to see you," he said at last. Despite their silence, their fingers continuously caressed and stroked their hands. He finally slipped his fingers out of hers and gently stroked her forearms. She gripped his and softly returned his touching.

She went lax and released his hands—he slid his off at the same time. She was blushing again—but this time it was a sign of conflict, tension. She wanted to look down but forced herself to look at him instead.

He lightly shrugged his shoulders and began moving away from her. Instantly she reached out for him and grabbed his arms.

"*No!*" she said urgently and he paused. "No," she repeated quietly. She gently caressed his arm.

She leaned back in her chair, obviously relieved. For some reason, he felt the same way—and that bothered him. Not to the point of disturbing him, but enough to give him pause.

"I still want to take you to the forest," she said. "At midnight," she added.

He smiled.

"Does that make sense?"

"Actually it does. That's safer for you. Not *that* way," he said quickly, seeing her expression, "I mean that's your home. You're the Dryad of the forest—it's where you belong."

She smiled.

"I'm having a hard time resisting you," she said, shyly.

"Me too," he admitted, but he made no move toward her.

After a while, he stood up, stretched and began walking out of her field of vision. She flinched a little but did not leave the chair. He moved to a position behind her. She could feel the warmth of his body close to her and then felt his hands on her shoulders—gently pressing and rubbing.

"Oh—!" she gasped and leaned her head back.

"May I touch you?" he asked.

She nodded. He pressed a little harder and she sighed. She leaned her head all the way back against the chair, her eyes closed. He leaned forward a little and gently kissed her forehead. She smiled but kept her eyes closed.

He continued massaging her shoulders and worked his way up her neck, gently holding her head as he turned it.

"I love this," she said softly.

He reached her head and began running his fingers through her hair, massaging her scalp and then slowly following the strands from their roots to the tips. She was leaning forward now, her breathing deep.

He stood up and moved away from the chair.

"Lie down," he directed, pointing to the bed, "I want to do your neck properly. It's got to be uncomfortable for you in that chair."

She slowly opened her eyes and looked at him steadily, then gradually rose from the chair and crawled on to the bed.

"No," he said as she headed for the pillows, "lie this way," and he moved a pillow to the opposite end. She adjusted herself.

"On my back or my front?" she asked shyly.

"On your back," he said.

She carefully lowered her body until it lay on the bed, her head on the pillow, staring up into his face. He looked at her with a tender, loving expression, reached out and gently touched the tip of her nose. She smiled.

He stood up and moved so he was behind her head. He reached out and began rubbing her shoulders again, slowly moving toward the center. She closed her eyes, breathing, deeply and lingeringly. He reached her neck and brought both of his arms together so her head rested on them. He rubbed the base of her neck for a while. Then, gradually sliding his hands upward, still supporting her head with his forearms, he rubbed her neck muscles, gently turning her head every so often.

She sighed.

Then, he slid his arms beneath her shoulder, along her back and gently lifted her off the bed with his forearms. He slid his hands up her spine at the same time, the pressure of her body causing him to pressure her back, all the way to the base of her neck. She gasped. He repeated the action.

"Oh my," she breathed.

"Is it good?" he asked.

"Oh, yes," she said. He continued this for a few more minutes.

Then he gently released her head and began stroking her face— massaging her temples, her forehead, her cheeks and even her lips in the same gentle but powerful motion. Her muscles gradually lost their tension and she shivered every so often.

"Under my spell?" he asked.

She nodded her head.

"Go ahead and turn around, so your feet are at this end," he said. Slowly, she shifted herself around and sank back into the pillows. He slipped her shoes off before she was aware of what he was doing. She opened her mouth to say something and then closed it, moaning. He had her foot in both of his hands, rubbing it, massaging out all the tension. She lay, enthralled with the sensation.

"Oh, if you only knew how good that feels," she finally said. He laughed.

"It's amazing how the foot connects to the body," he said. "We carry a lot of tension there; it's the best place to treat it."

She nodded her head.

He was now massaging her legs through her clothing. The heat of his hands penetrated the cloth; it felt pleasurable. He worked up to her knees, then walked to the other end and began with her right arm—from the shoulder all the way out to the fingertips. Then the left arm the same way.

After a while, she managed to find her voice.

"I—I—thank you for doing this," she said finally.

"You don't have to thank me," he said.

"Well—I feel I do," she responded.

"No," he said softly, "I'm getting just as much out of this as you are."

She opened her eyes.

"How is that?"

He smiled.

"This is how I make love—this is my way of intimacy. To surrender to my touch," and he squeezed her fingers.

She closed her eyes again.

"I see," and she flushed and went quiet.

"Turn over, love," he said. She looked at him briefly, then spun herself over so her face lay into the pillow. He reached up and stroked her hair, placing it like a fan around her head.

"Sorry, I couldn't resist," he said.

She laughed.

He slid his hands just underneath her shirt; she tensed up as he contacted the flesh of her back. She moaned again as his warm fingers met her skin and he carefully worked her neck, shoulder and arm muscles, then up and down the spine. At midpoint, he slipped his hands out and continued with his hands on top of her shirt. Each stroke was lower and lower until his palms came to rest just above her tailbone.

He paused, then began at her feet again.

"I always save the tension spot for last," he said, enigmatically.

A faint trace of anxiety came into her voice.

"The tension spot?" she repeated cautiously.

"Yes," he said reassuringly. "This spot right here," and, with both hands, he gently pressed down on the center of her back, just above the tailbone. She gasped and clenched her hands.

He released and returned to her legs.

"See what I mean?" he said.

"Oh wow—I had no idea—"

"That's where women carry all of their tension," he said.

She did not reply to this.

He slid his hands upward and began stroking her back, down toward the tension spot, pressing a little harder as he got closer. He finally reached it and she gasped, again and again, as she felt the heat and pressure of his hands.

"Now," he said in a whisper, "For this to have its full effect you have to breathe deeply, in rhythm with my pressing. Don't worry about being exact, just concentrate on the breathing," and he again pushed on the spot, holding it and releasing it.

After a few cycles, she fell into the rhythm.

"Keep breathing deeper each time," he advised.

She did so. An incredible feeling began to consume her. She felt as though she were an empty, deep pool, a deep well, a deep well slowly filling with water. With each press as she breathed, the water rose higher. Her entire body tightened and her breaths became more shuddering the deeper he pressed. She was shaking hard, burning with fever and still breathing deeply, filling up the well. It was getting harder and harder to draw her breath and she felt herself struggling.

Abruptly she tensed, paused and with a cry of release she collapsed, all the tension exploding out of her like a fountain gushing. She felt her throat tighten, hot water in her eyes and she sobbed—sobbed like a child, the toxins of her negative feelings and emotions pouring through her tears. And all the time there was the continual, gradually softening pressure of his hands, pressing up and down.

She finally collapsed, limp, senseless into the pillows, shaking with the aftershocks. He slowly lightened his pressure and gently ran his hand up her spine, then stroked her hair again. She continued trying to get her breathing under control. He did not intervene—he just kept one hand touching her, lightly, preserving the contact.

She rapidly reached out a hand and gripped his wrist, tightly. She still was calming down and gasping. He passively allowed her to hold his wrist and did not try to pull away. Her sounds became quieter and quieter.

Then she turned over, staring at him with her beautiful eyes, the tears sparkling, with a glance that shot him straight to the heart. It was his turn to gasp.

"Oh—oh," she said, at a loss for words, "How did you *know* that? Did you know that would happen?" she finally asked.

He smiled.

"You had a lot of poison to get out of your soul," he said. "I knew *something* was going to happen but I wasn't expecting it to be that intense."

He gently made to free his wrist but she shook her head and held him there. He looked at her, puzzled as she continued to calm her breathing.

Finally, she let out a final sigh and opened her eyes. They were still wet. The sight somehow triggered his own tears and his eyes glistened too. He tenderly reached out, grabbed a tissue from its box and gently wiped her eyes. He patted the tissue, then leaned over and gently kissed the closed lids.

As he moved to rise, she instantly grabbed both his hands, made a guttural sound and pulled him forcibly onto the bed into her arms before he could stop her.

He started to say something but her mouth locked onto his; at once, they were holding each other tightly, crying softly, caressing but not breaking their contact for what seemed like hours. He was having difficulty controlling his feelings; he did not want to take her somewhere she didn't want to go. But every time he tried to release himself, she would only pull him back harder—and soon he matched the intensity of her embrace.

At last, they both collapsed and he gently laid himself down next to her. She was still holding on to his hand; she carried it up to her mouth and kissed it greedily. He looked at her with blazing eyes the entire time, completely under the spell of passion. He kissed her tears away again, but this time he gently caressed them away with his tongue. She pressed her face into his mouth and gripped him hard.

Satisfied at last, they fell back, exhausted. Feeling dazed, she looked around her in amazement. Her clothes were still on, as were his. She was safe and so was he. He smiled at her and gently kissed her mouth again.

"*That's* how you make love?" she asked.

"Yes," he said with a broad grin.

"*Gawd!* Everyone else is doing it wrong," she blurted out.

"I love you," he said and she swiftly turned and looked at him.

"I love you too," she said.

The tears came into their eyes and they embraced again, although not with the same intensity as before.

"I am so glad we met each other," he said finally. She nodded her head.

"Me too. It's the best day I've ever had in my life."

"I only wish we had met sooner," he said in an undertone. Something in his voice caused her to look into his eyes and she paled.

It was a face of profound grief.

"What's wrong, darling?" she asked, quickly sitting up and pulling him toward her lap. She rested his head in her hands, the tears pouring out of his eyes.

"What's wrong, love? Please, please *say something!*" she cried out.

He reached up and gripped her hand.

"I don't know," he said miserably, "I don't know. It's been hitting me like this all day. I've had such terrible dreams…" and he shook. She gently kissed his eyes.

"It isn't *me*, is it?" she asked, almost too frightened to say it. He immediately pulled her close to him.

"No, no. Gawd no. You—" and he seemed to reach out to her with every fiber of his being, "You are the greatest thing that ever happened to me. You are my soul mate, my love," but he choked up again and couldn't speak for a few minutes.

"I am so happy I could die," he finally said to her, gently squeezing her hand. "This is the best day of my life too—but I have this terrible feeling. I'm scared. It's like I'm afraid if I kiss you for too long I'll wake up and find out this whole thing is a dream—that all of this is just a cruel trick, that you don't really exist."

He clung to her.

She gently rocked him in her arms.

"I'm not going anywhere," she said to him, "I'm not going anywhere. You're not losing me."

He looked at her again and she paused, transfixed by the intensity of his expression.

"It isn't *you*. I know *you* won't leave. I'm afraid I'll be taken away from you," and she immediately bowed her head as though stabbed in the belly. Terror, icy terror poisoned her blood.

That look in his eyes burned in her memory—it was like looking over the edge of the pit of death.

It often came back to haunt her dreams.

She collapsed on him and again they held each other—desperately clinging, trembling. She was frightened—too frightened to ask about those ominous words—*'I'm afraid I'll be taken away from you.'* It chilled her heart like a blast of Arctic wind.

They lay there for a long time, not wanting the moment to end and dreading the ending. At last, they both fell asleep for a few minutes in each other's arms and for once, his dreams were peaceful. They were both in bliss. When they finally opened their eyes again, the only emotion they felt was love—a love that somehow bound them, that would never die.

She stretched, looked over at the clock and started.

It was eleven-fifty.

IX—Invocation II

He did not feel afraid any more. His initial feelings of grief were gone—any remnants that came back to haunt him vanished when he felt the still-wet trail her tongue left behind on his face. Her scent. Her perfume. Other than that, he felt nothing. It was as if he knew the result was fated and didn't want to waste any energy fighting it. He just wanted the ordeal to end.

They drove through the dark streets and finally parked at a location she pointed out to him. He couldn't make out very much—he was starting to have difficulty seeing—but the distant loom of the wood across the field was obvious.

She carefully got out of the car, closing the door quietly. He did the same. They joined hands and slowly walked across the field toward the deeper black that marked the forest. They stealthily picked their footsteps as though fearing detection, their ears pricked and alert for the slightest disturbance. They reached the trees and passed into their shadow without incident.

It was very quiet inside the forest—as though a velvet cloth covered the ground, muffling every movement. No snaps came from the branches, no mysterious noises, no bats in flight—just silence. And darkness.

"Is it always this quiet?" he asked in a whisper.

"No," she said, barely breathing. "This is weird. I don't know what's going on," she added.

He tried to think of something to say but couldn't and they continued silently, their footsteps inaudible.

They finally reached a break in the trees and entered an open space in the middle of the wood. She stopped and spun in a circle, her arms outstretched and her head thrown back, making light, happy sounds.

"This is the place," she whispered, stopping and walking toward him, her open hands outstretched, "*This is my temple.*"

He stared at her for a moment, then fell to his knees and clasped his arms around hers. She pulled him close, stroking his head and held him against her legs for a moment. He gently kissed her knees. She raised him up and he stood on his feet again.

"You feel the magic?" she whispered.

"Yes, my goddess," he said, "I do feel it."

There was some subtle change in his voice that disturbed her. She looked toward him anxiously, but could not see his face in the darkness.

Calming herself, she turned to the camera she carried in her free hand and activated the switch. There was a sudden flash cutting through the darkness as the LED screen came to life, vanishing as the screen saver kicked in.

"Here," she whispered urgently, "Hold this," and he took the camera as she stepped a few feet away.

"Where are you going my love?" he asked.

"I'm getting naked," she replied.

He expected a thrill or shiver to run through his body at the thought of her getting naked—even though she was invisible—yet he felt oddly detached and emotionless. He had once again separated from his body and viewed the entire scene as if outside himself. Even the subtle rustle of her clothing sliding over her limbs did not tweak his emotions.

At last, the rustling ceased and she again spun on her toes in rapture.

"It feels so good to be naked," she breathed, "One with nature, the earth," she continued softly while he just stood silently—waiting. She stopped abruptly and came in front of him. He could feel the heat of her skin even though she was not touching him. His hands twitched.

"Are you ready?" she asked.

"Yes," he said, "Yes, I am."

She reached out, took his hand and he followed her lead as though dreaming. He reached out and felt her back, slid his hand down her spine and gently rested it on the curve of her tailbone. She laughed with pleasure.

"That feels wonderful," she said.

They stopped and he sensed they were in front of a tree—a large tree. A tree with twisting branches reaching out like arms and rough protrusions jutting out of the bark, like a gnarled satyr with rough skin. She sighed and flung her arms around the tree, holding it tightly.

"Get the camera," she whispered tensely, "let's get some pictures," and she began twisting her body against the trunk.

"I'm going to make love to my tree," she said.

An unexpected feeling flared up inside him at these words—boiling from his belly out to his throat. A smoldering, bubbling rage.

Jealousy.

She started to climb and he listlessly picked up the camera. The first flash was like a star exploding in his face and he flinched. He took another one and then another, straining to follow the sound of her and her voice as she moved up higher. His hands went slack and he felt as though he were about to faint—the numbness spreading up his limbs.

"Are you there?" he heard her saying.

"Yes," he replied—and even in the dark, she sensed something wrong with his voice. But she was caught up in the moment and paid no attention to the warning sensation shooting through her heart.

"Oh, my love, I'm so glad you're with me tonight," and again she passionately embraced the tree.

She failed to notice he was no longer taking pictures.

Then, she turned to him in the darkness and he could sense, even if he could not see, the intensity of her gaze.

"Get naked with me, my love," she said softly.

His heart froze.

"Naked?" he repeated, hardly daring to breathe.

"Yes," she said, with intensity. "Be one with me—be one with me and my love."

He did not reply to this but immediately put down the camera and started taking off his clothing, piece by piece. He noticed a rock nearby with a flat surface; as he removed each piece he carefully folded it and placed it on the rock. For some reason, this sight caused tears to well up in his eyes; for a moment, he felt as though he could escape from the doom he'd woven.

It wasn't until he was nearly finished it occurred to him he could see the rock and all of its details despite the absolute darkness. He also noticed that, although he had nothing on but his briefs, he did not feel cold. He did not feel *anything*. He tried to touch his arm and he felt nothing on his arm or fingers—it was getting difficult to move.

"Are you naked yet?" came her voice.

He pulled the briefs off his legs and added them to the pile.

"Yes, my Dryad," he replied and he heard her gasp as he turned around to face her.

It was pitch-dark. There was no light. There was no moon. Yet he could see her, see her clearly, a vision of pure alabaster, her skin glowing with a white luminescence bright enough to light the whole forest.

As though she had captured the light of the moon in her skin.

It was an unbelievably beautiful vision—her nakedness at once powerful and vulnerable. Her legs, the muscles stretched tightly, her arms raised over her head, her sleek neck and shapely breasts were shining, gleaming in the darkness.

He looked into her face and terror overcame him instantly.

Her expression was frozen in shock—frightened beyond screaming. He could see why: the reflection of his face in her eyes was a shapeless, menacing mass of black from which two glowing red eyes protruded.

She made a choking noise in her throat, cowering against the tree.

"Oh my Gawd," she whispered. "Oh—what—what—*what is happening?*" she cried out.

She cast herself out of the tree, landing hard at his feet. As she frantically scrambled to rise, she collapsed on her knees, looking up at him with horrific fascination. It dawned on him she could see him just as clearly as he saw her.

It was his last rational thought. A strange, powerful force that felt as though it was coming from outside him whipped through his body like a firestorm. He looked at her with his blazing red, firelit eyes, his soul filled with lust, ravenous lust and insatiable hunger. She cried out in terror, leaped to her feet and tried to flee.

It was useless.

He stretched out his arm to seize her without taking notice of its unusual length. Even the realization he could not move any other part of his body failed to rouse a response. He had completely surrendered to the force engulfing him.

She struggled desperately as his fingers closed around her neck, going limp as she felt him overpower her and lift her off the ground, higher and higher. She tried to cover her face with her hands as he forced her to turn toward him.

"No, no, no, *please no,*" she pleaded, crying out louder and louder until she burst into frenzied screaming—the echoes ringing off the trees. This only drove him wilder and he pulled her to him, forcibly pressing her to his body, the look of terror in her eyes; the tears; the mingled fury and sudden desire exploding within them wresting the last drop of humanity from his soul. His passion inflamed to a fever pitch, his eyes blazing. Her mouth went dry; her screams ceased; and she stared at him—unable to avert her gaze or make a sound.

He gripped tighter and slowly brought her toward his mouth, his vision rapidly obscured by red flames. She completely lost control, screaming and writhing frantically, with no vestige of sanity left in her—a frightened animal struggling in the predator's merciless claws.

He didn't really hear what she was saying. But he knew she was saying *something*...

Ἄρτεμις προστασία σου ἱέρεια!

A blinding flash seared him straight through his eyes to his feet. He tried to scream, but had no voice. There was a brief vision of a tall entity in white, a furious snarling like a pack of wild dogs, blazing flames, intense heat, the sound of her pleading for mercy, teeth tearing and flesh ripping...

A white-hot spear flew out of nowhere and buried itself cruelly into his heart. He swooned from the intensity of the pain. He heard her fleeing blindly through the darkness. In desperation, he tried to follow but could not move—not even his arms. The sounds of her crashing into the unseen trees, tripping over the branches, the brambles ripping at her legs, slowly faded to a terrible silence.

And somewhere, far, far away, there was the harsh, soulless laughter of an unseen demon accompanied by mysterious flute-like sounds.

He fell swiftly, slamming hard into the ground. A terrible, agonizing sensation of loss and grief that would have torn his throat if he had been able to scream exploded out of his heart, shot out to the end of his limbs and briefly crushed him in its icy, merciless grip.

Then, darkness—absolute, cold and permanent darkness— descended and he knew nothing more.

X—Elegy

She finished pulling on her top and unwillingly stared at her face in the mirror. Blinded by a hot flash of water at the expression in her eyes, she turned away angrily, wiping her tears and blowing her nose with a tissue.

She picked her coat off the bed, shrugged into it and zipped it tight. Her purse was still on the night table—she walked over and recovered it. She slowly gave the entire room a last searching glance, making sure she left nothing behind.

A fit of shaking seized her, forcing her to stagger to the edge of the bed and sit down, her head in her hands. It took a few minutes but she managed to calm herself without giving way to the feelings overflowing in her throat. With a deep breath, she rose, walked to the door, pulled it open and entered the corridor.

She passed by the nurses' station without a glance. The two at the counter looked up briefly, without interest and resumed their tasks. She fought to keep herself on an even emotional keel all the way to the elevator.

The doors shut and she leaned against the wall for a moment, her hands gripping the rail, pressing her burning forehead against the cold metal, her eyes closed. She heard the warning bell and slowly straightened up. The doors slid open, the chatter and muted noise of the lobby poured in. She took another deep breath and left the cage, turning to her left.

She was almost to the foyer doors when the voice broke into her thoughts. Startled, she turned swiftly toward the source, then felt her body tense at the sight of the speaker.

"If I could just have a word with you before you leave."

She gave a sigh of exasperation and tossed her hair irritably out of eyes.

"Make it quick," she snapped, whipping her fingers through her hair.

Tokasti looked at her stonily.

"Is there *anything* you can add to what you've already told me to help us find out what happened—" but she cut him off, tears welling in her eyes despite her resolve.

"No, no," she said, waving him aside, "I've already told you everything. We went into the forest. Something—*someone*," she hastily corrected herself, "scared us. I ran and lost track of him. I haven't seen him since. I have no idea where he is. I don't give a fuck where he is. He probably went back to Seattle—try there," and she glared defiantly at the officer.

His glance remained steady.

"We already have. They don't know where he is either."

He closed his notebook, bowed slightly and walked out of the hospital lobby.

She lingered for a few more minutes, her fingers nervously plucking her sleeve, her lip trembling and her eyes blinking. Then, holding her head high and looking straight ahead, she calmly walked out through the main door of the hospital into the cold sunlight.

* * *

Many hours later, as the sun was beginning to lower, she stood once more at the location where they'd parked, staring across the field at the wood in the distance, her heart pounding. She hesitated, gathering her courage and finally stepped off the curb, slowly walking through the field toward the trees. She managed to keep herself from faltering, even as she entered the forest, retracing that terrible journey. She had only taken a few steps in when she felt herself going numb and had to stop to control her trembling. She tried to resume and had to stop again.

She wasn't afraid, not in the daylight, but there was something wrong. This distorted scene did not match the one in her memory. A foreshadow of grief swept through her as she realized the peace and comfort she used to feel when walking through the forest was lost forever. It wasn't her refuge any longer. Exiled, unwelcome and disgraced, she shuffled forward, her head bent with shame, mumbling an old lullaby from some memory of her past—a childlike attempt to quell the fear in her heart. Her eyes grew damp for a moment but she viciously struck her sleeve across them and forced herself to keep going.

"*It must have been a dream…It was only a dream,*" she kept repeating. But her assurance lessened as she continued into the growing silence. When she reached the clearing, she was shaking so hard she could hardly stand.

She stood at the edge of the clearing and hesitated.

There would be no turning back if she took another step. It was her last chance to escape the truth.

Determined to find her answer and with a great effort of will, she forced herself to step into the clearing. She involuntarily closed her eyes as she entered—she could not reopen them at first.

Anger and shame at her weakness overcame her; she forced her eyelids open and stared, taking in the details with wild, wide eyes.

Her tree was there, mute and stark, its leafless branches splayed to the sky. She slowly turned in a circle, unwillingly counting under her breath. The rock came into view and she flinched—but she kept going.

Then she stopped with a faint, choking cry, unable to speak.

She rushed over to the remains, her mind fighting against the harsh truth she beheld. *She might not have noticed it before. It could have easily been there before and missed. She didn't pay much attention to details—*

But when she reached the remains, her arms went slack, her lower lip trembled and the tears came to her eyes.

Struck by lightning.

She heard the phrase—almost recognized his voice—but it couldn't have been him.

A lightning strike was the only possible cause for the tree's destruction. Viciously ripped down the middle, torn from the ground—the exposed roots obscenely gaping—broken up into a shapeless pile of shards, branches and splinters. All of it burned black.

She stared unwillingly, her lips moving in prayer.

She slowly backed away and her foot stepped on something that crunched loudly in the silence. She whirled in terror, lost her balance and fell down hard on the ground. It was a few minutes before she could breathe again.

She tried to pick herself up, failed and fell down again. Laying there, her whole body shaking, she felt something underneath—the item she'd crushed. Devoid of emotion from her sudden fright, she slowly got to her knees, mechanically reached for it, closed her hands around it and brought it to her.

She stared at it unbelievingly—paralyzed for a moment at this terrible confirmation.

Then, the tears pouring from her eyes, she pressed the object to her breast, hugged it tightly and wept, her hands caressing the lifeless twisted mass of steel and glass that had once sat on his nose—the framed windows through which she first saw his beautiful eyes looking at her when they first met at the restaurant...

Season's Greetings

He opened the door and shivered as the icy wind blasted through the narrow opening, peering at the two callers on the porch, tightening his ermine trimmed red robe. They were dressed in uniform, heavily insulated against the cold, their breath smoky and the condensation frozen on their microphones. He didn't waste time looking for the patrol car: he knew it wouldn't be visible from the porch.

"Yes?" he asked.

"Can we talk for a minute?" asked one of them.

He shrugged and pulled the door open, motioning the officers inside. He shut the door behind them and instinctively shot the bolts home; then, realizing what he had done, looked up embarrassed. But the officers did not notice so he left the bolts where they were.

"Here—you can use the couch," he said, waving at a badly stuffed sofa. The officers gingerly settled themselves, avoiding the myriad of holes, protruding insulation and occasional spring. The fabric might have been leather but its color had long since faded to black. It was, however, surprisingly comfortable and the officers relaxed once they sat.

For a moment they leaned toward the glowing woodstove, warming their hands, then began removing their gloves, outer coats and furred headgear. It was not until the second officer shook her hair free of her cap he realized she was a woman—striking, with vivid red hair and electric blue eyes.

After giving her a glance, he turned his attention to the other officer. This was a young man, with the inevitable beard so common in the northern regions and a taut, compact muscular body. He noted the clumsiness with which he retrieved his notebook and settled himself in a note-taking position. This told him the woman was the senior team member and, realizing this, he turned to her again.

She, in her turn, was glancing at him. Apart from flaring her nostrils briefly, she gave no outward sign of emotion.

"You keep this up every year?" she asked, as though not really interested in the answer.

He smiled tolerantly.

"I've already explained that—" but she cut him off.

"Yeah, yeah, I know. I've been briefed. You act the part, complete with costume and keep it up twenty-four seven," and again her nostrils flared.

"Ever think about getting that outfit cleaned?"

He responded politely without any sign of offense to the rude remark.

"I'm not allowed to wash it—" he began, but she wearily interrupted him again.

"I've heard all about *that* too. Family tradition and all that," was her cynical riposte.

The young man was staring at him with obvious amazement.

"Perhaps we should introduce one another?" he asked, politely as always. "My name is Sa—"

"Okay," the officer cut in hurriedly. "You don't have to *say* it."

He looked at her expectantly. She flushed and spoke up again.

"I'm sergeant Andrews. This is officer Schenk," she casually waved her hand at the young man who was furiously writing on his tablet. He knew better than to reply and merely nodded his head.

The young officer was having some difficulty writing due to the dim lighting in the room—the glow of the woodstove did not illuminate much beyond it. Andrews looked around with an annoyed expression on her face.

"Still no electrics?" she asked.

"It's too expensive to justify the cost," came the calm reply.

She gave an exasperated gasp, then glanced sharply at the young man, who was timidly raising his hand.

"Yeah?" she snapped.

"M'am," faltered the officer, "What do I put down for name?"

Her eyes gleamed dangerously for a moment as the young man bravely held his pen, steeling himself for what was coming. But she simply let out a heavy sigh and said, resignedly, "Santa Claus."

The officer stared at her.

"Santa Claus?" he repeated, disbelievingly.

Andrews flicked her fingers in annoyed dismissal.

"Yeah."

"Are you new in town, young man?" asked Santa.

The officer glanced shyly at Andrews who stared straight ahead, ignoring him. Hesitantly, he answered, "Yes, sir. I've only been here for about two weeks."

"Came up from Seattle or some such place," Andrews muttered, as though his decision to move caused her to doubt his sanity.

"Ah! Then you probably don't understand what's going on then," said Santa, leaning back in his chair.

There was a pause.

"Go ahead and get it over with!" snapped Andrews, crossing her arms over her chest.

"Well," said Santa with obvious relish, "I suppose you are familiar with the accepted, the, shall I say, *commercial* view of Santa Claus?"

Officer Schenk looked faintly bewildered.

"Most everywhere you go in the world," continued Santa, "there is some variant of the story. An old man or some avatar like him appears around the time of the Winter Solstice and everyone prays—I'm sorry," he said as a look of shocked surprise came across Andrews' face, "everyone *begs* or writes to ask him for a gift. It isn't exactly the same everywhere you go but they're all pretty close."

Schenk nodded his head, writing furiously.

"However, as you probably know, this whole identification with St. Nicholas and all that other nonsense is nothing more than an attempt by the early Christian missionaries to wean their flocks from pagan traditions. Christmas, as it is celebrated today, was originally the Roman rite of Saturnalia—a fairly wild festival with all kinds of drinking, celebrating, you name it," and Santa smiled as though seeing something funny in this.

"That's the reason why St. Nicholas got grafted onto the thing—to make it less, umm, barbaric. The actual St. Nicholas was Bishop of Myra and he had a reputation of helping the unfortunate. The most consistent *'gift'* legend tells of him flinging a purse of gold through the window of a house where the daughter was facing a life of prostitution because of her debts," and he laughed.

Schenk continued writing. Andrews yawned and glanced at her watch.

"How we got from that to *'coming down the chimney and leaving presents'* I don't know—but we did. In many ways, that strategy of the monks worked: few people remember the original Winter Festival before the White Martyrs replaced it when they set out to spread the Word among the pagans. Some of the original material is still there—the Evergreen tree for example."

"The Yule log," muttered Andrews.

Santa smiled.

"Yes, that was one of them too," and Santa leaned back, staring into the fire.

"But the original tradition was different. Very different indeed," and he shook his head.

"How was it different?" asked Andrews, unexpectedly watching him with sharpened eyes.

Santa laughed.

"No one knows for certain," he answered, "but one of the variants, the one my family has kept alive in memory, is the Winter Festival is actually a sacrificial rite, intended to placate the Demon of Winter so the world will live to see another Spring."

"Human sacrifice?" prodded Andrews.

Santa nodded affably.

"Oh yes. Doubtless. Likely a virgin, you know, all the usual trimmings," and he smiled to himself again.

"But no one believes that today, do they?" asked Schenk, with pen poised above the paper.

"Mmmmm," said Santa, "Well—I suppose you could make that argument. On the other hand, perhaps the only reason we haven't seen disaster befall the world is someone, somewhere, makes the sacrifice and keeps the world safe for at least another year. And as long as someone continues that tradition, the world will always be here for us."

"That's just sick," spat out Andrews.

Santa looked up at her, distressed.

"Why do you say that?"

"Well for one I can't think of a single virgin youth willing to offer themselves up, so to speak," she said, flatly.

"Ah," said Santa, shaking his head, "That is the point however. The sacrifice must be an *unwilling* victim."

"An unwilling virgin," repeated Andrews. She smiled maliciously.

"Good luck finding one," she tauntingly spouted.

Santa was unperturbed.

"There always is one," he assured her.

"How do you know that?" asked Andrews.

Santa smiled again.

"The world is still here, is it not?"

Andrews shook and spoke through gritted teeth.

"All of that stuff is just the usual male-centric garbage. Obsessed with virginity," she sneered disgustedly. "I wish they would come up with something new to drool over."

"I don't recall saying the victim had to be a female," remarked Santa.

"I think it's stupid. We need to get rid of these outdated traditions. This is the twenty-first century for Gawd's sake!"

Santa looked alarmed.

"I wouldn't say that," he said. "Asking for new traditions is dangerous. You might not like the answer. It could be worse, you know."

"I don't give a damn," she stated, glaring at him. "I can't see how people can worship a creep who gets off killing people every year. You see something deep, mystical and significant in all this but I just see it as over-the-top cruelty. Your Demon of Winter is a nasty slimeball as far as I'm concerned."

Santa sighed, shaking his head.

"I don't blame you for thinking that," he said, "but, think about this: What if the demon was *forced* to take part?"

She stared at him.

"*Forced?*" and she snorted. "How?"

"Well—what if a terrible event took place, so long ago there is only the faintest echo of its memory today. Suppose the demon originally was the guardian, the caring protector of the world and he did something foolish that offended the Powers, forfeiting the lives of his people."

Both of them stared at him, silently.

"And," he continued, "what if the only way he could save his people from a horrible death was to make a promise that every year he would give Them one victim and for that victim They would leave his people in peace for the rest the year."

"Sounds awfully convenient for the demon. I'd be more impressed if he offered himself instead," scoffed Andrews.

"I don't think it would happen that way. The Demon loved his people. He probably would have gladly sacrificed himself for them. Forcing him to sacrifice a victim taken from his own people by his own hand would cause him unbearable pain and anguish—it would be like a father having to kill his child! The suffering would be horrible. Unfortunately, the—those who made the agreement likely *demanded* suffering as part of his penance. The Demon is the *real* victim—all year he lives in dread of what's coming."

Santa's face became more and more distressed.

"How terrible to be doomed to living under such a shadow for all eternity," he said, looking up, with tears in his eyes. "Every year he has to seek out a victim and desperately hopes he finds one to spare his people incredible torture. Every year he brings a new person to the feast—his heart breaking, yearning to save them—and he, personally, has to tie them to the stake and horribly put them to death. Every scream is a knife across his heart and the echoes of those screams never die away. *Think about that!*" he finished, looking up at them with a heart-wrenching expression on his face.

Andrews softened for a moment—she briefly lowered her eyes—then the mood passed and she stood up from the couch with an angry gesture, pulling Schenk up with her. Taken by surprise, Schenk dropped his pad and pen and had to grovel on the darkened floor to find them. At last he stood up next to her, both of them flushed with their efforts.

"You really believe you are the Demon of Winter, don't you?" said Andrews sarcastically. "If I had my way, I'd have you locked up. You and your bullshit talk! You belong in a mental home somewhere, not running loose."

Santa gave a tolerant smile.

"It wouldn't matter after a year—" he began but Andrews lost control and screamed at him.

"*Don't start with that! Nothing* would happen after a year! The world would still go on—*oh forget it!*" and she regained her temper, breathing hard.

"Well then, arrest me," said Santa complacently. "Take me off the streets for my own protection," and he opened his arms in surrender.

Andrews glared bitterly.

"Don't play that game with me. You know as well as I do they have no legal reason to hold you against your will. Being delusional and crazy isn't enough to get you put away anymore—as long as you don't harm yourself or others. I—" she choked, fighting for control, breathing hard.

"You know why we're here," she said at last.

"Another young person has vanished, I take it?" asked Santa calmly.

"Yeah," said Andrews viciously. "You going to make me get a warrant?"

Santa smiled, shaking his head.

"Do I ever? No," he said, "Go right ahead. Search the house. There is no one here. There never is."

Andrews face went white and she bit her lip, drawing blood. Abruptly she began systematically going through the cabin, Schenk right behind her. They lifted rugs, sounded floors, explored the attic space, opened doors and rifled cupboards. Santa watched Andrews' growing annoyance with a sad smile.

"The keys to the outbuildings!" she snapped.

"They're on the hook," he said, with a sigh.

Andrews furiously yanked them off the nail, pulled her outer gear back on, stormed up to the door and shot back the bolts, Schenk following in her wake. As he reached the door, she turned around and exploded:

"Good grief! You want to freeze to death? Put your winter gear on! *Jeez!*"

Schenk rushed over to the couch and flung his gear on with alacrity. He rejoined Andrews who gave a final gasp of exasperation as they both walked out of the door. Santa winced as it slammed behind them.

A long time later, they both struggled back inside, the snow freezing to their faces and uniforms, shivering and stamping their feet. The cold slowed Andrews down but her anger still raged hotly.

"Found anything?" asked Santa, blandly.

She whipped around and faced him, her eyes blazing.

"Shut up!" she barked.

Santa smiled.

"Did you check the bookcase?"

She froze in mid stamp and looked at him intently.

"What do you mean, *'the bookcase'?*" she asked, warily.

Santa sighed, stood up and walked over to the large bookcase that stood along the inner wall. He waved her over, showed her the catch, unlatched it and swung the bookcase open. Andrews gaped, her face lighting up like a predator about to pounce.

"Ha!" she cried, forcing her way past him into the room, Schenk trailing behind as always.

There were sounds of items moved, dropped, dragged, a brief silence, then a final snort from Andrews. Both of them, emerged from the opening, covered with a thick layer of dust, coughing, wiping their eyes and shaking off their coats. A thin cloud of debris rose from their sleeves.

"Still nothing?" he asked in the same, bland tone of voice.

Andrews glanced at him venomously.

"No," she said, breathing hard, reluctantly admitting defeat. She pulled her cap off and shook her hair free for a moment.

"What does she look like?" asked Santa.

"Medium height, red hair, fair skin, green eyes—twenty years old. She's probably safe anyway," she added viciously, "hardly likely she's a virgin," and Andrews laughed hollowly.

She cut herself off, put her hair up and firmly clamped her hat on her head. Signaling Schenk to follow her as though he were a wayward dog, she made her way to the door.

"This isn't the last of this!" she snarled, whirling around to face him.

"I hope not," replied Santa, "I get so lonely out here—" but Andrews and Schenk had already left. Andrews tried to slam the door but as she twisted around, she missed her footing and slipped off the stairs, falling face first into the snow. She slowly raised herself up, spitting the snow out of her bleeding mouth, stared at Santa for a moment. She got to her feet and left, plowing her way through the ever-falling snow, holding her sleeve up to her mouth.

Santa sighed and then, very reluctantly, closed the door, shot the bolts home and stood for a while—an expression of intense grief deepening on his face. He took a few shuddering breaths and then, slowly, turned around and walked back into the room behind the bookcase.

The young woman lay naked on the steel table under the harsh lights, tightly bound with rope, a ball-gag fixed in her mouth, her green eyes wide with silent terror. She made a vain attempt to struggle but she could not move in the slightest.

"Ah yes," said Santa, opening a cupboard to reveal an assortment of knives, their long, thin, serrated edges gleaming coldly. He picked up one or two of them and tested them in his hand, occasionally looking back at his victim who followed his every move despite her inability to move her head.

"You see," he said, choosing a knife and slowly walking toward the table. "What a person sees through their eyes is not always going to be what is actually there. Things get in the way: perceptions, prejudices, all kinds of distractions. So," and he walked until he was standing right next to the victim, "even though they came in here and tore the room apart, they still could not see you."

He looked at her, tears in his eyes.

"I wish they had," he said softly. "I really wish they had."

Taking a deep breath, he picked up the knife and brought the point of the blade toward her eye. Her entire body shook, her face flushed purple and a faint sound, a muffled shriek of terror managed to make its anguished way past the gag. He stopped when he heard it, shocked into immobility.

He looked at her again.

"Please," he said, calmingly, bringing the knife back to her eye, "Don't make this harder for me to do."

He gritted his teeth, closed his eyes, the tears pouring out freely and pushed in the knife, twisting it as it plunged...

The Sabre-Toothed Rabbit

It was August 1992 at Mather Air Force Base California. The base was quiet and the mood subdued. Closing permanently within a year, most of the personnel were already gone or leaving within months. Buildings were shuttered, parking lots emptied, dust lay think and undisturbed on the deserted roadways and the wildlife, no longer repulsed by the presence of people, gradually began to take back their territories.

The upcoming closure cast its gloomy shadow over the base, affecting military and civilians alike. Although they wore the uniform according to regulations and strictly obeyed all protocols, there was an attitude of weariness and listlessness one never saw at a normal base. With the usual enthusiasm and *'fighting spirit'* muted; the expected frantic pace of life slowed to a crawl; this infectious ennui grew stronger and spread further as the final date approached.

The late afternoon heat of the Sacramento valley laid its stifling blanket across the fields, radiating fiercely from the ground and buildings like the blast from an open oven door. People wore short-sleeves—no ties or jackets visible. Between the gloom of the impending closure and the severe heat, it felt like time slowed to a standstill; no one moved fast outdoors and most stayed indoors, keeping company with the hum of the omnipresent air-conditioning.

Sarah, fresh out of uniform and wearing a white top with shorts to match was walking down the hallway of the dorm when she nearly ran into Mark, who was still in his fatigues. She came around the corner and had a one-second up-close view of his killer-blue eyes before she stopped herself in time. Mark, just as surprised as she was, threw himself backward to avoid a collision. They looked at each other for a minute, then laughed.

"Are you still working?" she asked, noting his uniform.

"No—just don't feel like changing."

This was no surprise to Sarah. Mark was rarely out of uniform. Many people assumed he was *'ate up'* (obsessed with the military) or a *'brown-noser,'* but Sarah knew the real reason was Mark had a limited wardrobe, no taste in clothing and hated making choices about what to wear. For him, uniforms were just easier to deal with.

Sarah was the opposite: she couldn't stand wearing the uniform any longer than she had to and removed it every time she had a chance. She smiled at him and they both took a breather in the hallway.

"Where ya going?" she asked.

"Over to the dining hall, try to get some food," he replied.

"You want to walk with me?"

Mark smiled. Despite his cold exterior and indifference, he thought Sarah incredibly beautiful and dreamed of being able to hold her hand and feel her fingers in his. He was also cruelly realistic about his chances with her and never even hinted any of these thoughts to Sarah—he didn't want to lose what little contact he could get. Sarah, for her part, suspected he might be interested in her and didn't care if he was. Mark had it right: He did *not* stand a chance with her.

He was still better than nothing for company as far as Sarah was concerned and Mark was never one to turn down an opportunity, so he nodded and they both headed toward the double exit doors. The savage heat rolled over them like a wave as they stepped out of the air-conditioned building; they both stopped for a minute to adjust themselves to the change. Mark immediately put his hat on as soon as they were outside. Sarah didn't care about protecting herself from the rays and enjoyed the feel of warmth on her skin, but the heat was intense enough to slow her down to match Mark's sedate pace. They both strolled slowly along the concrete swath that cut straight through the grassy field lying between the dorm and the dining hall.

The dining hall was about two hundred feet straight across from the dorm. There were no shade trees or bushes to break up the monotonous grass of the field between. The few clouds in the golden sky were too high up to provide any relief; the night wind had not yet started and the air was chokingly thick. The heat rising from the concrete was so intense Sarah felt it through her shoes.

All at once, she noticed Mark was continually looking behind him at something. She didn't pay much attention to this at first, but when she caught the look in his eyes, it startled her: his face drawn and his eyes furtively glancing about. It finally came to her he was *afraid* of something—that caused her to look back as well. But all she saw was the grass, the concrete walkway, the dorm and several grey, humped shapes scattered across the field, crouching close to the ground. She hardly gave the shapes a second thought—they were a common sight on the base: huge jackrabbits.

The jackrabbits were all over the base wherever there was grass available. These were not little fluffy cotton-tailed powder puffs; they were hares the size of a large wildcat; enormous compared with cottontails. They seemed to be endlessly grazing, their large ears flat to their skull, their eyes staring simultaneously to the right and left as they hunched over, chewing away, oblivious of anything else.

They did not look particularly appealing up close. They had formidable claws and their hard, cruel eyes did not have the sweet innocence of domestic rabbits. They did not look helpless by any means. They paid no attention to the people or animals around them and had good reason for this attitude: if anyone so much as tried to approach them, they would instantly break into a run. Although '*run*' is too mild a word to describe their motion—'*ground-flying*' would be a better description. Nothing on earth could catch up to a fleeing jackrabbit—their speed was amazing. The sight of them bounding at full throttle usually left pursuers, people and animals alike, dumbfounded with their mouths hanging open.

Between their eyes and their powerful ears, they had a nearly three-hundred and sixty degree view of what was going on around them—sneaking up behind them and taking them by surprise was impossible. On the off chance they didn't hear you approaching, there were always plenty of others in the area to signal a warning. They were sadistic in flight, often deliberately remaining just out of range of their frustrated predator, taunting them until their pursuer eventually dropped from exhaustion while they scampered coolly on. A newcomer to the base always found them fascinating at first—but there were so many of them that this first impression quickly wore off. People ignored them as part of the background.

Not seeing anything else, Sarah turned back to Mark and caught him in one of his backward glances. He seemed embarrassed but Sarah confronted him at once.

"What are you looking at?" she asked, bluntly.

"Keep going," he said, quietly, hunching his head down between his shoulders. "Don't stop."

She felt a chill of fear shoot through her. She looked back, despite herself, but there was still nothing to see except the rabbits.

"What are you talking about? What are you afraid of?"

"*Them,*" he answered, enigmatically.

Sarah was not known for her patience.

"What are you talking about? *Who? What?*"

He walked on for a minute. Then, stopping within a few feet of the dining hall door, he looked up at her.

"Them. *The rabbits.*"

Sarah stared at him dumbly, then broke out into hysterical laughter.

"The *rabbits?* You're afraid of the *rabbits?*" She could not believe what she was hearing.

Mark shook his head with a solemn expression on his face.

"You don't understand. They—they've *fooled* you like everyone else. They're *dangerous,*" he whispered at the last. Sarah was still smiling but a chill clouded her expression.

"What do you mean?" she asked.

He pointed to the crouched shapes in the field.

"You see them? Crouched down? Have you ever seen one that wasn't with its face low to the ground?"

"No," Sarah admitted.

He looked around again and came closer to her.

"They keep their heads down like that to hide their fangs, so people won't see them," and he stole a glance across the grass again.

Sarah went quiet for a moment. Then:

"*Right.* Fanged rabbits. Give me a break!" and she half-turned to go in the dining hall.

He caught her arm and she spun around to face him with a lethal stare.

"You don't believe it? Okay—have you ever seen one up close? Have you ever tried to?"

Sarah slowly and deliberately unloosed his fingers, one by one and slipped her arm out of his grasp, looking thoughtful.

"Well, no. I mean they run away as soon as—"

"Of *course* they do," said Mark, conspiratorially. "You know why? *So you can't see their fangs!* They don't want anyone to find out they've got them. Not until it's too late."

Sarah shivered despite herself. Then she laughed again—but anyone who knew her would have thought her laughter sounded forced.

"What do you mean, '*until it's too late*'? What's *that* supposed to mean?"

He looked at her as though disbelieving she needed this explained to her.

"It's simple. People are used to seeing them and they ignore them. No one knows about their fangs. No one believes they're dangerous. They're just *rabbits!* No one suspects they could attack you at any moment—and they're pretty quick, too."

Sarah shook her head but the expression in her eyes was in conflict with this signal.

"But they won't allow themselves to be seen moving; they can't let their fangs show. You always have to look back at them when you're walking. That way they can't rush you—you keep looking at them and they have to stay where they are, crouching down and hiding their fangs. Otherwise—"

"Otherwise?" she breathed.

He looked at her scornfully.

"What do you think? They catch you."

"And then?" she whispered.

"They *eat* you."

Sarah shuddered.

Mark shrugged his shoulders.

"They get someone once in a while—someone who doesn't know better. Sometimes they find traces, sometimes they don't. But they don't get it—they never do. They just cover it up and hope it doesn't happen again."

"W—w—what do you mean?" Sarah asked, her voice barely audible.

Mark looked annoyed.

"What do you think happened to Darryl? Or Marcy? Or Anita? You don't see them around anymore, do you?"

She felt her face flush.

"They went PCS (transferred to another base)," she hissed, "Everyone knows that."

"*Sure* they did," agreed Mark, mockingly. "And has anyone heard from them afterward? Marcy was a good friend of yours, how long has it been since she's written you? Darryl and I were pretty close; I haven't heard from him in ages. You ask around you'll get the same story. But they didn't go PCS. They're gone. *And they won't be back.*"

Sarah stood at the doorway staring at Mark in shocked silence. He turned on his heel and walked into the dining hall without another word. Sarah stayed for a while, trying to calm the thoughts racing through her brain. She finally went into the dining hall, but couldn't help looking behind her at the mute, hunched shapes keeping close to the ground as the entry door shut behind her.

The normal roar and clatter of the interior revived her and she shook off the shadow temporarily clouding her mind. She looked around and saw Mark getting his food, walking out into the seating area. She turned away, hoping he didn't see her. She didn't want to talk to him again. But Mark did not appear to be looking for her and she didn't see him after that.

Served her portions, she grabbed some salad, her drinks, a brownie for dessert and flashed her meal card at the cashier who waved her through with a bored expression. Stepping out into the seating area, nervously looking around to see where Mark was, she caught a glimpse of Melissa, sitting with some friends from work. They waved her over and she walked to their table, a grateful smile on her face, sank into a chair and forgot about her strange conversation earlier.

"See you got a new boyfriend," remarked one of them, teasingly.

Sarah colored up.

"What're you talking about?" she snapped, defensively.

"We saw you walking here with him. Is it *love?*"

"In his dreams," she retorted.

"But you two looked so *good* together," her friend continued with a malicious smile.

Sarah made a gagging noise.

"I'll never be *that* desperate."

They laughed, Sarah joining in.

They chatted about nothing in particular—events at work; the usual lack of reliable equipment; the idiocy of some of the decisions made by their sergeants and officers, the deplorable lack of desirable males and those endless details of personal lives always kept so secret but revealed so freely. She found herself laughing and smiling, feeling much better than she had when she first came in.

It was later, during one of the rare pauses in the conversation, a thought occurred to Sarah and she addressed Melissa.

"Hey, 'Lissa. Have you heard from Marcy at all?"

Melissa looked at her, her drink halfway to her mouth.

"No. Have you?" and she swallowed some of her drink.

"No," admitted Sarah, "How about Darryl?"

Melissa's face went a little cold and she stared straight ahead.

"Not a word," she ground out, placing her glass on the table.

Sarah's face filled with dismay.

"*Nothing?*" she responded in amazement. "But—but—but you two were so *close.* I mean he *proposed*, didn't he?"

Melissa stared straight ahead, her jaw muscles clenched and her eyes starting to blink rapidly.

"Yeah he did, but I guess he wasn't serious. He never replied to my letters and his phone is disconnected—" she stood up quickly, gathered her dishes from the table and race-walked over to the busing area. She left the dining hall wiping her eyes as she opened the door.

"Oh—my," Sarah gasped and she sat back in her chair. She was pained she had upset her friend so badly and even more dismayed at the news of her break-up. She was still trying to recover her thoughts when another voice from the table broke in and she started.

"Speaking of friends," it was the girl sitting opposite her, "Have you heard from Anita at all?"

Sarah was forced to shake her head.

"No. But, I mean, she's only been gone for—"

The girl shook her head in turn and started to gather her dishes.

"She's been gone a *month*. Darryl's been gone for nearly two. You'd think we'd hear *something* from them by now. My best friend went PCS to Germany and she promised she'd stay in touch. That was three months ago and I've heard nothing. It's like all those people walked out the main gate and never looked back," and she took her dishes to the busing area and left.

Sarah sat at her table alone for a long time in sadness. Her coffee went cold and she listlessly got up to refill it. She sat and reflected, trying to make sense out of her disjointed thoughts—but she couldn't catch hold of anything. On her third refill of coffee, she realized the dishwashing crew was going around to the tables, recovering any remaining dishes. Chairs were turned over and put on counters; vacuum cleaners started up; the gates to the serving area rattled shut.

The dining hall was closing.

With a sigh, she drained her coffee and absently handed it to the dishwasher who passed by her table. She stood up, stretched and looked around the dining hall. She'd forgotten about Mark until then. At first, she was afraid she'd seen him—but he wasn't there. Only a few people remained at the tables and none of them looked familiar. She sighed, stretched again, walked to the exit door and left the building. The door shut behind her with a deliberate, loud click.

She was locked out.

It was dark. The sun had gone down but the sky was backlit with a deep, dark, purple overlay. The night breeze was just beginning to puff lightly through the grass but the heat rose from the ground as before; the air was still stuffy. Sighing again, she ran her fingers through her hair and started walking back to the dorm.

She was maybe a quarter of the way across the field when she felt something tingle at the base of her neck—a shiver—and she whirled around and looked behind her.

They were there—they were always there. The rabbits. The hunched, crouching, mounds, barely visible in the fading light, grazing as usual.

She smiled and shook her hair and turned back toward the dorm.

Without knowing why she did it, she abruptly turned around after a few steps; her eyes widened and she caught her breath.

The rabbits were still there—as always. What made her gasp and her heart start pounding was they had moved. *They were closer.*

She angrily tossed her head and turned around, forcing herself to ignore her feelings, but she couldn't stop herself from looking around the field to see if anyone else was outside. She wasn't *afraid* of course; she just wanted to talk to someone, to—

Again, she whipped around and this time let out a little cry of terror.

They were even *closer.* She could see their eyes—for a moment, it seemed they all looked in her direction at the same time without turning their heads, their eyes gleaming red. Then they vanished from sight as they crouched down again in the growing darkness.

The night deepened.

"Oh—Gawd," she said to herself, in a barely audible voice. She was shaking. She looked around her again. She was halfway between the dining hall and the dorm. With the dining hall locked and no one else in the field, the only refuge for her was the dorm.

And they were still with her.

She started walking again, her knees nearly giving out from under her; again she turned around and again they had moved, always closer. She turned around yet again and they were even nearer. They were close enough by now she could see their features clearly: the gleam of their cruel eyes, muscles tensed and ears flattened, staring at her fixedly...what were those things just barely visible below their jaws? They *couldn't* be...

Terrified, she screamed and broke into a run, clattering down the sidewalk in a blind panic. Sobbing, her eyes filled with tears, her breathing painful, frightened, trying to ignore the growing sounds of pattering feet behind her, steeling herself to feel their claws slashing as they sprang upon her, the sting of fangs sinking deep into her flesh, the tearing, the rending, the pain, the desperate useless struggles...

She reached the dormitory, ripped open the door, flew through it, slammed it shut behind her and leaned back against it, breathing hard, tears in her eyes, trembling violently. Mentally she knew she was safe but her body refused to accept that fact and she continued leaning against the door, trying desperately to calm the pulsing of her blood, the pounding in her head.

At last, she managed to push herself off the door and walked unsteadily across the lobby to her hallway. As she turned the corner she saw a flash of killer blue—but this time she couldn't stop and crashed into Mark, falling into his arms as she closed hers instinctively to protect herself. Surprised, he tried to move back but he wound up pulling her closer instead. She pulled away in turn and threw them both off balance. They crashed to the floor entangled in a clutching embrace, struggling to get free of each other.

They finally separated and looked at each other; Sarah, scrambling to her feet with a flushed, tear-stained, face, her breathing ragged, still trembling; Mark, rising as far as his knees, with a similar expression. Conflicting emotions chased themselves across his face; he was dazed from the wonderful feel of her soft body in his arms and frightened by what he saw in her face.

They only stayed like that for a moment.

Then her face flushed dark and she lunged at him in a fury.

"*You son of a bitch!*" she screamed, slapping him so hard he fell against the wall and slumped to the floor. Bursting into tears, she ran down the hall, up the stairs and into her room where she collapsed sobbing with her face buried in her pillow, not bothering to close the door behind her.

Mark, dazed and angry, watched her departure with disbelief in his eyes, struggled to his feet, rubbed his face and shook himself angrily like a soaking-wet dog.

"Bitch!" he muttered to himself and continued scowling down the hallway.

Outside, the darkness complete, there was the faintest suggestion of a collective sigh of disappointment. It likely was just a trick of the wind blowing steadily across the field. The rabbits continued their endless grazing, crouching a little closer to the ground so their fangs could not be seen.

Trapped in Boirac's Coil

1st Spiral—Apogee

Rain. Relentless, unceasing, merciless rain. Pouring from a gloomy grey sky, framed by silent, dark sentinels of evergreen, pounding a never-ending tattoo on the roof of the car, gurgling into overworked storm drains, flooding the roadway, cold, wet…

I am driving along the Steilacoom road from Dupont. The beat of the raindrops, the roar of the defroster and the swish of the wipers are nothing compared to the deafening silence in the car. My jaws clench as I force my eyes to stare straight ahead. But I can still feel her sitting next to me, her face as grim as mine, her arms crossed over her breasts, her fingers drumming furiously.

As an oncoming car throws its spray onto the windshield, blinding me momentarily, she bares her fangs and hisses, "I can't believe we're doing this," and shakes her head.

I refuse to respond out loud to this statement, although I mutter, "I can't believe it either," under my breath. The forest closes in as the road bends sharply to the left, cutting through a forgotten corner of Fort Lewis—North Fort Lewis to be accurate. Even with the windows closed as tightly as we can make them, the water somehow manages to trickle through. There is already a faint coating on the floor mats and the door armrests are soaked. Raye shifts position and explodes in a profane rant as she unwittingly puts her sleeve in the pool forming along the edge of the window. Her hoodie sucks in the water like a giant wick and she angrily shakes her arm, glaring at me as though it's all my fault even though the car does not belong to us.

We plunge down the steep hill into Steilacoom proper in icy silence, the rain continuing without change. The rolling waters of Puget Sound almost immediately come into view—slate colored, perfectly matching the sky.

And our moods.

I waste a few minutes wondering if maybe there *is* something to those stories I've heard about Seasonal Affective Disorder when Raye gasps involuntarily and wordlessly points to the left. I nod my head grimly: far across the water sprawls McNeil Island Penitentiary—a concrete nightmare coated with paint in a color that reminds one of butterscotch. *Or diarrhea,* I glower, as my thoughts darken to match the image before me.

The speed limit slows to 30, then 25. Downtown Steilacoom, which claims to be the oldest settlement in Washington, has a wealth of restored houses and little shops. It has a small-town feeling that has long since vanished from similar places up and down the Sound. Perhaps this is because Steilacoom does not have the specter of unemployment and shuttered industries hanging over it—although such things exist here, they are hidden from the casual tourist.

The beauty of the downtown is lost on us. We do not see the buildings or the neat little café at the landing.

I make the right turn onto Starling Street and pass through the main part of the town, its beautiful houses—both modern and restored—climbing the steep hills above. The scenery vanishes as we plunge into the dark woods and turn away from the Sound.

We traverse the valley, climb to the top and emerge from the woods as we pass the turn-off for Oakbrook—a subdivision whose winding streets are notoriously confusing. Taxi dispatchers refuse to send someone to that locale at night unless the driver has been there before during the day. On my own ventures into that labyrinth, I always managed to make my way out with no blundering but it wasn't easy.

We get to the traffic light. The name of the road is now Steilacoom Boulevard. On the right is a large park—mostly a blank grassy field huddled under the shadow of a cliff directly behind it. A few pathetic picnic tables and a play area—all deserted in the never-ending deluge still falling from the sky. Both of us shudder involuntarily as the building on the left comes into view: Western State Mental Hospital. The asylum, the snake pit, the grim facility that houses those exiled from society because of their behavior. The last stop for people who have lost touch with reality so far they'll never make it back—along with the criminals who cannot be held mentally responsible for their violence.

It actually isn't that frightening—simply a set of strait-laced brick buildings with no barred windows or other stereotyped icons visible. But the dark red mixed with the gloomy sky and pouring rain adds an extra touch of desolation so strong it's as though we're sucking it in through our skin. Terrible things happened to the inmates before the reforms of the 1950s. I force myself to drive straight ahead—ignoring everything but the road.

"Oh my Gawd!" gasps Raye, pointing at the same time with a shaking finger.

I'm more startled than I'd like to admit and my stomach is churning as I follow the line of her finger. Then it's *my* turn to go into shock.

"Is that...*Jerrod?*" I whisper hoarsely, not liking the possibility.

Raye's white face is confirmation enough.

"It's him," she states, coldly.

Jerrod: a bad name out of our past. In high school, he was notorious for his athletic prowess, his ability to seduce anything in panties— willing or not—and his bullying of those he considered inferior. When he got to his senior year, his arrogance was out of control. Everyone resented him and no one felt sorry when his whole life came crashing to the ground. I'm amazed he survived the prison sentence. I didn't think he'd last more than a few months behind bars.

But there he is, hunched over with a rake scraping up leaves in the rain with a poncho so full of holes he might as well have not bothered with it. His movements are jerky and shaky as he awkwardly gathers the leaves in his arms and flails them toward the garbage can. A few of them make it inside but most of them just blow back on to the ground. He either ignores this or just doesn't care—as long as he has something to do, I suppose...

As we come up to him, he suddenly raises his head and stares straight into our eyes. We both make a sort of choking sound. Despite the grey overtones outside, his eyes are blazing—almost glowing— stabbing us straight to the heart with their intensity. Grief? Anger? Sorrow? No—the curl of his lip and the snicker I see him spit out shows only one emotion: *contempt.* The only thing missing is the middle finger. He continues to stare at us as we get closer.

He's expecting us to just drive on, I think to myself, fighting a feeling of shame for refusing to recognize him with even a wave. The sneer on his face grows nastier as we draw up alongside him, his eyes following our passage.

Fuck this!

"What are you *doing?*" cries Raye in horror as I slam into the curb, screech to a halt and yank on the parking brake.

What am I doing? I don't know—but something in me is perversely refusing to do what Jerrod knows we are going to do. It's like he's telling *me* what to do.

The look on his face as we halt is worth it—for a moment he is at a loss and uncertain. But he quickly recovers and when both of us slowly get up out of the car, shut the doors and begin walking back to him, I'm not so sure who is leading and following. He laughs shortly.

"What are you doing here, Jerrod?" I ask—I have to say *something*.

He doesn't look any better up close—pale, haggard, wheezing, snot running down his nose, red eyes and filthy skin, blackened nails, his face a black mask of stubble. His breath and body exude a poisonous stench that grips your nose and stomach with iron claws. Prison time and life on the streets can do terrible things to a person—even if we never were friends, it's harsh to see someone you know after they've fallen that far.

He grits what teeth he has in a tight grimace, sucks in his breath with a harsh sound and answers my question.

"Having fun watching assholes go by," he replies.

It's obvious we're included in that description.

I shake my head sadly—not willing to take the bait at this point.

"Probably better than staring at bars and guards all day," I fling back.

He draws himself back in mock anger—then snickers again, an ugly sound.

"Yeah—but at least there aren't any stuck-up pansies in there to deal with. Fucking bullshitters who strut their goody-two-shoes faces there get shut down pretty quick. It's kind of fun to watch—especially when I think of it being *you.*"

I still refuse to take the bait.

"It sounds to me like you're going to be able to enjoy that pleasure again soon with *that* attitude," and I start to walk away.

"Haven't you got anything to say to me, Raye honey?" he says in a heavily mocking voice, ignoring me for the moment. "I don't recall you being so cold the last time I held you in my arms."

Raye flares from frozen to boiling in less than two seconds. Jerrod can't help himself: he straightens up and moves back a pace.

"Guess your memory is about as good as your dick Jerrod—fucking useless," Raye spits out.

He quickly recovers and deliberately sticks his tongue out with an exaggerated licking motion. Raye gags and turns away. I follow.

"What's the matter?" I hear behind me. "Can't take it?"

I turn back around.

"We haven't got time to waste on you. If you got nothing to say then we're out of here."

"Awww," he says, the sarcasm heavy in his voice, "I thought we were friends."

"If this is how you treat your friends I'd rather be your enemy," I shoot back.

"Don't you worry, Dirk," he continues with oddly strong confidence, "I got *all* kinds of friends."

Even as he says it, I hear a shriek of terror from Raye. I'm not too far behind imitating her. From the other side of the garbage can, a shape rises—a shape I thought I would never see again: *Her.* What on earth is She doing here—and with *him?* Unlike Her follower, She hasn't changed at all: the deadly white skin, glaring eyes, fangs, claws—and that cold stare that freezes you from the inside out. She looks at me and flares Her nostrils but I return Her stare until She finally drops Her eyes. The power is still with me.

It isn't until then I realize something else: *Raye can see Her too.* Not sure what that means at this point.

"Oh, of course," Jerrod nods his head, "Of *course.* Dirk and Raye can't waste time with an old friend—they're too busy to waste time with *anyone* except themselves. Far be it from them to pull their heads out of their selfishness and think about other people."

Jerrod doesn't know how lucky he is. If I punched his face as hard as I'd like to right now, he'd never wake up. But he continues.

"Must be nice Dirk, you and Raye with your life together. Just what you always wanted isn't it? A lifetime of bliss with your perfect soul mate and nothing to spoil it for you," and he lowers his voice.

"But what about your *friends,* Dirk," and he comes down hard on the word *'friends.'*

"What about the people you supposedly care about? What happened to all that bullshit talk you used to spew about loyalty and trust and all that? It's dangerous to forget people who care about you Dirk—very dangerous. Especially when they're so far away—they could wind up getting in trouble and you wouldn't hear their cries for help. They'd scream and scream and you'd never hear them. But that doesn't matter to *you,* does it? You don't *want* to hear them."

She reaches his side and slips Her arm into his: he shudders despite himself but doesn't try to pull away. After a moment of silence, She tears open Her blouse and both of us stare in horror.

The names Trevon and Misty are carved in blood across Her chest.

With a grim smile, She closes Her blouse and turns away, walking off arm and arm with Jerrod.

Both of us are sick, sick and dizzy. I am disgusted—horrified that despite all my power I let Her in. She got through to me—and I didn't even have a chance to stop Her.

Raye and I look at each other wordlessly with frightened eyes. She takes my hand in hers and bends her head close.

"How long has it been since we've heard from Misty and Trevon?" she asks, a tremor in her voice.

I blush.

"I can't think—I don't know. I don't remember the last time we heard from them. I know we got that postcard in September—" but I stop, ashamed of myself. *My best friend—the one who stood by me in that ugly last year at school and I haven't thought about him or wondered about him for almost six months.*

Jerrod's taunting words echo through my head and burn painfully in my stomach: 'They'd scream and scream and you'd never hear them. But that doesn't matter to *you*, does it? You don't *want* to hear them.'

I can hear them now.

1st Spiral—Perigee

The City of Seattle is a depressing place. Even the full sunlight and heat of the summer cannot drive the shadow away. It lingers like the stench in a dog run. It is crowded with unhappy and impatient people who clog the narrow streets and sidewalks. Even a short visit leaves me in a bad mood.

The rain does not let up as we travel northward. We follow the eastward swing of the freeway through Fife, up the Hogback to Midway and down into the Duwamish valley where the city proper begins. We crawl under the convention center, limp along the side of Capitol Hill and finally, after crossing the high bridge over Lake Union, leave the freeway at 45th Street.

I find myself saying repeatedly: *I cannot believe we're here.* It sounds like the same litany I used earlier but the mood is very different. Raye has a worried look on her face that probably matches mine. She leans forward in her seat, as if that might make us get there faster. It takes forever.

After taking twenty minutes to crawl two blocks, I find myself homesick for the casual pace of Shelton, nearly two hours away from this nightmare. We reach the corner of 11th Avenue, turn left and roll to the north toward 65th Street.

Raye is drumming her fingers anxiously. I'm singing the same song—I'm surprised the steering wheel doesn't have holes by now; I'm gripping it so tight. The numbered streets slowly slip by: 47th, 50th, 62nd and finally, 65th. I turn right and then right again two blocks later. The street I'm on now is so narrow I'm forced to drive down the center—otherwise I might hit the parked cars that line the sidewalks.

As I try to keep the car from disaster and watch out for oncoming traffic, Raye is looking around outside to see if she can pick out their apartment building. She spots it just as I recognize it from the photograph. Now the only trick is to be able to park.

There is no break in the line of parked cars—and up ahead it looks like we'll be shortly running out of road—a dead end. At the last possible second, two blocks past, there is a space just before the red lines of a fire zone I might be able to squeeze in. After a few tries I manage to do it but I hope the guy behind me isn't in a hurry to leave—I'm forced to block him in.

Raye jumps out into the rain and starts running back up the street. I follow her and catch up just as we reach the apartment house. It isn't really an apartment house, now that I can see it clearly. It's an older house cut up into apartments. For the student trade from the nearby university, no doubt.

The rain has already soaked us to the skin as we reach the base of the house. We look at the room numbers on the doors—the one we're looking for is 28 and none of the numbers are higher than 13. I waste a couple of minutes venting and then Raye pulls my arm and points to a stairway I hadn't noticed before. We start climbing to the second floor.

The stairway is wooden, the wood spongy and the paint mostly peeled off. Up close, the house seems very old with a musty smell like blankets left outside too long. The stairway feels like it gets narrower as we get closer to the top and I try to avoid looking down.

I had no idea I had vertigo.

We finally reach the top floor and stop for a moment, trying to catch our breath. The silence is starting to get to me. Since we turned onto this side street, there hasn't been a sound. No people. No cars. Even the apartments are quiet.

Quiet. That doesn't sound like Trevon and I feel like I'm afraid of something. *Why can't I hear the freeway traffic?*

The 'hallway' is an outside balcony that circles three sides of the house. We go to the left and pass 24, then 23. Since we obviously won't reach 28 this way, we turn around and go the other way. 28 is the apartment at the end of the balcony.

There is a picture window opening into their apartment right by the doorway. The curtains are up and we can see inside. It is dark and lifeless—no lights, nothing. A closer look and I find myself cold. The whole place is trashed: stuff thrown all over, chairs upside down, broken dishes on the floor, a serious mess. The same thought occurs to me and Raye and she pounds on the door. I look through the window but there is nothing moving inside.

I come up beside her while she's pounding again and press the doorbell. I can hear it through the wall but there still isn't any sign of life. For the hell of it, I reach down and grab the doorknob. To my surprise, it turns and the door slowly swings open with a long creaking sound.

Raye is paralyzed for the moment and so am I.

Then the smell hits us: a horrible nasty smell that reminds me of something I don't want to think about. Raye retches and I have trouble keeping myself from doing the same. We breathe some good air into our lungs from the edge of the balcony and rush inside.

The damage looks worse up close: it's like a gang of vandals broke in and just went ballistic. At the same time, I find myself thinking: *that can't be possible. Vandals would have also broken the windows.* All the windows are shut; none of the glass is shattered or missing.

Raye has gone into the back of the apartment and I nearly shoot through the roof when I hear her scream. It is loud enough to leave my ears ringing. You don't often hear a girl scream like that and I hope I never do again. I run to the back, tripping over all the junk and halt at the bathroom door.

Now I *am* sick. I grab my stomach and fall to the floor, retching and vomiting. *At least we know why it stinks in here and* as that thought crosses my mind, I throw up again.

I stagger to my feet and try to keep cool as I look inside the room. Raye is hugging the toilet, her arms shaking, tears pouring out of her eyes. I'm right there with her and I can feel my throat getting painful. But not because of Raye. It's because of the other things in the room: the naked bodies of Misty and Trevon sprawled in the bathtub like they were thrown in. I barely recognize them—their faces slashed to ribbons, the ugly gashes all over their bodies, Misty's sweet eyes ripped out of their sockets...

I can't look anymore.

I sort of stumble over to Raye, lift her up from the toilet and half drag, half carry her out to the balcony. She is crying hard and so am I. And instantly, like a brick hitting my face, the words come back as if Jerrod was speaking:

"They'd scream and scream and you'd never hear them. But that doesn't matter to you, *does it? You don't* want *to hear them."*

I think about those words, I think about how they must have screamed when it happened and I almost throw up again over the edge of the railing. The guilt is killing me: *if only we had done something different this wouldn't have happened.*

I've already whipped out my cell phone and punched in 911. I try to report this in a calm voice but I cannot finish my sentences without screaming. The dispatcher is annoyed and keeps shouting at me to calm down—but I can't help myself and just scream—loud enough to rip out my vocal cords.

I never hear any sirens. There is a sound of doors slamming; faint flickers of electric blue light flashing off the walls; and the thunder of the police storming up the stairs. They rush past us, into the apartment, go berserk when they find the bodies and I hear orders barked, radios crackling, and, finally, sirens. Louder and louder.

Out of the blue, I feel myself grabbed by the arms and slammed against the wall. I flash open my eyes and catch sight of a huge buff dude in a blue uniform looking at me like I'm a pile of maggot-infested dog shit. He backhands me one across the face and I just go numb with the pain. I hear something similar happening to Raye and she screams.

"Fucking scumbag!" I hear someone shouting.

I come back to life and I shake myself loose of the jerk holding me.

"What the fuck are you doing? *We* didn't do this! Those are our friends! We're the ones who called—" but a pair of heavy hands comes down hard on my shoulders. Before I know it, my arms are pulled behind my back and I feel cold steel as the handcuffs snap.

"Get these fuckers out of here!" I hear someone shout and I'm dragged down the stairs, limp and stunned, across the yard and thrown into the back seat of a police car. The door slams behind me. I look around but there is no sign of Raye and I feel tears coming into my eyes. I try to wipe them but my hands are cuffed. I struggle a bit and then sit back.

I don't like being helpless but there isn't anything I can do about it.

* * *

The police station appears. I'm yanked out of the car, dragged through the crowded lobby and down a long hallway. Everything echoes loudly off the stone walls. The lobby is full of people shouting, at the clerks, at each other, some of them in lines, some of them just standing around.

We come up to a door. With no warning, I'm thrown against the wall again, my head slamming against the concrete. I hear a moan and look over to my left. Raye is standing next to me, blood caked in her hair.

I writhe in the cuffs but, to my surprise, they are unlocked and my arms are loose. I flex them, trying to work the circulation back in. Raye touches me and we fall into each other's arms, clutching each other tightly.

There is a cough and I finally look up through my tears. There is a uniformed cop staring at me without really seeing me. At least that is what runs through my mind. He turns to another cop and I recognize the second one as the jerk who cuffed me. For a moment, I have thoughts of revenge but I somehow hold myself back. The two of them mumble to each other and finally they split up: the one who cuffed me goes through the door, the other one comes up to us.

"You two okay?" he asks with no sympathy in his voice.

Raye snuffles and nods her head. I say nothing.

"This way," orders the officer, motioning us to follow.

We follow him back down the hallway to the lobby, which is still a chaotic riot. He turns and steps into an open elevator. He punches for the third floor. The floors crawl by on the display and the doors finally open.

This time we find ourselves in a room full of desks, telephones, police officers and people who might be suspects. The room is ringed with offices, some of them with their doors open. The cop escorts us into a large one where an older police officer sits behind a desk and leaves us there.

"Why don't you two sit down?" growls the older officer.

My head is pounding, pain is shooting through me and I feel myself fighting a dizzy spell. Raye looks like she's feeling the same. We somehow manage to sit down in the two chairs he points out. Raye leans against me and holds my arm tightly; I flex my fingers and try to comfort her.

The officer looks at us for a moment, then picks up a huge pile of papers and starts reading them. This takes forever. As he keeps going through page after page, I have this weird feeling no matter how many pages he reads, the pile isn't getting any smaller. I start watching him closely to see if this is for real but he unexpectedly throws the papers down and looks right at me.

"You have anything to say?"

He sounds—*annoyed?*

I find my voice.

"About what?"

The police officer gives me an irritated look and replies, exaggerating his words, "About the *murders,*" and he looks at me as though I've said something wrong.

I reply in the same tone.

"All we know is we drove up here to visit our friends and we found them murdered in the bathroom. The door was unlocked when we got there."

He leans back in his chair with a scornful look in his eyes.

"So," he repeats, a little sarcastically, "You suddenly decided to drive all the way up from Shelton to see friends you haven't bothered to talk to for nearly three months and—"

"Wait a minute!" I interrupt in a sharp voice. He stops and looks at me.

"How did you know we came from Shelton?"

"Didn't you tell them already?" he replies, *a rather strange choice of words,* I find myself thinking.

"No one's asked us anything—not our names, nothing," and I know I'm starting to get an attitude.

A funny look comes across his face—*is he embarrassed?*—and he lowers his voice.

"Sorry, I forgot where I was. You keep messing me up."

I look over at Raye and she looks right back at me. We both are kind of weirded out.

"I don't get what you're saying," I find myself mouthing—the words sounding unnatural in my ears.

Now he leans forward with his elbows on his desk. I can't figure out what the look on his face means.

"I don't get it either."

He stands up.

"I can't believe they're dead," I hear Raye saying, "I just can't."

"I can't believe *any* of this is happening."

The police officer is smiling—*smiling?*

"You know *that's* not true—at least if you know *anything.*"

I stare at him and everything fades out.

2nd Spiral—Apogee

Rain. Relentless, unceasing, merciless rain. Pouring from a gloomy grey sky, framed by silent, dark sentinels of evergreen, pounding a never-ending tattoo on the roof of the car, gurgling into overworked storm drains, flooding the roadway, cold, wet…

I am driving along the Steilacoom road from Dupont. The beat of the raindrops, the roar of the defroster and the swish of the wipers are nothing compared to the deafening silence in the car. My jaws clench as I force my eyes to stare straight ahead. But I can still feel her sitting next to me, her face as grim as mine, her arms crossed over her breasts, her fingers drumming furiously.

As an oncoming car throws its spray onto the windshield, blinding me momentarily, she bares her fangs and hisses, "I can't believe we're doing this," and shakes her head.

I refuse to respond out loud to this statement, although I mutter, "I can't believe it either," under my breath. The forest closes in as the road bends sharply to the left, cutting through a forgotten corner of Fort Lewis—North Fort Lewis to be accurate. Even with the windows closed as tightly as we can make them, the water somehow manages to trickle through. There is already a faint coating on the floor mats and the door armrests are soaked. Raye shifts position and explodes in a profane rant as she unwittingly puts her sleeve in the pool forming along the edge of the window. Her hoodie sucks in the water like a giant wick and she angrily shakes her arm, glaring at me as though it's all my fault even though the car does not belong to us.

We plunge down the steep hill into Steilacoom proper in icy silence, the rain continuing without change. The rolling waters of Puget Sound almost immediately come into view—slate colored, perfectly matching the sky.

And our moods.

I waste a few minutes wondering if maybe there *is* something to those stories I've heard about Seasonal Affective Disorder when Raye gasps involuntarily and wordlessly points to the left. I nod my head grimly: far across the water sprawls McNeil Island Penitentiary—a concrete nightmare coated with paint in a color that reminds one of butterscotch. *Or diarrhea,* I glower, as my thoughts darken to match the image before me.

The speed limit slows to 30, then 25. Downtown Steilacoom, which claims to be the oldest settlement in Washington, has a wealth of restored houses and little shops. It has a small-town feeling that has long since vanished from similar places up and down the Sound. Perhaps this is because Steilacoom does not have the specter of unemployment and shuttered industries hanging over it—although such things exist here, they are hidden from the casual tourist.

The beauty of the downtown is lost on us. We do not see the buildings or the neat little café at the landing.

I make the right turn onto Starling Street and…

…and then, I begin to pay attention to an uncomfortable feeling that's been getting stronger and stronger for the last—*how many minutes? Hours?* I don't know—but I can't ignore it. I pull over to the curb and shut down the engine. The rain drums monotonously on the roof; we can hear the water gurgling in the gutters.

We turn and look at each other.

She has the same look on her face that I do.

"Raye?" I ask, almost whispering. "Didn't we just do this?"

She swallows and nods her head.

"Yeah—I think we did."

"Baby," I whisper to her as a strange thought comes to me. "Do you remember how we got here? I mean, do you remember anything about this morning?"

She shakes her head.

"No—I don't. I don't remember anything before—before we were driving," and now she *is* afraid. So am I—*because I can't remember* **anything** *about this morning either. I don't remember what I ate, starting the car, driving through Olympia—it's like my past is shrouded in fog. Grey fog.*

What really bothers me is I'm even having trouble remembering Shelton, what it looks like. I can't even picture our *house.*

This is getting a little too intense for me.

I look up from my thoughts just in time to see Jerrod swaggering down the sidewalk toward the car, with Her right alongside. He looks even cockier this time and something in his sneer sends shivers through me. He walks up to the window and waits. Waits for me to roll it down. I just stare at him.

When he figures out I'm not going to talk to him, his sneer widens into a smile and She starts tearing open Her blouse again. I can just see the beginning of the blood...

...and all of a sudden, I decide I really don't want to talk to this slimy creep after all. I turn on the ignition and burn rubber as I shoot back into traffic. Jerrod and his companion, with Her shirt half open, look at me with surprise—*but why is he still smiling like that?*

Behind me. I can hear him shouting, loud enough to hear through the window.

"Hey lover boy! Can you hear them *now?*"

* * *

The City of Seattle is a depressing place. Even the full sunlight and heat of the summer cannot drive the shadow away. It lingers like the stench in a dog run. It is crowded with unhappy and impatient people who clog the narrow streets and sidewalks. Even a short visit leaves me in a bad mood.

And—

"Raye!" I shout, suddenly focusing. She is already staring at me, her eyes wide, tightly gripping my arm. I'm right there with her.

"How did—how did we get here?"

But I already know the answer: she doesn't know. *And neither do I.*

Oh well, at least I don't have to waste time looking for the house—I know exactly where it is. As I park in the same spot as before, I can't help feeling if I had taken my feet off the gas and my hands off the wheel the car would have driven itself here anyway.

We sort of halfheartedly walk up to the house. Seeing those stairs— they look so steep—I don't really feel like climbing them again, dealing with the vertigo; and besides, then we'll have to go through the police scene. My head is already hurting in anticipation. And I really don't want to see the bodies again—*it's too harsh to see Misty like that...*

"Well?" she asks, one foot on the stairway, looking back at me.

I start at her voice—she derailed my train of thought. I clench my fist and slam it into my palm. "Screw this—we already know what's up there, let's go!" and she comes back down, walking toward me, worried.

"Dirk, what the hell is going on?" she whispers, clinging to me for a moment. It's been a while since I've held her close and it always feels so good. For a moment I'm fine—and everything's at peace.

Then I break free of her and start to run.

"Let's get out of here!" I shout back over my shoulder and she runs out of the yard, following me. Stupid move—I am running the wrong direction, toward the main road instead of the car. Even so, I don't turn around—the silence is starting to bug me and I have this need to hear some noise and see some people.

Was it really this far back to the main road? It's taking forever...

I need to stop making wishes without thinking about what I'm wishing for. I didn't like the silence but I sure didn't want to exchange it for sirens. They're getting closer and we both stop, breathing heavily, looking desperately at each other.

I pull her into this sort of passage between two houses and we flatten ourselves against the wall, out of sight. I see the police cars go flying by in a blur of flashing lights and squealing tires. When the sirens go silent, I start to step out.

Raye pulls me back sharply, terror in her eyes.

"Dirk!" she hisses. I turn back at her with my eyes blazing.

"What's the problem?" I hiss back.

"Dirk—why are the police here?"

I look at her like she's lost her mind.

"You know why—because Misty and Trevon were murdered—" and then I figure out what she's really trying to say and I run out of breath.

How did the police know to come to the apartment if I never called them in the first place?

"Come on!" I urge her, "We've got to get off this street and get to the main road," although I don't know why I say that. She still hesitates and I lose my temper. I reach out, grab her hand and cruelly pull her out onto the sidewalk. It's a wonder I don't break it off her arm. She shakes her hand free and rubs it, tears in her eyes.

Only then do I realize that I just did something unforgiveable. I am white with shame. *What have I done?*

"Oh my Gawd Raye—I didn't mean to hurt you," but the words are going sour in my mouth. I try to take her hand to kiss it but she snatches it away and backhands me across the face. It hurts but I stand to it.

"Do it again, baby," I croak, my voice hoarse, "I deserve it!"

She swings her hand again and then stops—her lip trembles and we both fall into each other's arms, our tears running down our faces. I finally gently take her hand in mine and kiss it, caressing it with my fingers.

"Surprise!" a voice shouts in my ear.

I jump so hard it's amazing I'm not airborne. *Where did they come from?* Their cars are here, the lights are going, the engines are running, the radio chatter—*how was it I didn't hear them approach?*

I start to go sullen—and then notice all of them are laughing. *No— not just laughing; they are going hysterical.* Two of them are falling on the ground, holding their ribs, laughing their heads off. All of them.

The *'arresting officer'* from before, the one who slammed my head, is in front of me, laughing with the rest—but then he looks at me strangely—*like his feelings were hurt.*

"What's wrong with you?" he asks, his voice genuinely concerned. "Did you get lost?"

I don't know what to say to this. I don't like what's going on. And I'm getting tired of not knowing why. I'm especially tired of being pushed around—it feels just like that. Figuring I might as well make it worthwhile, I sucker punch the officer in the jaw with my left hand and kick him in the crotch as he falls over. He goes down hard, in a painful crouch.

"Hey—hey—what are you *doing?*" I hear shouted around me from various voices—their laughter gone.

I look around, fist at the ready for the next enemy—but instead of enemies I see the policemen all backing away from me toward their cars, whispering to each other, not taking their eyes off me.

Are they afraid? What the hell—they've got guns. Why don't they shoot or something?

The officer I hit moans and staggers to his knees, then his feet. He's having trouble standing. He shakes his head and sees me. That look again—yes, he *is* hurt. His feelings are hurt. *Are those tears?*

"What did you do that for? You didn't have to do that!" I am speechless. He's sniveling just like a little kid in elementary school.

And then, crying hard, he runs to his car and takes off with squealing tires—just like the bully's victim fleeing the playground.

The other officers are watching me, nervously.

I look at Raye and she is just stunned, her face white. Part of it must be because she's never seen me do violence—*that's got to be scary for her.* It's just about as scary for me—*I can't believe I did that.*

Now the officers are leaning against their cars, looking at their watches, shrugging their shoulders. It's like they're bored.

I'm too tired to deal with this.

"All right," I start, turning toward them. They instantly come to attention. I walk over to the nearest car and open the back seat door. I hold the door open for Raye and start to slide in after her.

"Let's get this over with," I snap impatiently and they immediately break ranks, walk to their cars and leave, one by one. One of the officers comes over and slides into the driver's seat, shuts his door and starts the car.

He looks over his shoulder at me.

"Where are you supposed to go?" he asks.

What?

"The damn police station of course. What's wrong with you?" I growl at him.

He shakes his head and starts driving.

"There's nothing wrong with me," I hear him saying, "But for sure there something wrong with *you.*"

2nd Spiral—Perigee

The police station is crowded. *Well, that's no surprise. It was the same way last time.* But this time we walk in together without wearing handcuffs and no escort. It almost feels like I'm naked without them. It doesn't help that, although the same chaos is going on, I feel everyone is looking at us uncomfortably out of the corners of their eyes.

We just get to the elevators when a police officer stops us.

"You two—follow me. *Now!*" and he turns and motions us into an open elevator.

I toy for a minute with the idea of repeating the scene back at the street but I'm tired and I don't want to frighten Raye anymore. It's bad enough I hurt her wrist. *I will never do that again.*

That reminds me—I recall I punched an officer in the jaw. Hard enough to knock him off his feet. *Why doesn't my hand hurt? Where are the bruises?*

The elevator halts at the third floor and once again we thread our way through the crowded room to the Interrogator. I don't know what else to call him—I'm getting tired of just saying *'officer'* all the time. However, this time he isn't alone. The police officer I punched in the street is there too—still sniffling, standing next to the Interrogator. For some reason his tear-stained face grates on my nerves and I am glad when he turns away, refusing to look in my eyes.

"Why don't you two sit down?" the Interrogator growls.

I shake my head.

"I'm going to stand," I challenge.

"See what I mean?" the voice of the other officer breaks in. "He isn't playing fair!"

"Shut up!" the Interrogator barks harshly.

Playing fair? This isn't a game, is it?

"What did you have to hit him for?" the Interrogator asks me.

I shrug my shoulders like I really don't care.

"He didn't have to hit *me* last time—I guess I wanted him to know how it felt."

"I hit you because it was in the script!" the outraged voice of the officer shrieks. "It's *your* fault I hit you! *You* wrote it in—" but the Interrogator actually smacks him one across the back of the head and pushes him hurriedly out of the office.

"Take a break for Gawd's sake!" he shouts after him and, shaking his head, returns to the office.

Script?

"He's got a point, you know. It *was* in the script he backhand you—" but I don't have time for this.

"What script are you talking about? I didn't write a script!" I shout.

To my surprise, the Interrogator winces and looks around in alarm.

"Keep your voice down!" he whispers, urgently.

This has me totally confused now.

"I think *you* need a break, too," and he gets up from his desk, takes both of us by the arm and leads us across the big room to a metal door marked "ACCESS FORBIDDEN" in red letters on a white background. I'm a little concerned since this door is obviously on the outside wall. *Perhaps there's a fire escape or something?* There is a key-combination knob and he punches in some code. A buzzing noise sounds and he steps through, pulling us with him.

Now I'm even less sure about where we are.

Like I said, the way that door was placed it looked for all the world like it was on the outside wall. I was expecting to see a three-story drop behind it. But that's not what I'm seeing and I'm looking around just—confused.

The first thing that comes to mind is a locker room—I mean there are all these tall metal cabinets arranged along the wall with wooden benches running the whole length alongside. There are people either standing against the walls or resting on the benches. Some of them are napping, some of them are reading and some are just staring off into space, not moving.

It's funny—but I can't help feeling I know these people. They all look familiar—yet I can't place them.

The Interrogator, now that I take a good look at him, has that same cast to his face. I know he's a total stranger and yet—

"Oh Christ!" I hear him mutter in exasperation. From the far end of the room (which is so huge I can't see the end of it), I hear the whining voice of my victim, rattling on and on about not playing fair and it sounds like we're getting closer to him.

"Just what we needed," the Interrogator mumbles and shakes his head.

I finally see the officer in the distance, still talking non-stop and waving his arms. He's got someone else with him—a strange looking guy now that I can see him. He's wearing a white outfit—kind of like surgeons scrubs—and a green eyeshade hat just like an old-fashioned accountant. He has a clipboard in his hand and jots down notes, nodding his head.

Seeing the Interrogator, he stops writing and motions the officer to stay put. He walks up and I notice he also is wearing what looks like a pair of headphones around his neck but I'm not sure. I have a lot of trouble seeing him clearly.

"What's the problem?" asks the man, crisply.

The Interrogator shakes his head and points at me.

"This guy isn't following the script."

The man with the clipboard looks at me like I just punched his sister in the face. He's shocked.

"Why aren't you—" but, as I said, I'm kind of short on patience right now and I interrupt him.

"Who are *you*, first of all?"

I see the Interrogator shaking his head and the clipboard guy looking at me strangely.

"I'm the Area *Supervisor*," he answers, although there's something odd about the way he says it.

Having announced that piece of news, he just looks at me. I guess he feels he answered my question—and I suppose he has—but I can't help feeling there's something else behind the words he thinks I should be catching. But I'm not.

"What is this *'script'* everyone keeps talking about? I know nothing about it," I finally say when the silence gets boring.

"Well—usually we don't use a hard copy. I don't have one to lay my hands on," says the Supervisor earnestly, "But you should at least know the basic—"

"I don't," I snap.

If I was confused, the Supervisor is worse off.

"I *told* you," says the Interrogator.

"This—this is really strange," mutters the Supervisor and he looks over his clipboard as though expecting to find an explanation.

"There's something wrong," the Interrogator insists.

"There can't be," the Supervisor replies, "If there were it would show up here and we wouldn't be having this conversation."

The Interrogator shrugs his shoulders and looks back at me.

"If you need to take a break go ahead—although we usually don't allow it *here*. You need to get with the program or word might get back to the Master," but the Supervisor interrupts:

"The Master? No—the District Manager. Why would the Master get involved? That's pretty high up," but the Interrogator gives a snort of contempt and just sits down on one of the benches.

"He's certainly well on his way there," the Interrogator says, lying back on the bench.

"Anyway," continues the Supervisor, "You two need to play fair or I'll have to refer you. I've never had to do that—I don't *want* to have to do that," that last phrase he says to himself.

"Forget it!" the Interrogator growls as he stretches out on his back. "I'm telling you, he doesn't have a clue what you're talking about."

I'm losing interest in this out-of-body conversation—and once again, the room goes black.

3rd Spiral—Apogee

Rain. Relentless, unceasing, merciless rain. Pouring from a gloomy grey sky, framed by silent, dark sentinels of evergreen, pounding a never-ending tattoo on the roof of the car, gurgling into overworked storm drains, flooding the roadway, cold, wet...

I am driving along the Steilacoom road from Dupont. The beat of the raindrops, the roar of the defroster and the swish of the wipers are nothing compared to the deafening silence in the car. My jaws clench as I force my eyes to stare straight ahead. But I can still feel her sitting next to me, her face as grim as mine, her arms crossed over her breasts, her fingers drumming furiously.

As an oncoming car throws its spray onto the windshield, blinding me momentarily, she bares her fangs and hisses, "I can't believe we're doing this," and shakes her head.

I refuse to respond out loud to this statement, although I mutter, "I can't believe it either," under my breath. The forest closes in as the road bends sharply to the left, cutting through a forgotten corner of Fort Lewis—North Fort Lewis to be accurate. Even with the windows closed as tightly as we can make them, the water somehow manages to trickle through. There is already a faint coating on the floor mats and the door armrests are soaked. Raye shifts position and explodes in a profane rant as she unwittingly puts her sleeve in the pool forming along the edge of the window. Her hoodie sucks in the water like a giant wick and she angrily shakes her arm, glaring at me as though it's all my fault even though the car does not belong to us.

We plunge down the steep hill into Steilacoom proper in icy silence, the rain continuing without change. The rolling waters of Puget Sound almost immediately come into view—slate colored, perfectly matching the sky.

And our moods.

My mood especially. I realize what's going on and turn to Raye; she figures it out at the same time.

"Not again!"

For a moment, I'm tempted to turn the car around—*fuck the traffic behind me*—but that doesn't work does it? We always wind up going where we don't want to be anyway. Still, it is tempting and I find myself gripping the steering wheel tightly, knuckles going white, ready to make the move—

Well—let's not do that. Let's test our boundaries instead.

Raye gasps as I take both hands off the wheel, pull my legs up to the seat and wind up sitting on my knees. I catch a glimpse of my face in the mirror—it isn't pretty.

"Dirk! What are you *doing?*" she screams—loud enough to make me put my hands over my ears.

The car veers toward the edge of the road—and for a second I can feel my blood pressure skyrocketing, my head pounding as the adrenaline rush hits. A strange feeling comes over me—it's like watching a movie in slow motion. *Ultra slow motion.* I watch, detached, as we run off the edge of the road with a lurching crash, into the ditch and crunch to a dead stop. I can feel the seat belts strangling me for a moment and Raye's scream of fear and pain takes possession of my senses for what seems like forever. I can't help letting out a sound myself—*this wasn't supposed to hurt.* It feels like I'm spinning, dust flying everywhere, noises, tires squealing, metal screeching…

…and the movie goes back to normal motion, the dust vanishes, I'm painfully crushed against the steering wheel—hardly able to breathe. I struggle a little but I'm seriously pinned in—can't move a muscle. I go cold as I realize there isn't a sound from Raye. No breathing. No moaning. Nothing.

What a terrible way to find out my guess was wrong.

I thaw free of the deep-freeze I've plunged into and a hot tear drops out of my eye. But I can't even breathe enough to sob. My body goes limp as the pain begins to scream through me…

…and we are instantly standing on the sidewalk along Lafayette street in downtown Steilacoom, in front of the café, the car at the curb. Raye is standing next to me. She is white as a sheet, just staring at me. *She's still too frightened to be mad at me—but that won't last.*

I turn, wincing with anticipation but the pain is gone. I can breathe. Everything seems normal.

As I suspected, the car shows no signs of damage.

Raye starts to shake; the color is coming back into her face. I see the tears forming and her lip trembling and I quickly reach out and pull her close to me. We cling tightly for a few minutes.

Then she viciously pushes me away and I fall to the ground on my back. It jars me pretty hard, but I'm grinning inside—*it only took her five minutes to explode.*

I look up at her—she is really torked. Breathing hard, tears running down her face, fists clenched, with a look that would probably make an ice cap out of Waikiki beach.

"You stupid son of a bitch!" she screams at me. "What the fuck are you trying to do? *Kill us both?*"

I climb back to my feet. I walk toward her but she crosses her arms across her chest and turns away.

"Babe," I say and touch her back but she flings my hand off and turns away again.

I give her a few minutes and then start again.

"Baby, listen to me: I'm not trying to kill us. I'm trying to get us the hell out of here."

Silence. *Well, that's a good sign.*

"I just wanted to see what would happen if I let go of the wheel. I thought the car would drive itself—I didn't think we'd really crash. But we wound up here anyway, didn't we?"

I reach out and hold her from behind. She leans into me and swiftly turns around and all at once, we are kissing—deep kissing—totally into each other.

"Yo, Lover Boy!" a voice rudely cuts into my consciousness. "You coming or what? I haven't got all day!"

I angrily turn to Jerrod and give him the finger. *Petty of me I suppose but I'm about sick of this.*

I turn my back to him, take Raye's hand and we walk into the café. I turn around as the door shuts behind us—Jerrod and his familiar have vanished. I shrug my shoulders, not really sorry about it.

To my surprise there's someone actually working the counter—generic female type espresso jerk. I notice her lip piercings with a kind of horrified fascination.

"Yeah?" she asks, looking bored.

I am about to order when I remember I have no money with me—and I'm not low enough to ask Raye for money. I can feel my face reddening up as I turn on my heel and head for the door.

"Yo! Wait up dude!" the espresso jerk shouts. I turn around, my hand on the door.

"Whatcha dashing for?" she asks.

"No cash—left it at home," and, having said enough to make my point, I pull on the knob to open the door.

"Hey! It's okay—don't worry about it!" and I turn around, the surprise showing on my face. *This is a first for sure—a sympathetic espresso jerk?*

"Are you serious?" I ask, walking back toward the counter.

"Yeah," she says, "You can pay next time you come through," and with this, she breaks out in hysterical, stomach-shaking laughter. She's laughing so hard she actually falls on the floor, tears in her eyes.

What is so funny about this?

Wait a minute—where is Raye? I look up quickly and she's still standing at the counter, staring at the espresso jerk in disbelief.

Probably the same look I have on my face.

After about five minutes, the girl is still in the throes of her laughing jag. It's getting old.

Paying no attention to her, I come around the counter, find a cup and pour myself a cup of coffee. I look at Raye and raise my eyebrows.

She nods.

I pour one for her and hand it to her. I step out from behind the counter and we both hit the milk station. Then we collapse at one of the tables and drink our coffee without saying a word—the espresso jerk's laughter still in full swing.

Like a broken record.

It eventually occurs to me this has been going on for about fifteen minutes and I'm getting bored with it. I stand up, drain the cup empty and walk, heavily, back up to the counter, lean over it and stare coldly at the girl rolling around on the floor.

"You've made your point!" I don't exactly shout but my voice is ringing off the walls. She still keeps laughing.

"I wonder if she'll keep laughing if I throw some hot coffee on her?" I say out loud, actually looking at the pot.

Instantly she falls silent and stands up, looking at me warily. Something in her eyes tells me she's still laughing inside.

"I've made my point?" she repeats my words, softly, shaking her head.

"Maybe—but you aren't even close to getting it," and she stifles another giggle attack as she takes my empty cup to the sink.

It's a damn shame there aren't any cups on the counter—or she'd be getting the cup and *the hot coffee coming at her.*

I walk back to the table and look at Raye. She's finished her drink and is already standing up, looking very uncomfortable. Without another word, I take her hand and we walk outside of the café onto the sidewalk.

I'm not quite sure what to do next. I know what I *don't* want to do. Be damned if I'm getting into the car.

Raye is looking at me, the same question on her face.

"Let's just keep walking. See how far we get before something happens."

She looks troubled but we start walking along Lafayette, northbound from the café, the old restored houses lining each side of the street and hanging from their perches on the hill above.

We've gone maybe a block before I realize something's wrong. In another second, I figure it out: *where is everybody?*

It is deathly quiet, not a sound. No wind. No traffic. I look around—not a person in sight and not a car on the streets.

And this is Steilacoom in the morning on a weekday? Impossible! There should be trains on the tracks, waves crashing on the beach, people on the sidewalks—and traffic. *Lots* of traffic.

But there is nothing.

It starts to get a bit stuffy after a while. We are both breathing hard, sweating and exhausted. Like we've been swimming for hours against a stiff current or something. We've only gone a few blocks on a level street and it's like we've been going up a steep hill. A bench appears in the distance and we drag ourselves toward it and collapse.

"Dirk?" asks Raye in a small voice, afraid to break the silence.

"Yeah, babe?" I reply, putting an arm around her.

"We can't break out of this, can we?"

That was a surprise.

"What do you mean?" I ask her.

"I don't know," she says, uncertainly. "But I'm so tired—I feel like I've been walking for hours," and I nod my head wearily—I feel that way too.

"I wonder what would happen if we walked back? If it would be— you know—easier?"

I still don't get it—and then I do. *We're being pulled back to the car— and the further we try to get away the stronger the pull. We can't jump off the track.*

"I don't want to go back there," I say out loud, staring at the ground.

Her hand tightens in mine.

"I don't either. But I don't think I can go much further—it's so hard," and she leans her head against my shoulder. In a few minutes, she's out of it, snoring and snuggling against me.

The thought of going back, getting in the car, driving all the way up to Seattle is just too much for me to think about and I lean into her—ready to fall asleep myself. And then I violently pull myself up and shake my head.

Don't fall asleep you idiot!

I look around angrily but I know I can't hold out much longer. I'm in the grip of something stronger than myself—and I have no idea what it is. There must be someone watching all this—someone controlling it—but I see nothing. Silence. That's all there is.

*Well, I am **not** going to look at Misty's body again. No fucking way.*

I pick up my cell phone. Amazingly, there *is* service available—guess they missed that one—and I dial 911. Why not let *them* do some work for a change?

"911 Dispatch—what is your emergency?" the voice barks.

"Just come and get us—we're tired and don't feel like walking," and I end the call.

3rd Spiral—Perigee

I guess they came and got us—I don't remember. At any rate, we're here—back in the office.

The Interrogator stares at us, coldly, but also uncertainly. He runs his hand through his hair and breathes deeply for a minute. *I guess we're a challenge to deal with?*

"Look," he says, "Why are you screwing this up? You aren't making this easier for anyone—least of all yourself. I mean—*you* set this up. Why not follow your plan? This is just making it tough for everyone else—" and he stops, as if unsure of himself.

Then he looks at me directly.

"At least you didn't beat him up this time around—he almost didn't show up on stage," and he shakes his head.

On stage?

I casually stand up, walk up to his desk and then, suddenly furious, wipe my arms across the desk, taking everything movable over the edge. It's a satisfying sound as it all crashes to the floor. I deliberately stomp on the pen set and do some serious damage to a picture.

"Oh, Gawd!" he ejaculates and gets to his feet, losing patience at last.

He grabs both of us by the arm and hustles us to the doorway in the wall.

And we're back in the locker room. Everyone stops what they're doing—talking, reading, whatever—and look down at the floor, away from us. I can catch the expressions on their faces: they are tired. Exhausted. *And they aren't real happy with me.*

Fuck 'em.

The Supervisor appears again, writing in his clipboard as the Interrogator lists his grievances.

"I told you this guy doesn't get it—didn't I?" he spits out.

The Supervisor nods, soothingly.

"Yeah, yeah, I know. But—"

"But nothing!" and at his tone the Supervisor looks up at him, surprised.

"I'm tired—the whole damn crew is tired. We're sick of this. *We want to go on to something else!*"

The Supervisor flips through his clipboard.

It almost feels like they don't know I'm here.

The Supervisor looks up, as does the Interrogator, with exasperated glares.

"Oh we know you're *here* all right," the Supervisor says, shocking the hell out me when I realize they can read my thoughts, "We just don't understand why you're *doing* this."

"Doing what?" I shout out.

The Supervisor has difficulty keeping his temper but he answers me as though speaking to a wayward child.

"You're not following the script—and considering *you* wrote it—"

"I did not write any fucking script! **I don't have a clue what you're talking about!**" and this time I'm screaming. Everyone is looking at me, with—*fear?*—in their eyes. The Supervisor takes a step back, wide-eyed, clutching his clipboard to his chest like a shield. The Interrogator stares for a minute in disbelief, then shrugs his shoulders and collapses on the bench again to take his nap.

"I guess you're right," the Supervisor finally says. I think it's to the Interrogator but I'm not sure. He actually *looks* at me and Raye.

"Follow me," he says, resigned, jerking his head toward the back of the room. I figure we have nothing to lose so I take Raye's hand and we start walking down the length of the locker room. The Supervisor is shaking his head and muttering to himself the whole time.

"A referral," he keeps saying, "A referral. I can't believe I am making a referral," and he keeps walking, not even looking to see if we're behind him.

I suppose he'd know if we weren't without having to look.

It takes a *long* time to get to the end of the room—a very long time. Most of the other people in the room are stretched out on the benches and relaxing.

Taking naps?

"Well, what else would you expect them to do?" the Supervisor says, again breaking into my thoughts. "They have nothing to do between scenes," he adds. *What is* that *supposed to mean?*

We finally get to the very end of the room. There is another door—this one has a keypad *and* a combination lock. It looks pretty substantial—solid metal and all that—but at the same time, it seems...*impermanent?* It almost looks like you could just walk through it even though it's solid.

The Supervisor, busying himself with the locks, once again reads my mind.

"It does look kind of strange, doesn't it? But, you know, no matter what you *think* it looks like, that isn't what it really *is*. It doesn't look the same to everyone—it looks like what you *expect* it to look like—"

The door opens, swinging back soundlessly. I hesitate for a minute: *there is nothing but darkness beyond the threshold.* I snap a look at Raye and she is staring at it too—round eyed. *I don't want to go in there*—I feel myself digging in my heels—but the darkness sort of—how shall I say this?—*reaches out,* wraps itself around me and pulls me through the door with the sound of rushing winds—like I'm traveling over a hundred miles per hour—

I was wrong—it *isn't* dark in here, although I'm still having trouble seeing. I can't get a clear glimpse of anything—everything is blurred and run together. It's like I've lost control of my vision. I close my eyes for a minute and take a deep breath—and when I open them again, I nearly stop breathing.

It is a long, long, endless hallway—like a platform at a railway station. Actually, like *several* platforms at a railway station. There are no windows—the walls, floor and ceiling are unpainted grey concrete. There are banks of cold, shielded incandescent lights hanging from the ceiling in rows that run up and down the length of the platforms—the shields are glass, reinforced with steel bars. There is a yellow line running right underneath each row of lights. And on each side of the line are rectangles, huge rectangles, outlined in yellow. The rectangles are marked at three of their corners with bright orange stanchions linked with yellow rope. They are open at the end that parallels the yellow line.

Each rectangle contains cardboard boxes, neatly stacked, with nothing indicating their contents. Some of them have what might be packing slips in plastic sleeves but I'm not sure from this far away.

There are rectangular signs next to the open edge, attached to a stanchion at one of the corners. I'm standing next to one of these and I stare at the letters—not understanding them:

Chalk XVD1477S5
AS Kandle

There is another line underneath that last one but I can't make it out.

"Step off the chalk!" a crisp voice breaks the silence and we both simultaneously step out of the yellow rectangle and stand on the yellow line. I notice a sign hung from the lights, yellow on black, informing us we are standing on row 94E991. I can see similar signs on the other rows of lights—row 94E992 is to our right, 94E990 is to our left.

"Well, Mr. Kandle?" says the voice.

I look around but I cannot see anyone else in the room besides us.

"I have to refer these two," says another voice—but I recognize this one—it's the Supervisor.

Wasn't the name 'Kandle' on that sign?

"What's wrong?" asks the first voice—at least I *think* it's asking. It doesn't sound like it has an expression.

"Failure to track, sabotaging the script, attempting to trash the set," says the Supervisor in a quavering voice, "But—I didn't mean to bring this direct to you. I was going to take it to the District Manager—" but the other voice cuts in.

"I intercepted and diverted you here. It would have come to me anyway."

"I—I see."

If I didn't know better—I would swear the Supervisor is *afraid* of this other person.

Where is he?

"Hmmm," says the first voice and there is a sound of—pages turning? I'm starting to get a little freaked out, turning around and around trying to figure out where the voices are coming from.

"Oh!" says the Supervisor just as the first voice says, "See this? *That's* why."

"My goodness," the Supervisor says, in a hushed voice, as though in awe.

"What on earth are we going to do?" he asks, almost whispering.

"That's up to *him,*" says the first voice.

"I don't know if that's fair," the Supervisor says, half to himself. "I mean—he isn't really aware of what—" but the first voice cuts in coldly.

"He has the key—he's going to have to figure it out for himself. But he will. He just has to start doing his own thinking."

A pause.

"You can go, Kandle. Don't be so hard on yourself—this is a bit out of the ordinary."

I don't know why—but somehow, I know Kandle, the Supervisor, is no longer with us.

This is getting way too strange for me.

"What is going on?" I ask, my voice echoing off the concrete walls.

"Nothing, really," says the first voice. I frantically look around but still can't see the person speaking.

"Where are you?" I finally ask, starting to get a little frightened—and my voice shows it.

"You can't see me?" the voice asks.

"No!" I reply.

Raye's hand is starting to sweat. She's gripping me tightly.

"That's strange—I wonder why that is," the voice sounds puzzled. Then, "Oh—*I* see. Your mind is very unique—you don't have any preconceptions," and I shake my head, more puzzled than ever.

"Preconceptions?" I repeat, not understanding.

"Expectations," the voice says.

I still don't get it.

"Well—I don't expect you to get it. You're in a material sphere and can't see me in my—I guess you could say *'real'* form—but—" and then the voice stops for a moment.

"You wouldn't understand it even if I explained it," it finally says.

I believe it.

"I'll tell you who I am—or at least tell you what I might mean to you—you might be able to see me after that."

Now I'm *starting to sweat. What is this person talking about?*

"Who are you?" I ask, my voice getting smaller and smaller.

"I am the DreamMaster."

I jump—damn near out of my skin. *How was it I didn't see him before?* He was right in front of me all the time! A tall, sturdy old man with blazing eyes, white hair and a beard, dressed in some kind of white robe with a gold belt. He's holding a thick, gold tube or rod with a round thing at the top. The robe is almost too bright to look at.

"No," he says, shaking his head with a strange smile on his face, "I *wasn't* right in front of you the whole time. I'm not in front of you *now*. That's just how you choose to see me—" and again he stops himself.

"Never mind all that," he continues. "You cannot see me unless you have an idea of what I look like—a preconception," and, seeing the uselessness of explanations, just stops.

I think I know what he means. But I'll never understand it—I just have to accept it.

He nods.

"You get it—or get it enough anyway."

I look at Raye. She's deathly quiet, white to the lips.

I'm afraid too—but not in the same way. *Is it because I understand this person and she doesn't?* At least I feel comfortable asking questions.

"What is going on? What is this place? Who are you?"

He laughs.

"Who I am would make no sense to you—you would get the wrong idea if I tried to tell you. I am no more or less than I told you: the DreamMaster," and he nods his head to me. I can't help but do the same thing in return—bowing I guess it is.

Raye does not move.

"She cannot see me," the DreamMaster says in explanation.

"Can she hear you?" I ask.

"Yes," Raye says, in a very frightened voice.

"She will not hear me as you do. All I am doing is frightening her—I do not wish to," and I quickly put my arm around Raye reassuringly. She's trembling like a leaf.

"It's okay," I whisper to her. She quickly nods her head and buries it in my neck, clinging to me.

"You mind telling me what's going on?" I ask, stroking her hair.

"Well, I am, as I told you, the DreamMaster. I am responsible for all dreams, past present and future," and he waves his arms, indicating the huge hall around us.

"*All* the dreams?" I repeat, not really believing it.

"Oh yes," he replies, nodding his head.

"Each one of these rectangles in this hall is a dream—a dream created by a person's imagination. They write the script, we assemble the materials, put them on the chalks and then set their dream in motion. You can see they are endless," and I look up and down the hall, following his hands.

Is this what they meant by the script?

"That's impossible," I find myself saying.

"In a way you're right—it *is* impossible. But it's the only explanation that will make sense to you. It's the same way with how you see this room and me. There aren't *really* yellow lines and rectangles and signs and all that. The reality—if you want to call it that—is very different. But there is no way I can describe it to you. It is beyond your understanding. What you see around you is only the smallest part of what is really here."

I find myself shaken to the core with this speech—I understand the words but the words aren't what he is really trying to say. I'm not sure I *want* to know what he's trying to say. I *am* frightened.

Poor Raye! I can see why she's terrified.

"That doesn't explain what's going on," I finally say to him.

He nods again.

"Well—you are in a strange situation. You see, in your case and I don't know how this happened, you are not in control of what's going on."

My blank stare tells him I don't have a clue what he's talking about. He sighs and tries again.

"This isn't *your* dream. You've stumbled into someone else's dream. I don't know how, but you have. You don't know what the script is because you didn't write it. Take a look at the sign on your chalk: can you read the third line?"

"No," I hear myself saying, "I can't. It's blurred out or something."

"Well," the DreamMaster continues, "If this were *your* dream you would see your name on that line. But it isn't there. And," and here I start to shiver, "your name and your companion's name are not in the master listing. As I said, you're trapped in someone else's imagination and under *their* control. Unless they release you voluntarily—"

Now I *am* scared. Scared shitless.

"What do you mean, *'trapped in someone else's imagination?'* What's— whose imagination is this?"

The DreamMaster shakes his head.

"I do not know. I'm concerned because even *I* can't read the name on the sign. The only thing I know is you've stumbled into someone else's dream and your name is not on any of the other dreams in this hall."

This can't be happening.

"My name has got to be in here somewhere! It's got to be!" and I'm screaming now.

He gets a little stern at this.

"Why do you doubt my word? I should think you'd believe what I'm saying by now," a funny look comes into his eyes.

"However," he continues, "go ahead—search the chalks. Try to find your name. You won't be able to," he turns away and vanishes.

I'm not quite in panic mode yet but I'm getting close to it. I gently detach Raye and stroke her face—she is about on the edge of collapsing with fear and I know her sanity is strung to the breaking point. That's even *more* frightening than the other stuff going on.

"Raye," I whisper to her, "Can you read the third line on this sign?" and I point it out to her. For some reason, I have this strange feeling she can't see it—or can't see it the same way I do. But, her voice shaking, she quavers out:

"No, Dirk, I can't read it."

I look up and down the hall. There seems to be no end to the chalks—there must be thousands, millions of them—*can these really be all the dreams that will ever be?* There is no way I can search them all.

But I've got to try.

We spend hours—days—weeks—I have no idea how long; it's like there isn't any time in this hall. We walk up and down the rows—there seems to be no end to them—I never actually reach the walls even though I can see them. We never get less than one row away. We look at sign after sign after sign; but none of them are legible. I don't feel tired; I don't feel exhausted; I don't even feel hungry. We keep searching and still the nightmare shows no sign of ending.

"Dirk?" asks Raye unexpectedly. I stop and look at her.

"Yeah, babe?" I answer.

"Dirk, why can't we see any of the dreams? I mean, we can see the *signs*—why can't we see the dreams?"

From out of nowhere, the DreamMaster's voice sounds out.

"You can't see the dreams from *here*—that would take more mental power than you could handle. It would destroy you to try. But, believe me, you *don't* want to be able to see those dreams. You wouldn't be able to survive what you would see..." and the voice falls silent. He doesn't need to continue. *I'm* frightened at the thought of what those dreams might look like—

"It's okay Raye," I find myself saying, feeling her trembling violently. "We don't want to see those dreams anyway."

After a while, there is an unexpected change in the scenery. We are approaching what looks like the end—or one of the ends—of the hall. A blank gray concrete wall, just like the sidewalls and ceiling, cuts across the rows, blocking any further progress. However, the lights and the yellow lines keep going past it—there are little spaces at the top of the wall for the banks of lights to pass through; the yellow lines run straight to it without a break. It's obvious they continue on the other side. As we get closer, I can see doors—one door for each line with the line running right to the center of each doorway.

The doors don't look out of the ordinary—they are grey like the concrete, with ventilation louvers on their bottom halves. They have the same strange look the door coming in here had—that sort of solid but not solid feeling—but these don't have combination locks or keypads. It looks like you just turn the knob and walk through.

However, there is something about these doorways that—that—is just *scary*. It's weird because there isn't anything freaky about the doors by themselves. It's almost like something is slipping through the cracks or the louvers you sense—like a bad scent. The closer they get the more frightening it feels—and it isn't just an ordinary feeling of fear. This is the kind of fear where you fall to your knees screaming for mercy—a blind, crawling, mindless terror. Raye is starting to shake violently and I'm right with her. We keep pressing forward as though unable to stop ourselves, but our bodies are starting to ignore our minds: we can only go so much further before we're going to have to stop. No—not just stop. Turn and run. Flee.

All at once, Raye can't go any further and she halts, rooted to the spot. She's shaking so hard her teeth are rattling—there are tears in her eyes, her lips are trembling and she can barely breathe. I feel the same way as the doors get closer. I'm growing—*younger?* Younger—that's right. I'm morphing into a little boy, terrified of the dark—hiding under the blankets. I go as cold as ice as I watch my unwilling hand slowly reach out to the knob, my hair rising…

"No Dirk, *don't!*" I hear her cry but I can't stop myself—

Then she screams. And so do I.

A hand—a thin, bony hand, a huge claw, a horrifying skeleton hand, dripping with blood, pieces of rotting flesh peeling off it, is reaching out and grabs my wrist. Raye collapses on the ground; I turn around, feeling everything going black…

…and, all at once, there is the DreamMaster again and we're standing in front of our chalk. He releases my wrist and I notice, to my surprise, his hand is an ordinary hand. No claws. No bones.

I am shaking like a leaf. Raye is cowering on the ground.

"What—what was *that* all about?" I finally gasp, helping Raye to her feet. I'm still having trouble breathing. "What's on the other side of that wall?"

"Beyond that wall are the dreams of the Dead," says the DreamMaster and I shudder. I don't even want to *think* about what that might mean—it's a lot more than I can deal with.

"The dreams of the Dead are not for the living," he finishes.

"But," I quaver, "the doors were locked, weren't they?"

"No," says the DreamMaster sorrowfully, "They aren't. There is nothing stopping you from going through. But once you go through, you cannot return. Those who cross to the other side never can go back through the door. It's closed to them forever."

I am so tired. Weariness permeates my blood and I stagger.

"Stand back on the chalk," says the DreamMaster. And I drag poor Raye back with me.

Before the darkness takes over, I manage one last question.

"How do we get out of this?"

"You have the key," he says inexplicably, "You need to *think*."

And the darkness is complete.

4th Spiral—Apogee

Rain. Relentless, unceasing, merciless rain. Pouring from a gloomy grey sky, framed by silent, dark sentinels of evergreen, pounding a never-ending tattoo on the roof of the car, gurgling into overworked storm drains, flooding the roadway, cold, wet...

Not again. Enough. Fucking enough of this bullshit!

Raye already looks terrified—both because she recognizes what's going on and because of the look on my face. She tenses, white as a sheet and I hear her pleading voice:

"Dirk—please don't—it hurt so bad last time—"

Tears come into my eyes at the sound of her voice—but I'm not going to be stupid this time. I slam on the brakes and the car skids noisily to a stop. I manage to steer the car to the shoulder so we get off the road in one piece—without getting hit from behind.

As the screech of our tires dies away into silence, I hear Raye breathing softly and catch a faint, "Thank you, baby."

I don't say a word. I just fling the door open and so does she. The rain is pouring down in buckets—the shoulders are like a sea of mud and our shoes make a strange sucking sound as we slog through it. We're about to step out on the road when it occurs to me to check for traffic *before* we start crossing.

Sure enough—two cars, one from each direction, flash by—they must be doing at least a hundred—with a roar of noise and wind. Then—silence.

Absolute silence.

I take her hand and we dash across the road. It isn't until then I try to see where we are. The dark wall of evergreens on each side tells me we are in the middle of Fort Lewis (or, as they now call it, 'Joint Base Lewis McChord').

I hesitate. Walking along this part of the road is dangerous—no shoulders at all. Not that I care if we get hit—I know we'll survive—it's just it still hurts as though it really happened. A person can only take so much of that—and I'm not putting Raye through that bullshit again.

Walking back won't work—we tried that before, remember? That just wore us out. But plunging through the woods of the north Fort is not exactly for the timid either: they do training exercises here—often with weapons. True—they fire blanks, but anyone who thinks blanks can't hurt you should take a look what happens when you fire blanks at a pop can. Tears it up. *I would hate to be that can.*

Still, falling into the hands of the Army would be a nice change from the police. Might even be interesting.

I look back at Raye. She is nervous about plunging into the dark forest—I don't know if she knows how dangerous it is, or why—but I give her a reassuring look and she takes my hand, grips it tightly and we step into the forest.

Right away I figure out this is a bad idea. The rain manages to find its way underneath the needles and we are dripping wet after only five minutes. It is cold—and after the first few shivers, I sneeze. Then again—and it isn't a light sneeze either. Raye is starting to hold her arms to her sides, shivering.

I forgot this forest is pretty much as it was over two hundred years ago: tons of undergrowth, bushes, spider webs, deadfalls, tangles of brambles, slippery branches—all of it sopping wet and all of it sitting on top of a slimy layer of sucking mud.

We flounder through this for a while and finally reach a clear spot, breathing hard and leaning on each other. This place isn't much better though—the rain is pouring straight through the break in the trees, hitting us hard. There are a couple of concrete shelters—but the roofs leak and there's nowhere to sit that isn't covered with water.

She looks at me. She is too tired to deal with this. She is cold, shaking and fading out. I'm not upset with her—I can see my reflection in her eyes and I know I look the same way.

I'm too tired to deal with it too.

"Okay," I say, out loud, "I give up. I just want a cup of coffee or something before we keep going."

There isn't enough left in Raye to gasp as I feel warm—*and dry????*—with the sweet smell of coffee blowing through my nose. I don't even have to look to know where we are—the coffee shop again. The jerk is still working the counter and she still has the same teasing expression on her face—but she looks worried too.

"I guess you're right," I say to her, "I really *don't* have a clue what is going on."

The teasing vanishes from her eyes.

"I'm sorry. I wish I could help you out of this," and I see she looks…sad? *That* wasn't expected. But she shakes this off and waves us to a table.

"You two must be wretched tired. Have a seat—I'll bring you some coffees," and, with no fight left in either of us, we drag ourselves over to the table and sink down in the chairs.

When I get some strength, I finally look outside the window. There is no sign of Jerrod but I know, somehow, he's not far away.

Waiting for us.

Jerrod, I think to myself and instantly go hot—furious. This is *Jerrod. He's* the one fucking with us. That *bastard!*—I jump as I feel a hand on my shoulder, then relax as I hear the coffee cups hitting the table.

"Take your mind off that for now," says the jerk soothingly, "you need to take a break. Save that for later," she releases her hand from my shoulder and drifts back to the counter.

Raye sighs and drinks her coffee gratefully. I can't help doing the same. At least the coffee is good anyway. We both get calmer the more we drink—and the jerk gives us a couple of refills without asking—but we both are still tired—fucking exhausted. I look out of the window and—as I expected—Jerrod is standing in the parking lot below. Jerrod and *Her.*

I thought I was done with Her but it doesn't feel like I am. I wonder where I went wrong on that?

Well—no sense in putting it off.

"I guess we should go," I finally say and stand up slowly. Raye does the same and gives a long, drawn out yawn.

It's funny—I'm trapped in a dream and I can't get any sleep.

The jerk gives us a sympathetic look and waves us out the door. We stand on the sidewalk again—in that strange silence.

I know Jerrod is waiting for us in the parking lot; I know that's where the car is—but I just can't bring myself to go there. Raye says nothing but I can tell she doesn't want to either. We both just stand there for a minute.

Then, not knowing what else to do, I pull out the cell phone to call 911 for a ride. Maybe the Interrogator will take us to lunch or something.

I stare at the phone. "NO SERVICE." For a moment, I just freeze—stunned.

"Oh Gawd, Dirk," I hear Raye breathe as she looks at the phone in my hand.

'You are not in control of what's going on,' the DreamMaster's voice echoes in my head.

I'm *not?*

Then who is? *Jerrod?*

I feel rage instantly boil up inside of me and I damn near crush the phone in my hands as I thrust it back into my pocket. Raye looks at me, frightened at what she sees in my face.

"Dirk?" she quavers, but I break in, my voice cold and hard.

"The DreamMaster said I'm not in control of what's going on. They won't let me speed things up by calling the cops? Fine," and I look up the street.

The Victorian houses are only a block away.

"We'll see who's in control," and I break into a run, up the street toward the houses.

"Get back here!" a voice shouts out—it might be Jerrod—but I don't have time for him. I'm concentrating all of my energy to get to that first house. That's all it will take. *Get to that house,* I say over and over as I struggle forward. *Get to it!*

Yes—it is hard. I can feel myself slowing down—like the stream from a water cannon is smashing my chest—but that only makes my anger worse and I roar out like an animal. I push harder. *I am taking control,* I keep chanting. And the houses, slowly, painfully, get closer.

It wasn't any surprise She got a hold of Jerrod. But I never expected them to work *together.* I should have known though—he couldn't have done something like this on his own. I fucked up on that one—I didn't think he'd get over being terrified of Her.

Well—I have no use for either of them running my life. I am *not* going to surrender.

Two feet from the house—and I can't get any closer. Stopped right at the stairs going up to the door. I lunge forward and grip the rail tightly. I reach back with my other hand and feel Raye grab hold.

And now our bodies leave the ground until our feet stick straight out behind us, whipping around like flags in a hurricane. I keep listening for the wind—because it sure *feels* like we're caught in some kind of wind—but there's only the roaring silence. I have to keep tightening my hold because whatever force is trying to suck us backward is putting on more strength. We start to levitate again until we're almost facing the ground head on. My hand is starting to ache, muscles are cramping—I know I'm not going to be able to hold on much longer. My fingers will slip and we will go sailing backward and slam into something if we don't fall straight down and smash our faces into the ground.

I can feel Raye slipping out of my other hand and I squeeze tighter.

It's a struggle but I can hear her screaming out.

"Dirk! What the fuck is going on? What's happening?"

I can barely find the strength to answer. I have to shout—as loud as I can—even though it is still deathly quiet. Like I'm in a soundproof room.

"It's fucking Jerrod," I scream back. "Him and Her. They're fucking with us. *They're* doing this!"

I feel Raye's grip tighten on my hand—then her anger flares up and flashes through her hand into mine, continuing right up my arm to my brain like an electric shock.

"Fuck that asshole," I hear her roar at the same time—and with that last second boost of power we shoot up the stairs like we've snapped out of a rubber band, crashing into the door so hard it breaks open, slamming violently against the inside wall. It hurts like hell and we both fall over ourselves on the floor. But we instantly get untangled and scramble to our feet.

We haven't got much time.

I grab the door and slam it shut—Raye shooting the bolts as fast as she can. I don't know why—and I don't know why we *both* know this—but I know once that door shuts, we're out of danger. We've broken free.

For a moment.

I pull the cell phone out. Still "NO SERVICE." I fight the urge to throw it though the window and savagely cram it back in my pocket. I turn to Raye. *Excellent!* She isn't pale anymore. She is glowing with anger. Power.

That's what we need. *Power.*

"That son of a bitch," she keeps repeating, "I'm not playing games for him," and I grip her shoulder.

"Don't fall into that," I warn her. "We got stuff to do."

She glares at me for a moment—then lets it go.

"Come on!" I hurl over my shoulder as I run into the interior.

Is there a phone? Yes. Does it work? No—why should it? But I dial 911 anyway. Silence of course. But I go ahead and scream into the receiver, "Come and fucking get us or we trash the whole fucking city," and slam the phone down.

I already hear things breaking. Raye got the rolling pin from the kitchen and she is swinging it like a baseball demon. Antique glass, shelves, oil lamps, figurines, bell jars, clocks, snow-globes; anything she can hit is smashed to atoms. The look on her face frightens and thrills me at the same time. She isn't afraid anymore. And she isn't a wuss either—some of that stuff is solid, thick, glass and she's grinding it to powder with just one blow. *Good for her!*

Meantime, I've got two or three knives. They're razor sharp and I put them to use immediately. Tables made of antique wood? Forget it—they all are getting *deep* scratches. Carpet? Slashed to ribbons. Curtains? Where there are two, there will be at least six when I'm through.

We manage to get the first floor done pretty quickly. She starts working on the ornate wood railing on the stairway and I start adding my own artistic efforts to the oil paintings hung above the steps. I'm amazed those knives are still sharp. Then we both freeze as we hear the noise we were waiting for: running footsteps. Shouts. Thundering on to the porch. Pounding on the door.

Pound your fucking knuckles bloody.

I look around quickly. The bottle I'm looking for seems to be on the mantelpiece. I rush over and, yes, it is oil for the lamps. *Ah!* A bonus close by—a box of matches! I run back with them just as they manage to kick the door open. They freeze in the doorway as they see me finish pouring out the oil on the stair carpet and pull the matches out of their box.

"What are you *doing?*" someone shouts in horror.

"You guys fucking built the set," I shout back as I drop the match onto the carpet and the flames spring up, licking greedily at the wood of the stairway.

"You can fucking fix it," I finish. I grab Raye by the waist and we both vault off the stairway, which is now in flames. The crowd at the doorway screams with rage but they can't chase us through the growing wall of fire as we run toward the back of the house.

"Call the fucking cops you wimps!" I scream back at them. "I *dare* you!" and, reaching the back door, we rip it open and dash across the lawn to the next house.

Obviously *that* move wasn't expected either. We run into no kind of resistance and quickly reach the next house. I don't waste any fucking time on this one. We scoot around back to the shed. The door is locked but I just kick the thing in—Raye helping. We have it down in seconds. Just as I thought—I spy the gas can and grab it. It's full. *Nice of them.*

The crowd just manages to reach us as I finish pouring the gasoline all over the side of the house. They stare in disbelief as I throw a match to it and the walls instantly vanish in a sheet of roaring fire. Bad thing about those old houses. All that wood siding. Just like kindling.

The crowd isn't frightened anymore. They are getting angry. But for some reason they can't get to us—they can't stop us. We bolt from that house and this time head straight up the hill, vaulting over the fence into a maze of blackberries. I don't even feel the thorns as we push our way through and struggle toward the obnoxious modern glass and steel castle that sits at the top.

But we are too late. They are already there waiting. The crowd. Sullen. Angry. And no police.

I should probably be afraid but I'm not.

Who's in control now, Jerrod?

"Didn't you fuckers hear me? Call the police."

No response. They are glaring at us.

"Call the fucking police, you cowards," I repeat with a little more strength.

Still no response. I lose it.

"Call the police or I blow this house up where it stands!"

Raye gasps at that.

"Dirk—how?" but the crowd interrupts her in several shocked voices.

"You can't tell us what to do! You're out of line! You're breaking the rules! *You can't blow up that house!*" I don't even care to see who says this or listen to the rest.

They have a point. I'm not a wizard—I can't wave a wand at a house and make it blow up. I wouldn't know what to do with dynamite if I had any.

But I am in control now and I believe I can do it.

"Watch *this,* fuckers!" I spit out, pointing my finger straight at the house with a thrusting gesture.

When the explosion blows me and everyone else off their feet I don't know who is more surprised—them or me. It's a satisfying sight though—flames shooting out, the roar and the whole thing vanishing in a glowing red fireball with nothing left behind but ashes and smoke.

The crowd is silent now. They are picking themselves up off the ground and starting to back away. They are afraid of me. I scramble to my feet and start picking off houses up and down the street—all of them exploding spectacularly. The fires spread rapidly. I make a complete circle and realize the entire city of Steilacoom is burning to the ground.

Now *that's* why I call vandalism.

I turn and point my finger at the crowd—and someone screams out, "You win! The police are here!" and they bolt, vanishing down the flaming streets. The police come roaring up right on cue and step out of their cars to face us—although they are watching my finger (which is still extended) with a great deal of concern.

"We're here," a voice shouts out through a megaphone, "What do you want?"

I change my pointing finger into the bird and flip them off, laughing ferociously.

"Fuck you," I shout back. "We don't need *you* to get to Seattle."

And, just like that, we are there.

4th Spiral—Perigee

We stride through the station lobby yet again—but things are very different this time. The crowd panics at our approach and runs screaming from the building—tripping over themselves, scrambling in blind fear. I guess they've got cause—Raye still has the rolling pin in her hand and I've got one of the knives. It didn't help that she took some swings and contacted a few people before they figured us out. No one even came close to me—the knife is nasty looking.

It's worse on the third floor. I don't think I've ever seen people jump out of their chairs and over their desks before. Really noisy. I knock a few of the desks over myself and can't resist slashing some of the telephone lines.

The Interrogator slams his office door shut—he must have seen us coming—but it doesn't slow us down. Raye smashes the knob off the door just as I point my finger at it and we literally blow our way into the office. The impact knocks him on the floor; I can't see him at first through the dust and smoke. I start trashing his desk and throwing things around.

Bad move. I should have located him first. I feel a hand grab me from behind and both me and Raye are frozen in place. For a moment, we just hang there—breathing hard.

"You two," he finally growls out, "have stepped into some seriously deep shit. Who the hell do you think you are?" he roars but he recovers quickly and starts dragging us toward the door.

I only lose it for a moment. Then, remembering this is a dream and anything goes, I shake free of his grip, effortlessly vault him over my shoulders and now *we* are pushing *him* toward the door in the wall. Before he can recover, I hear myself saying:

"And who do you think *you* are? Stepping out of a doorway opening on a three-story drop? You suicidal or something?" and I reach out to the knob.

He is calm but I can feel his tension.

"You can't open that door. You don't have—"

I reach out, grab hold of the knob and wrench the door open with a nasty sound of grating metal. He instantly goes slack with terror.

"You're right," I agree. "I can't open *that* door. But I can open *this* one," and he starts to struggle. I can understand that. Instead of the locker room, we're looking at what should have been there to begin with: a nasty, three-story drop onto Third Avenue, which is full of traffic.

"You go first," I say with grim courtesy and start to push him through.

"No!" he screams out, but for some reason that only makes me angrier. I push harder. He fights back harder.

I don't know how it happens—but, all at once, we are all falling to our deaths together. The wind is rushing past my face, whipping my hair around and freezing me through my clothes. It's interesting. It doesn't feel like I'm falling. It feels more like I'm standing still and the buildings are moving upward.

I should be scared but I'm laughing. Laughing my head off. I look over at Raye—and she is doing the same thing. The Interrogator is screaming like a woman. The ground rushes up to meet us and I close my eyes. Yes, I know it will hurt. It will hurt like hell. But I just don't give a damn anymore.

My face smashes into the concrete. It hurts, but not as bad as I thought. But before I can relax, it happens again. And again. I find myself starting to wave my arms around, fighting back whatever is happening.

Now I am terrified. What is going on? I'm losing it, getting dizzy, screaming and yet...

"What the hell are you doing? *Stop it!*" a familiar voice breaks through the darkness and I instantly open my eyes.

I am staring into the Supervisor's face. He is trying to separate me from the Interrogator, who, still furious, raises his fist to smack me across the cheekbones again. I growl, he tenses, but the Supervisor violently pushes us apart and we both stare at each other.

"Take a break! Get the hell out of here! *Move it!*" screams the Supervisor.

The Interrogator looks at him, coldly. Then, silently, he slowly turns and walks down the rows of lockers, vanishing into the distance.

Fuck him anyway.

I try to turn and see if I can find Raye but my face is really hurting. I wince and moan. I reach out and a soft hand grips mine. Raye. She's okay. Good.

"I cannot believe you," the Supervisor says, disbelief in his face and voice. "What on earth drove you to *do* that? You've destroyed the set. You've got everyone worked up to the point they aren't going to play with you anymore. What are you thinking?"

"I'm thinking they'll have to fucking get over it," I snarl. "Like the man said, this isn't *my* dream. I can do whatever I want to. *You* all will just have to deal with it."

The Supervisor is shocked.

"Well there isn't any need to be an asshole about it!" he finally spits out, exasperated. "*We* didn't force you to come here either. We tried to make it easier for you. And you already *know* how to get out of it! You figured it out! But did you go? No—you had to stay here and fuck with everyone! That makes you just as bad as whoever got you into this!"

I hang my head at this. He's right. Then I look up at him, puzzled.

"What do you mean, *'I already know how to get out of it'?* I *don't* know how to get out of it. Do you think I'd still be here if I did?"

"*Jeeezas!*" the Supervisor looks as though he wants to backhand me himself. "You aren't thinking! You—" and he stops abruptly.

What does that look on his face mean? Did he say something he shouldn't?

I start to point my finger at him but he just sneers.

"*That* doesn't work *here*. This is a sterile area," and again he falls silent.

I thrust it at him anyway and he flinches but, of course, nothing happens.

"For someone who thinks they've taken control, you sure don't have any. You're not even *close* to being in control. You're still dancing on a string—even if you're too stupid to see it," and he just turns and walks off.

We are alone. No one is in the entire locker room except us.

Raye collapses into my arms and buries her face into my neck, sobbing her heart out. I try to comfort her and gently stroke her hair—but something is bothering me. *What did that last remark mean?*

Am I really in control? I thought I *was*—at least at first. And then I wasn't. When was that?

But I can't think. I'm way too tired.

I stagger toward one of the benches slump onto it, pulling Raye onto my lap and just hold her, feeling the wetness pour out of her sweet eyes.

Don't fall asleep! I keep saying to myself.

But it doesn't work.

Impact!

Rain. Relentless, unceasing, merciless rain. Pouring from a gloomy grey sky, framed by silent, dark sentinels of evergreen, pounding a never-ending tattoo on the roof of the car, gurgling into overworked storm drains, flooding the roadway, cold, wet...

I am driving along the Steilacoom road from Dupont. The beat of the raindrops, the roar of the defroster and the swish of the wipers are nothing compared to the deafening silence in the car. My jaws clench as I force my eyes to stare straight ahead. But I can still feel her sitting next to me, her face as grim as mine, her arms crossed over her breasts, her fingers drumming furiously.

As an oncoming car throws its spray onto the windshield, blinding me momentarily, she bares her fangs and hisses, "I can't believe we're doing this," and shakes her head.

I refuse to respond out loud to this statement, although I mutter, "I can't believe it either," under my breath.

I already know it's started over yet again. She knows it too. We both know we're trapped with no escape from this noose tightening around our necks. And we're both tired—we're both ready to admit defeat and surrender. An icy chill comes into my brain and starts freezing my thoughts.

"I can't believe this is happening," I mutter to myself.

And then *I get it.*

They're right—I *was* stupid. It *was* right there the whole time and I couldn't fucking see it. What an idiot.

I waste time on this for about two minutes. Then I turn to Raye—my eyes blazing and she just stares at me—amazed.

"No," I shout out, "That's wrong! '*I can't believe this is happening?*'" and I violently slam the brake to the floor, throw the transmission into park and even pull up the parking brake. Raye screams and we grind to a halt, stopped dead in our tracks.

"'*I can't believe this is happening,*'" I slowly repeat with a smile. Raye is watching my face—and all at once, a smile breaks out on hers too. *She knows.*

"Then," I say, slowly and deliberately, "***It's not.***"

Diana's Pact

Thursday

...the crowd is going wild. The Captain of the Reds has seized control of the ball and is rushing down court like lightning. The Wildcat defense is in hot pursuit but Kasly is untouchable. She shoots...

"Hey, Captain!"

She shook herself free of her daydream and glanced toward the voice. Her face wrinkled.

Maybe if I keep going she'll go away, flashed through her mind.

She continued running, her heart pounding, feet slamming into the ground, her breathing painful and her senses on overdrive. *Running. Coach said that's the key. If they can't catch you, the game is yours to control.*

She began her fourth lap, trying to keep her breathing regular, ignoring the painful glow in her legs and chest. *It's always like this at first,* she thought. *Just have to keep going.*

"Captain! Wait up a second!"

She's still here?

She glared at the owner of the voice. Somehow, she found the breath to shout out, "I'm busy!" and continued to her fifth lap. The pain was already numbing out and that strange euphoria—the *'runner's high'*—was beginning to pour through her bloodstream. She gritted her teeth and tightened the pace.

"Andy! I *gotta* talk to ya!"

Doesn't she get it?

Andy shook her head at the other woman's pleading face as she approached.

"I'm busy!" Andy snapped.

"But it's important!" wailed the other.

This will get rid of her for sure.

"I can't stop to talk. You want to tell me something, you gotta run with me!" Andy gasped out over her shoulder as she ran past.

That, she chuckled with a grin, *should take care of her.*

She started when she heard the sounds behind her: wheezing, laboured breathing; heavy footfalls; moaning...

She didn't! *Oh Gawd...*

She winced as something crashed heavily to the ground behind her and the noises ceased.

She kept going for a moment, out of either anger or denial and then, with a sigh, stopped and turned around, hoping her fears were unjustified.

No such luck.

The other woman was not standing by the track any longer. She lay flat on the ground; face down, her arms extended over her head, her fingers clawing into the track.

Andy looked around quickly. There was no one else in sight. She sighed.

Great.

She walked quickly over toward the other woman, her body glowing hotly from the aftershock of stopping, her heart pounding in her ears as she tried to keep her breathing under control. The pain returned full strength.

I am NOT doing CPR on this girl! she vowed, fiercely.

Reaching the other woman, Andy stooped down, took her by the shoulder and turned her over on her back. She quickly withdrew her hand, disgust flooding her face.

Oh Gawd!

She stared at the moisture dripping from her hand and shook it off as though it stung. She shuddered.

Nerving herself, she reached down, gingerly touched the woman's sweat-soaked neck and pressed in, gritting her teeth.

There was a steady pulse.

Andy shook her again. This time there was a moan.

She stood up quickly and ran over to a gym-bag lying at the edge of the track. Zipping it open, she pulled out a water bottle and dashed back to the unconscious woman. Trembling, she tore off the cap and squeezed the contents all over the woman's face.

A gasp. A shudder. Then a sob.

"Come on, Spivey!" she barked, sternly. "Wake up! Snap out of it!"

"Oh...Gawd..." mumbled Spivey.

"Come on! Get to your feet!"

Spivey flailed her limbs convulsively and half raised herself, then collapsed back to the ground.

Andy did not relent.

"Come on! Put on your big-girl panties! Get up!"

Andy reached out and gripped Spivey's shoulders. Spivey moaned again. Andy pulled her up as far as she could—then held her in place while Spivey scrambled to get her legs under her. Then, between the two of them, Spivey rose to her feet.

She shook as Andy let go of her and reached out a hand to steady herself. Andy looked at her contemptuously.

"Jeez, girlfriend, what's *wrong* with you? You seriously think you could *run* with me? Get *real!*"

Her face flushed crimson, the sweat pouring off her skin, her breath gasping, Spivey trembled and started to cry.

"Come on! Get over it!" snapped Andy, shaking her by the shoulders again.

Spivey wiped her eyes with her sleeve and stared at Andy for a few moments, snuffling.

"Don't look at me like that," warned Andy. "You did this to yourself. Quit giving me that *'why did you hurt me?'* stare!"

Spivey rubbed her eyes again, speaking in a subdued voice and staring at the ground. "I had to talk to you."

"It can wait," said Andy, firmly.

"No, it *can't!*" snarled Spivey sullenly, stomping her foot on the ground like a child in a tantrum.

"Okay, okay," said Andy, resignedly. Taking Spivey firmly by the arm, she walked her off the track and over to a bench nearby. Spivey collapsed on the seat and leaned forward, her head in her hands. Andy immediately began doing some leg stretches.

Last thing I need right now are cramping legs.

After a few minutes, with no response from Spivey, Andy gave a gasp of impatience. "Look—if it's *that* important you need to tell me. *Now.* I still got to finish my run." She stopped stretching, stood and crossed her arms over her chest, staring coldly at Spivey.

Spivey looked up, with tear-stained eyes.

"Well?" prodded Andy.

Spivey sunk her face back into her hands.

"I found out something you need to know," Spivey began, talking through her fingers.

"Okay," said Andy, straining hard to keep her temper in check. "What is it?"

"It's about Cara."

Andy stiffened slightly.

"Well?" she prodded again.

Spivey snuffled and looked up.

"Guess who she's going out with tomorrow night?"

Andy shrugged her shoulders indifferently but her jaw muscles clamped tight. It took her a few minutes to force them open. She tried to keep her voice calm.

"Get off it. Her parents never let her outside the house except for school," she stated.

Spivey grinned through her tears.

"She got permission this time."

"Who says so?"

"She does."

Andy still looked doubtful but with less assurance than before.

"Okay. So she's going out tomorrow night. Who's taking her?"

Spivey smiled faintly.

That's not a good sign.

"You'll never guess," said Spivey with a slight overtone of teasing.

"Just tell me, okay?" Andy snapped.

"Derek."

Surprise flooded Andy's face for a moment. Then anger. She was about to respond when her expression grew thoughtful, as though something disturbing occurred to her. The colour vanished from her face and her arms fell limply to her sides.

"Derek," repeated Andy, softly.

"Yup," giggled Spivey, enjoying herself, "Derek."

"That's impossible..." but Andy fell silent.

Spivey watched her closely, puzzled at what she saw in Andy's expression. Instead of the raw fury she had expected, she saw concern. Concern blended with a tinge of fear. Spivey was just about to call attention to this when Andy's face changed back to a blank mask.

"Well—it doesn't matter to me," Andy finally said and she resumed stretching.

"What do you mean, '*it doesn't matter*'?" sputtered a very surprised Spivey. "You and she—" but she stopped at the look on Andy's face.

"It doesn't matter," repeated Andy, firmly. "We're not together anymore."

Spivey's jaw hung open in stunned disbelief and amazement.

"When—since when?" she demanded.

Andy continued stretching with no sign of emotion.

"Three weeks ago," she said flatly.

Spivey looked confused.

"Is that all?" asked Andy, pointedly as she ended her stretches and stood up.

Spivey nodded, clearly disappointed in Andy's reaction.

"Okay," said Andy, "I'm outta here. And *you* had better take it easy walking back. At least try to do some stretches or your stuff is going to lock up pretty tight after a few hours. You won't be able to move."

Andy turned around and walked toward the track. She looked back for a moment toward the bench.

Spivey was struggling to her feet. It took a few tries. Andy watched with a mixture of pity and disgust as Spivey slowly shuffled back toward the main building, her excess weight shaking with a life of its own.

Gawd! That girl's lucky she didn't have a heart attack or something.

She stared straight ahead at the track and suddenly launched back into her run, debating whether to count this as the sixth lap or start over...

* * *

It was lunchtime and the Commons was full of students; some of them eating and some just relaxing before the afternoon classes began. It was a large room with a skylight, glowing in the afternoon sun. A separate glow came from the students themselves—the euphoria of knowing only two days lay between them and summer vacation. Enemies were making up and friends were reaffirming their alliances; the radiating joy and anticipation was nearly tangible enough to reach out and touch.

At one of the tables sat a group of friends, chatting sociably. They had long since finished eating and were taking advantage of the extra time to enjoy each other's company. There was nothing to distinguish them from the cliques at the other tables, except the focus of attention involved only one of them: a young man sitting apart from the others.

They weren't the only ones watching him. Other people in the room were either listening to him or else pointing him out to others. Some of them laughed with him; some were blushing shyly; some looked at him with contempt. And some of them looked at him with a mixture of disgust and horror—when they looked at him at all.

Their adulation wasn't surprising. He was an incredibly good-looking young man—although his build was slight rather than muscular. His perfectly chiseled face with hard blue eyes like amethysts, his words chosen carefully and gestures wrapped in the same aura of confident arrogance. His clothes matched his social position—it was interesting to note how many others mirrored his style in the room.

He paid very little attention to the people at the other tables and only occasionally acknowledged a passerby with a nod or smile. He was in that enviable role where everyone wanted him to be their friend—and what enemies he had kept their thoughts to themselves or at a distance.

Even without his presence, people would have still looked toward his table. The young woman who sat next to him was getting her own share of scrutiny—although in her case no one showed disapproval. It was more like amazement.

She was strikingly beautiful—but in a very different way than her male companion. Her appearance was only a small part of her impact; her clothes—simple and bright white—heightening her allure; her glowing eyes; her golden hair and porcelain skin were the perfection of beauty. At first glance, the sight of her literally took one's breath away. A second glance, however, disclosed something discordant in her bearing—flawing the purity of her sweetness with a faint bitterness that lingered in memory. It was impossible to pinpoint the reason for this second reaction—but it was there, beyond doubt.

She had eyes only for the young man at her side and either did not notice or did not care about the observation she was under. The young man, on the other hand, was basking in the heat of the spotlight shining on him. The sudden silence that fell in the room and the odd look in the young woman's face failed to register with him in time. It wasn't until a pair of hands landed heavily on his shoulders he realized something was wrong. Whoever it was clearly had social rank at least equal to his own; no one said a word of warning or caution.

After a moment's confusion, he turned around in his seat, shaking off the hands at the same time and found himself staring at a tall, young woman with a presence exuding an aura of strength and power far beyond his abilities to match. She was as beautiful as he was handsome and equally alluring as his companion—but there was not a hint of vulnerability in her. The respect she commanded clearly applied to him as well as the others: his voice was calm and quiet as he spoke to her.

"Yes, Andy?"

"We need to talk," said Andy, coldly.

"Well, have a seat," he said, grandly pointing out a chair at the table, "Let's talk."

"No witnesses," she snapped.

There was a brief moment of uncertainty. The woman sitting next to him patted his arm reassuringly and looked up at Andy with an amused expression Andy deliberately ignored. He stood up, made his excuses to his friends at the table and left them with a friendly wave and a smile. Andy, impassive as ever, turned around and walked toward the outside door without bothering to see if he followed. The conversations and noise in the room resumed before she left but his table remained silent.

His companion leaned back in her chair, a silent smile in her eyes as the young man straightened his clothes and followed Andy through the outside door.

It wasn't until they reached the parking lot that Andy abruptly turned around to face him. If he had not been watching closely, he would have slammed into her. He caught himself just in time.

He smiled, a little grimly. She had no expression.

"Derek, why do you want to kill Spivey?" she accused.

The surprise on his face was genuine.

"Kill Spivey?" he repeated.

"Yeah," she said, flatly. "She damn near killed herself this morning because of you."

He shook his head, puzzled and annoyed.

"I've got nothing to do with Spivey."

"Yeah—she isn't *your* type at all," agreed Andy. "But that's not the point. Why did you tell her you were going out with Cara tomorrow night?"

He looked confused at this.

"What's *that* got to do with anything?"

Andy snorted. "Give me a break! You know as well as I do and everyone else on this campus if you want to get a secret out, the quickest way is to tell Spivey not to tell anyone. When did you tell her?"

Taken off guard, he replied, "On the bus this morning."

Andy laughed, bitterly.

"Yeah—well, she couldn't wait until gym class to spread the word. She came over to the track and tried to chase me down during my run."

Derek had the grace to look shocked.

"That wasn't nice," continued Andy. "She's hardly in shape to go *walking* around the track—let alone run. I thought she was going to croak right there."

"Jeez. What an idiot!"

"No, Derek. *She's* not an idiot. *You* are. You *must* be to think I'm going to fall for *that* bullshit. No—you told her because you *wanted* to make sure I found out about it," and she glared at him, ferociously.

"Listen," Derek began, placating, "It wasn't my—"

"'*It wasn't your intention?*'" mocked Andy, "Oh, p*lease.*"

"What does it matter, anyway?" exploded Derek, throwing his mask aside. "You two aren't together anymore, are you?"

"No," affirmed Andy, through gritted teeth, "We're not. But we're still friends and I care about what happens to her."

"So we're going out," said Derek, defensively. "So what?"

"So *what?*" repeated Andy, stepping closer.

Derek, terrified, shrank back.

"You're taking her out tomorrow night, right?"

"Yeah."

"Tomorrow night is Prom night, right?"

"Yeah."

"And what's the great tradition on Prom night?"

Derek looked annoyed.

"I don't know what you mean."

"Oh yes, you do," sneered Andy. "I even heard you say it once: '*Prom night is the one time when you're* **guaranteed** *to get some.*'"

Derek blushed and looked away.

"What are your intentions?" demanded Andy.

"What do you mean?" he stammered.

"Do you do frustration well?" she asked, again through gritted teeth.

"What's that got do with this?"

"Plenty. Because if you're planning on getting any from her—it isn't going to happen," and with that, Andy crossed her arms over her chest and stared him right in the eyes.

Derek laughed shortly.

"Why? Are you going to be there to stop her or something?"

"I know her better than you do," Andy reminded him. "And I know for a fact the only person she's ever going to give it up to is the person she spends the rest of her life with. And no *way* are you that person."

"They all say that—at first," replied Derek, equally coldly.

"She won't do it," said Andy, positively. "You'll be lucky if her parents let her out of the house—let alone go to a dance."

"They already told her she could."

"It doesn't matter—she won't do anything with you."

"She will," Derek assured her. "I'm pretty good at persuading—and I haven't failed yet."

"Proud of that reputation, are you?"

Derek grinned mirthlessly.

"So you want to go from being the biggest man-whore on campus to being a rapist?"

Derek flushed.

"Rape? Who said anything about rape? You can't rape the willing."

"Uh huh," replied Andy. "And she isn't."

"She will be," he repeated, firmly.

"If you force her—yeah."

"I haven't had to use force yet!" he snarled.

"Oh? What about Monika?"

Derek turned pale.

"What about her?"

"Was *she* willing?"

Derek's face and eyes froze in a cold mask.

"They dropped the charges. Remember?"

"Yeah, I do. But not because it wasn't true. The reason they dropped it was her parents didn't want her dragged through the slime in court."

"They never would have dropped it unless it was false!" rejoined Derek, doggedly.

"That's not what it said in the court filing," Andy snapped, a wicked gleam in her eyes "I'm going for a law degree. Remember? I help at the clerk's office all the time. And I read all the briefs she files."

"Oh!" said Derek, with exaggerated mockery. "A jock with brains. And *reads* yet—" but he stopped, cowering as Andy lunged forward, grabbed him by the shoulders and pulled him nose to nose with her.

"Listen," she said, in a quiet, deadly voice, "Don't push your luck. And don't you *ever* talk that way to me again. It so happens I got an academic scholarship—*academic*. Not athletic. That school I got accepted at (and you know which one I'm talking about) only gives out two of those a year to freshmen—I got the first one. There were three hundred other people applying. Having a four-point is the *least* hard part of getting it!" and she stopped, breathing hard.

"I took advanced Calculus in my sophomore year. I've been in Running Start for two years now. Did you ever pass Algebra?" and she pushed him away in disgust.

"Yeah, I did," he muttered.

"How many tries?"

"What does that matter?" he burst out in anger. He clenched his fists and jaw—trying to calm down.

"Anyway," she continued, "I know what I'm talking about. That girl isn't going to give up a damn thing to you—unless you force her."

"Oh yes she will," said Derek, grimly.

"You really think you can talk her into it?" challenged Andy, contemptuously.

Derek sniggered.

"You say that," he spat, "Every one of you plays that stupid game. You all want it just as bad as we do—but you can't admit it because you don't want to look like a *slut*. So we have to talk you into it so you'll have an *excuse*," and he sniggered again.

Andy remained unmoved.

"I don't waste any time on useless bullshit. Cut to the chase—do it—and move on. I get what I want—they get what they want," and he snapped his fingers.

"Tell me something," said Andy, with a terseness in her voice that made him pick up his ears.

"Do you have any *feelings? Any* feelings at all? Did you ever think your victims might see things differently? Do you care about *anyone* except you?"

"*Feelings,*" he mouthed as though the word disgusted him.

"Feelings," he repeated. "What feelings? What do feelings have to do with it? *Jeez!* People need to get over that shit. Always whining about their fucking feelings. Wusses looking for pity—too weak to get with the real world. Girls don't have feelings any more than I do. They got needs and they're gonna get them met—they don't give a shit about who they're with. All they want is to get fucked just like the rest of us. If they have a good time, they don't give a damn. If they get hurt or get the guilts then they have *feelings* and turn on the tears for pity. And everyone falls for it. They know how to work the system. It's all they're good for. Girls are nothing but brainless Tits and Cunt—fucking cum dumpsters."

Andy stared at him.

"*Tits and Cunt?*" she repeated in disbelief.

"Oh—did I forget *Mouth?*" he snarled, "Oh—and *Ass,* too. Yeah."

Andy stared at him in shock. She opened her mouth to say something—then pushed him away and spat on the ground.

"*'Tits and Cunt'*" she repeated with heavy sarcasm. "Oh—for*get* it!"

She turned and started walking away.

Derek looked puzzled.

"I thought you said you wanted to talk," he reminded her.

"Forget it! Forget I ever said anything," muttered Andy without turning around.

Derek drew himself up in mock anger.

"Thanks for wasting my time. *Oh Gawd—*" and he stepped back, white-faced with fright as Andy whirled around, ran back to him and grabbed him by the shoulders again, pulling him so close their foreheads touched.

"I already told you," she said, grimly, "Don't push your luck. I'm *not* going to tell you again," and she thrust him away. They both stood, staring at each other, breathing hard.

"Waste your time? Okay—I'll make it *worth* your time, then," she said harshly.

Derek winced as she continued, deliberately enunciating each word: "*Don't make promises you can't keep!*"

She turned away again.

"What?" asked Derek, completely nonplused.

Stopping, she looked back over her shoulder at him, saying, "*That's* what I wanted to say to you. And I'd keep it in mind, if I were you. It could save your worthless life," and she walked away without looking back.

Derek stood there for a few minutes, uncomfortable, frightened and angry all at once. He finally muttered something poisonous under his breath and began walking quickly back to the main building.

The woman from his table was waiting for him at the door.

"You okay?"

He glared at her.

"I don't wanna talk about it right now," and he stormed off, pushing her aside.

She shrugged her shoulders, watched him disappear into the hallway with an amused expression. Then she laughed and walked down the hallway toward her locker...

Friday Afternoon

"You wanted to see me, Coach?" asked Andy, standing in the doorway of the office.

The formidable looking woman seated at the desk looked up. Her face softened but she did not smile as she waved her in.

Andy stood in front of the desk uneasily. Sensing this, the Coach deliberately suppressed the edge in her voice as she beckoned, "Just take a seat, Andy."

Somewhat reassured, Andy sat down reluctantly on the edge of the chair. She looked expectantly at the Coach who regarded her with an unreadable expression.

"I understand you had a fight yesterday," the Coach said, at last.

Andy flushed—then turned pale.

"A *fight?* I wasn't in a fight—I haven't done that in—" but the Coach raised her hand for silence.

"Not with Derek Wenlok?" asked the Coach, blandly.

Andy reddened again and responded with an angry glare, "No. We didn't have a fight. I didn't touch him."

"The way you called him out of the Commons it sure *looked* like you were going to fight," was the dry riposte.

"I didn't want to talk in public. *That's* all," Andy growled.

She looked down in surprise at her clenched fists. Forcing them open, she leaned back in the chair, staring coldly at the Coach.

Unruffled, the Coach continued, "What did you have to talk about that couldn't be said in public?"

Andy stiffened.

"I don't see why I should have to tell *you*," she said, defiantly.

There was only the faintest tinge of anger in the Coach's voice but it was enough to cause Andy to tense in the chair.

"I'm your Coach, remember? It's my job to see to it you succeed and keep you from wrecking your future. On *and* off court."

Andy bowed her head and said nothing.

"We didn't fight," she said, at last.

"I heard you grabbed him a couple of times."

"Okay," Andy sighed, "Yes, I did grab him a couple of times. But I didn't hit him. I sure wanted too, though," she added, tersely.

"Why?" asked the Coach, coldly.

"He," and Andy flushed as she stammered, "He was saying things about girls. Said they were—were—*'cum dumpsters,'"* she raised her eyes but the Coach did not show any sign of emotion at her confusion.

"Well, I wasn't going to listen to him rant about how girls are nothing but *'brainless Tits and Cunt!'"* she finally spat out.

The Coach sucked in her breath with a hissing sound; then leaned back in her chair with a look of resigned amusement, shaking her head.

"That sounds like Derek, all right," and she laughed shortly. Then she looked back at Andy who was staring at her furiously.

"Listen," continued the Coach, "*You* know that isn't true. You know what kind of person he is. Let it go and get over it. If you plan to get into the law, you're going to get a lot of that garbage thrown at you. Just duck and don't throw it back."

Andy nodded her head, her clenching jaw muscles visible as she did.

"Andy?"

"What?" she replied, defensively.

"You weren't upset with him about Cara, were you?"

Andy sighed and leaned back in her chair as though exhausted, shaking her head slowly with her eyes closed.

"No, Coach, no. I don't care about that—Cara and I aren't together anymore so why should I get mad about it?"

The Coach's eyes opened wide.

"You two aren't together anymore?" she repeated, incredulously.

"No."

The Coach looked at her, astounded.

"But—but—but *why?* I mean, you two—" and the Coach stopped for a moment, swallowing hard before continuing.

"You two were the dream couple. You've been together since elementary school, almost. You both talked about getting married. You—"

"I know, I know," said Andy. "But things change, sometimes."

"Why did you break up with her?"

Andy's eyes blazed.

"I don't want to talk about it!" she snapped, then stopped in surprise at the look on the Coach's face.

If I didn't know better, I'd say she was about to cry.

"I'm sorry," she continued, in a calmer tone. "First, *I* didn't break up with her—and she didn't with me. It was mutual."

The Coach did not look as though she believed this.

"We both are going in different directions," Andy began again, then stopped and took a deep breath.

"She doesn't want to go to Seattle with me. She doesn't want to leave here. She wants to stay in this town the rest of her life. She won't change her mind and neither will I. I love her," she continued, trying desperately to keep the tears out of her voice and eyes, "I love her more than anything but I can't give up my dreams for her. I—" and Andy fell silent.

The sad look on the Coach's face deepened.

"I'm sorry, Andy," she said, at last. "I just wanted to make sure that—"

Andy nodded her head. They both understood each other. The Coach stood up from her chair and Andy followed suit, turned and began to leave.

"Andy," said the Coach as Andy reached the door. She froze without turning around.

"You know if you need to talk or anything—"

Andy turned and smiled at her.

The Coach nodded and Andy left the office, her footsteps echoing in the deserted locker room. The Coach sat down at her desk for a moment and buried her face in her hands. She could hear Andy's footsteps fading away followed by silence.

The Coach sighed, stood up, grabbed her bag and headed out of her office, snapping off the light switch as she passed through the door. Navigating cautiously through the locker room, she steadily shut off all the lights until nothing but the security lights remained burning. After a last look around, she walked out through the locker room door into the foyer of the gym, the automatic lock clicking behind her.

Without breaking stride, her posture straight as a broomstick, she marched steadily out of the gym, across the field, through the quadrangle and into the main building. She was barely through the door when she caught sight of a man leaning against the wall with a quizzical smile on his face as he watched her approach.

"You win," she said to him.

"I *told* you," he replied, gently.

He accompanied her to the faculty lounge. A line of inboxes was placed along one of the walls with a bulletin board just above. The main room contained several round tables in the center and a few small square ones along the edges. Another wall consisted of a battery of refrigerators and a coffee bar with cupboards placed just above it. A microwave oven squatted in the center with some utensil and napkin dispensers. A cup rack was close by, hung with individual ceramic, plastic and metallic coffee cups, neatly arranged.

The man took a seat in the dining area while the Coach walked over to one of the inboxes, picked up some papers, exchanged them for some in her bag and placed those in the outbox. She gathered her bag and walked back into the dining area.

"Dinner?" asked the man, hopefully, as she entered.

She sighed.

"Mr. Kell—" she began but he broke in immediately.

"Mr. *Kell?*" he repeated, smiling.

Her face colored up but she laughed, depreciatingly.

"Brett," she began again, "I really don't feel like going out tonight. It's been a rough week."

"Goodness, Sue," he responded, "It's been rough for *all* of us. How about just some coffee?"

She sighed.

"Okay—okay," she replied but there was a smile on her face. "I'll meet you there," and she gently squeezed his arm as she left the lounge.

* * *

The coffee bar was crowded that afternoon, but the atmosphere inside was a welcome relief to the severe heat outdoors. She let out a sigh as she passed through the door and felt the air-conditioning blast in her face. Even the sight of the long lineup at the counter didn't dampen her spirits.

She ordered her drink, picked it up and carried it gingerly into the seating area. Brett saw her at the same time she saw him. He waved and stood up as she approached his table.

"What?" she asked, noting the look on his face as she sat. She realized he was staring at her drink: a Grande mocha sundae with fudge sauce and whipped cream.

"Hey—it's Friday, okay? I need a break!" she protested with laughter. He smiled at her and reached out his hand. She met it with hers and squeezed for a moment. They both took a sip of their drinks and leaned back in their chairs with a sigh.

"Yeah, you were right," she said. "I should've known better than to listen to Spivey and Derek."

"*I* could have told you that," he responded. "That girl overreacts to—I'm sorry," he said, noting her raised eyebrows, "That *young woman* overreacts to everything. As far as Derek goes—" he waved his hand dismissively.

She nodded her head approvingly.

"I'm getting better," he added, sheepishly, taking a swallow of his drink.

She smiled.

"Did you know she broke up with Cara?"

"What?" Brett looked up sharply from his cup. "I didn't know that."

She giggled triumphantly.

"Got one on you!"

He laughed indulgently.

"I shouldn't be surprised," he continued. "I'm amazed it took this long."

"What do you mean? I thought those two were madly—"

"They *were*. But they haven't been for a while."

"Since when? The start of the school year?"

"No," said Brett, thoughtfully. "No—everything was okay until about the end of the first quarter. It was right around—" and he closed his eyes for a moment.

"Early November or something like that. Yeah—about then. I didn't think they'd drag it out through the school year—I thought for sure they wouldn't last through Christmas."

Sue stared at the table for a moment, absently stirring her drink.

"I wonder what happened. Those two were really close," she mused.

"Did Andy mention anything about it?"

"Not really. She said something about Cara not wanting to leave for Seattle with her."

Brett nodded.

"Yeah—that was part of it."

"What?" she asked, "Do you know anything different?"

Brett leaned back for a moment.

"I think it had more to do with her not being able to deal with Cara's new persona than anything else."

"*New persona?*" repeated Sue, cautiously.

"I noticed it right away at the beginning of the school year. She's—she's *changed* somehow."

"Well, like *how?* More assertive? Different outlook on life?"

Brett looked troubled.

"It's hard to explain it," he said, slowly. "She's just—different," and he shrugged his shoulders, as though dissatisfied with his answer.

"How big of a change is it?" asked Sue.

Brett looked up at her.

"If I didn't know better," he said, carefully, "I'd say she's an impostor."

Sue stared at him for a moment in silence.

"What does *that* mean?" said Sue, her voice skeptical and sarcastic. "Possessed by aliens or some dark inner—"

Brett did not smile.

"No—no," he stated. "I have no idea what's going on. But every time I talk to her it feels like the person I'm dealing with is someone else," and he paused, as though unsure how to continue.

"It's more like someone who *looks* like her has taken her place," he finished, although his face showed he was not satisfied with this answer either.

"Does she have a twin sister, maybe?"

"No. She's the only child. If there *are* any relatives she's never mentioned them."

"What does Cara say about it?"

"She doesn't like to talk about herself—it's hard to get her to do that," admitted Brett. "But I knew something was funny at our first advisory meeting. Last year, she was all eager to get into Running Start, plan for college, all that. When I asked her about it *this* year she said she wasn't interested anymore," he finished with an expression of disbelief.

"Wow," said Sue. "That's quite a change in only three months. Any clue what's going on?"

"Nothing definite. At one point she *did* mention something happened over the summer—"

"Between her and Andy?" Sue broke in.

Brett looked at her, annoyed.

"No. Andy had nothing to do with it."

"Well, what *did* she say?" prompted Sue after the silence started getting awkward.

Brett started as though he had been sleeping.

"She said," and he frowned, "she said she'd had an '*Enlightenment*'—whatever *that's* supposed to mean."

"Doesn't sound like she got '*Enlightened*' to me—not with dropping out of Running Start and going to college here instead of Seattle," remarked Sue, more to herself than to him.

"Not quite," said Brett, sadly. "She *is* staying here—but she isn't going to college. She—she said she isn't worried about that anymore."

"*Worried?* That was how she said it?"

"Yeah," admitted Brett. "I couldn't believe it when she first told me. I asked her how she expected to survive on her own with no skills."

"What was her response to that?"

"She just laughed. You know," he continued, "That's one of the things different about her this year. She acts like she's in on some secret—or some joke giving her an edge over everyone—" but he faltered again.

"Well?" Sue prodded.

"No—I thought I could explain it but I can't."

"Sounds to me like a cult got a hold of her," Sue remarked.

"I suppose," said Brett, thoughtfully. "Although I don't see how that could happen. She never leaves her house and her parents keep a close eye on her."

"What about the Internet?"

He snorted, derisively.

"They don't have Internet. By choice."

Sue, shock in her voice, asked, "No television either, I suppose?"

"Nope."

"Jeez," Sue's voice was acid. "Maybe—" and she stopped as another thought struck her.

"Brett? Why do her parents '*keep a close eye on her?*'"

Brett looked surprised at the question.

"Oh," he said finally, "That's right. You don't know about that part. She has some kind of mental condition. Autism or something like that."

"Good Gawd Brett!" exclaimed Sue in disgust. "Autism? If her autism is *that* severe, she wouldn't be in the mainstream student body. Is there an IDP on file?"

"No. You're right. It isn't autism. I can't remember exactly what it is. Whatever it is, though, it's pretty serious. She was hospitalized for a while over it."

"When was this?"

"Her freshman—no, her sophomore year. She was out of school for nearly three weeks."

"How on earth did she pass her classes?"

"Turned in her stuff by mail," responded Brett. "Or had Andy bring it in."

Sue looked down at her cup for a while, pondering.

"Did Cara say anything about the break up?"

"She mentioned it once—well, she didn't say they were '*breaking up*'—she said they were '*drifting apart.*'"

"Pretty torn up about it?"

"No," replied Brett, to her surprise. "She was sad, but it was more like she was sorry—sorry—" he stopped for a moment.

"It's like she was sorry she failed to convince Andy about something. Regretful but accepting. I don't know," he finished irritably.

"That happen around November?"

"It might have. I can't remember without my notes in front of me."

Sue sat back in her chair for a moment, her eyes closed.

"You know," she said, opening her eyes, looking at him and leaning forward, "Something weird happened to Andy about that time. She actually *missed* a game!" The look on her face showed this still shocked her.

"When was that?" she continued, leaning her head back and raising her eyes toward the ceiling. "Must have been—it was either the last October or first November game. Funny I didn't think of that before," she lowered her eyes and took a drink from her cup. "Yeah—it was then."

Sue brought herself back in a normal seating position, picked up her cup and took another sip. She swallowed it and looked up at Brett, asking, "Have you noticed anything else?"

"Yeah," responded Brett, in a lower voice. "There is one thing. Really weird too."

"Well?" demanded Sue impatiently.

"People are afraid of her."

Sue, stunned at this revelation, said nothing.

"Funny, isn't it?" he said, although his smile was a bit forced.

"Afraid of her? She's about as threatening as a cream puff! Why are they afraid of her?"

"Well—they don't come out and say it, not directly. But nobody—" he paused.

"No one will talk about her when she's not there—they won't even mention her *name*. It's like they're afraid she'll hear them."

"Really?"

"And it isn't just the g—the women," he amended with a grin. "The men are the same way. The only thing I could get out of any of them was they'd also noticed something was different about her but they couldn't explain it any more than I could."

"I wonder why Derek asked her to the Prom if everyone is so scared of her?" Sue pondered.

Brett laughed, sarcastically.

"*That* kid," he said, contemptuously, "has absolutely *no* self-awareness. He can't see past his nose. He wouldn't have a clue if there *was* something different about her this year—and even if he noticed, he'd ignore it."

"That's highly likely," admitted Sue.

"It's going all over the school about those two," remarked Brett. "Everyone is convinced he's going to get her in bed tonight."

"What do *you* think?"

"No way," he said, flatly. "She may have changed—but she's not weak or shy. Nothing like that. He isn't going to get her in bed—not in a hundred years."

"Unless he forces her," reminded Sue.

"He'll be in for a surprise if he does," said Brett, with a grin. "She swings a mean left hook," and he stood up from the table.

"How do you know *that?*" asked Sue, sharply, looking at her watch and standing up with him.

"I worked at the Middle School before I came over, remember? Didn't you hear about that fight?"

"Ah!" Sue snapped her fingers. "Yeah—that one kid wound up in the hospital. I remember."

"Well," said Brett, as they approached the exit. "Hopefully Derek doesn't find out about that the hard way."

They shared a brief embrace, then parted company, Brett with a smile on his face; Sue with a grim, concerned look in her eyes.

Friday Evening Part One

Da Minimis *(formal: Da Minimis Non Curant Lex). This axiom is usually translated as: 'The Law is not concerned with trifles.' A modern vernacular rendition would read: 'The Law doesn't care about the small stuff.' This concept is frequently referred to in cases involving illegal or unauthorized use of employee assets. A good example is a public sector employee who uses their computer to browse*

Internet sites unrelated to their job while on duty. Some references can also be found...

Andy looked up suddenly at the woman standing at her door. "Yes?"

"Andrae? You have a visitor at the door."

"Okay, Mom. I'll be down right away," she replied, adding under her breath, "And don't call me *Andrae* in front of my friends."

Leaving the book on her bed, she slowly got to her feet, stretched, ran her fingers through her hair, then walked into the hallway and down the stairs.

To her surprise, the foyer was empty and the front door shut.

"Mom? You didn't let her in?" asked Andy as she descended the stairs.

"She must've gone back to her car for something," came the reply as her mother passed through the kitchen door.

Andy rolled her eyes at this but did not reply. It wasn't until she had her hand on the knob it struck her she wasn't expecting any visitors. She hesitated for a minute, then pulled open the door.

"Yes—?" and she was immediately seized in a tight embrace. Taken off guard, she shrank back, staggering. Despite her desperate attempt to keep her balance she fell backward on to the floor, taking her visitor with her with a *thud!* that shook the house.

"What are you *doing* out there?" came an annoyed shout from the kitchen.

Andy, struggling to disentangle herself, managed to work in a "Sorry!" as she regained her feet. The visitor, meanwhile, had managed to get free and helped her up with the sound of laughter.

Andy finally looked at the visitor. Annoyance crossed her face.

"Lisa? What the *hell?*"

"Hey, girlfriend!" was Lisa's laughing response and she reached out to her again. This time Andy eluded her, grabbing her by the shoulders.

"What are you doing here?" asked Andy.

Lisa laughed again.

"Come to console you in your loneliness, of course," said Lisa, mockingly.

"What?"

"Oh, come on! Don't tell me you *planned* on skipping Prom, missy!"

Andy shook her head, wearily.

"I never was going to go, Lisa. Seriously."

"Whatever," was Lisa's skeptical response.

"No—I mean it."

"That's not what you said earlier," teased Lisa.

Andy flushed but did not waver.

"Yeah—I know. We only broke up three weeks ago."

"Oh!" responded Lisa, dropping her teasing tone.

"Well—I figured since you weren't doing anything tonight, maybe—"

"Oh Gawd Lisa!" Andy exploded. "I don't *need* any extra tr—"

"I just thought you might want to watch a movie or something since you weren't busy," said Lisa, with wide-eyed innocence.

It was Andy's turn to say, "Whatever.*"*

Lisa laughed again.

"I don't have bad intentions," she emphasized.

"It doesn't matter—you still have *intentions*," came the cynical response.

"Come on!"

"Look, Lisa," said Andy in a very calm, quiet voice. "I'm really busy. I got reading to do for that class I'm taking this summer and a lot of other stuff on top of that. I can't waste any time—" but Lisa reached out, squeezed her shoulder and just giggled in response.

Andy gave an exasperated sigh.

"Look, it's a Friday. We're done with Finals. You need a break. You need to celebrate! You *know* you'll catch up on that other stuff," said Lisa, with a knowing grin.

Andy laughed and smiled despite herself.

"Look, I got the movie right here with me," continued Lisa, holding out the cover so Andy could see it.

"I *did* want to watch that," said Andy, with some reserve.

"You still can," reminded Lisa.

Andy hesitated for a few minutes more.

"Okay," she said, finally, deliberately ignoring the joy blooming in Lisa's eyes and face.

"*Kewl!*" shouted Lisa, gleefully.

"Come on up," said Andy, heading for the stairs.

"Hold up a sec," said Lisa. "You got anything to snack on while we watch?"

Andy sighed.

"I should have known," and she led the way to the kitchen followed by the still-grinning Lisa.

They burst through the door into the kitchen and then stopped when they heard the gasp. Andy quickly turned toward the sound and said, "Sorry, Mom. Didn't mean to scare you."

The woman sitting at the kitchen table laughed and waved her excuse aside.

"No problem, Andr—" and she smiled, "Andy."

Andy smiled gratefully.

"Who is this? Oh! I'm sorry Lisa, I didn't recognize you."

"Is that a good or bad thing?" replied Lisa with a broad grin.

"You're actually looking really good," admitted Andy's mother, glancing at her with a critical eye.

"It took a lot but I'm not letting it go this time," was Lisa's earnest response. A faint blush lit up her face and she giggled again.

Andy, unwillingly, looked her over in turn.

"Yeah—you're right," she said, enigmatically.

Andy's mother looked at them with a puzzled expression. Andy caught it right away.

"Mom, Lisa's going to watch a movie with me. Is that okay?"

Her mother shrugged her shoulders but she was smiling.

"Sure," and, rising from the table, "You two need anything to chew on?" she asked.

"Oh, *Mom!* Sit down!" admonished Andy. "I can take care of it," and she busied herself with the cupboards, refrigerator and plates.

"Well—if you want to," and her mother reluctantly sat down again.

"You have any ice-cream?" asked Lisa, eagerly.

Andy and her mother both laughed. Lisa blushed.

"I thought you said you *weren't letting it go?*" reminded Andy.

"Oh—I can still have *some!*" growled Lisa in mock anger, blushing furiously.

"That's right," said Andy's mother with a smile. "Andy wouldn't think of ice-cream as a snack!"

Andy, her back to her mother, laughed but Lisa noticed she was gritting her teeth and unsmiling. Lisa gave her a puzzled glance but Andy did not respond.

At last, loaded down with several plates, glasses and bottles, the two friends made their way out of the kitchen.

"Thanks, Mom," said Andy.

"Yes, thank you very much Ms. Kasly," added Lisa.

Andy's mother smiled, shaking her head in amusement.

The dangerous thing about Lisa, thought Andy, as they struggled up the stairs, *is her damn laughing. I think it's catching.* Despite her resolve, when Lisa chuckled, Andy caught herself chuckling back, which only further encouraged Lisa until they were both laughing like lunatics. As they desperately tried to keep from dropping their burdens and laughed even harder at their frantic maneuvers, it was an even bet whether they'd make it to Andy's room without collapsing in hysterics with the dishes and food.

They made it to Andy's room without a single disaster. Lisa glanced around curiously as they entered.

"Where do you want this?" asked Lisa.

"The desk is fine," replied Andy.

Lisa spied the desk and carefully made her way to it, setting down the plates and glasses with exaggerated care. Andy followed suit and between the two of them, they soon arranged their feast on its surface.

Lisa, fascinated, gazed around the interior of Andy's bedroom.

"Did you set this up?" she asked.

"Yup," replied Andy with a smile.

Lisa nodded approvingly.

"I *knew* it wouldn't be pink," she laughed.

Andy looked disgusted.

"Yuk."

"Yeah," affirmed Lisa. "White is really cool."

Lisa took in the severe simplicity of the coverings, noting a complete absence of frills and fluffs and the bare walls without picture or poster. She nodded, as though all was as expected.

"I'll put the movie in," said Andy.

"Excellent!" said Lisa.

"I don't have another chair in here, though. I'll have to get one," said Andy as she busied herself with the player.

"Oh get off it, missy!" said Lisa. "We can sit here just fine."

Andy turned around. Lisa was sitting on the edge of her bed, a mischievous smile on her face. She stiffened.

"Lisa—" she began, but Lisa broke into convulsive laughter and Andy couldn't help but join in.

"It's *okay,* Andy," said Lisa, with mock seriousness. "It's just more comfortable than sitting—"

"Oh, p*lease,*" responded Andy, rolling her eyes, but laughing despite herself. She slipped the movie in, grabbed the remote and walked over to the light switch.

"Light out?" asked Andy, her fingers on the switch.

Lisa thought about it.

"Naw—not until we finish the food," she said, firmly. "I could just see myself tripping and falling in the dark," and she laughed at the thought.

Andy walked over to the bed and, with some hesitation, sat next to Lisa. Lisa reached out and gave her shoulder a reassuring squeeze, then concentrated on the screen. Andy sighed and worked the remote.

* * *

As the credits began to roll, Lisa raised herself up on her elbows and looked at Andy, dimly visible in the darkened room, still staring at the screen.

"Wadja think?" asked Lisa.

Andy raised herself up as well.

"That was really cool. Really. I'm glad I watched it."

"Me too," said Lisa.

They dragged the pillows to the foot of the bed as the evening progressed, lying face down to watch the movie, their original position of sitting on the edge too uncomfortable to keep up. They'd finished the food and drinks, a companionable silence between them.

Andy stirred herself further, stood up and made her way over to the light switch. She flipped it on and glanced at her clock radio.

"Wow. It's nearly one," she noted.

Lisa turned around.

"It doesn't feel like it," she said.

Andy nodded as she removed the disk, boxed it and shut down the TV and player. She sighed and then looked at Lisa.

Lisa looked right back at her.

"Lisa—" she began, but Lisa broke in pleading, "Don't send me away yet! Can we just talk for a while? I really don't want to go home."

The tone in her voice was a little too realistic to be her usual mocking. Andy raised her eyebrows but smiled.

"Sure—but I gotta get some tea if I'm gonna stay up."

"You got coffee?" asked Lisa, warily.

Andy laughed. "Yeah. You want some?"

"It isn't decaf, is it?" countered Lisa, suspiciously.

Andy smiled.

"Nah. It's leaded."

Lisa nodded.

"You want to come?" asked Andy as she headed for the door.

Lisa stirred and sat on the edge of the bed, her fingers drumming on the blankets.

"Naw—I'll wait up here. Gotta use the bathroom anyway."

"On the left down the hall," said Andy and she turned to leave the room.

Lisa's smile and bubbly manner instantly vanished. A bleak look appeared in her eyes just as Andy turned around, remembering the dirty dishes from their snack. Lisa quickly resumed her usual expression but not before Andy caught the change. It shocked her—she'd never seen Lisa show any sign of emotion other than joy—and she paused for a moment.

She let it go and made as if she hadn't noticed. Without a word, she crossed over to the desk, gathered the dishes and left, her footfalls on the stairs gradually fading to silence.

Lisa sighed and got to her feet, a little unsteadily. Keeping as quiet as she could, she made her way down the hall and into the bathroom, sinking gratefully on the toilet with a sigh.

She glanced up at the mirror as she washed her hands and looked annoyed. She looked down at the sink, then on each side of it. Then laughed.

You're not at home, girl, she rebuked herself.

Drying off her hands, she carefully made her way back to Andy's bedroom. Andy had not returned, so she sat on the edge of the bed and waited, looking around restlessly.

She noticed a mirror on the dresser with an assortment of necklaces and bracelets. Intrigued, she rose and then recalled something she'd forgotten.

She spied her purse on the desk where she'd left it earlier, grabbed it, fossicked around inside it. She drew out a miniature makeup kit, and, armed with this, walked over to the mirror, opening the kit.

She critically examined her face in the mirror, touching it up here and there and finally, although not completely happy with the results, snapped the kit shut.

While she was engaged in repairing her face, she had been examining the assortment of necklaces that caught her eye. She gently laid the kit down on the dresser and, absently, began picking out earrings, seeing how they looked on her, along with the bracelets and a few of the necklaces.

Lisa was impressed. With admiration and approval, she looked over the entire assembly, nodding her head as various items caught her eyes. At least two of the rings looked like antiques; although their stones gleamed, Lisa couldn't identify what they were.

Probably emerald, to match her gorgeous eyes, she decided after a moment.

With a sigh, she made to turn away from the dresser when her eyes caught sight of a necklace she'd overlooked somehow—at least she didn't remember noticing it *before*—and found herself staring intently at it.

Why is this so interesting? flashed across her mind. She drew her head closer, examining it carefully, as though attempting to identify what caused her to notice it in the first place.

It was not like the other accessories. For one thing, it didn't appear to be metallic—it looked more like leather. Not at all in keeping with the rest of the collection. Almost without realizing it, she found herself reaching out to touch it with her fingers. She gasped and pulled her hand back quickly, her heart pounding.

The room wasn't warm. The window was open, the heat turned off and she could feel the faint sting of the night chill against her skin. *But the necklace was almost too hot to touch.*

She looked at it again, fascinated and repelled. She cautiously reached out and touched it again; she gasped but this time did not withdraw her hand. It was hot but not too hot to touch once she knew what to expect. Stroking her fingers along the material, she decided it must be metal after all. At least it *felt* more like metal than leather. However, if it *was* metallic, why didn't it gleam or shine in the light like the others?

A closer look revealed it *was* shining—although *glowing* would have been closer to the truth. It was a faint, mere suggestion of radiance, hardly visible at first, but the longer she looked at it the stronger it seemed to become. Slowly, almost without being aware of it, she grasped it and picked it up from the dresser.

The glow intensified. She tried to look away from it but all she saw was darkness. Utter darkness. The only thing visible was the necklace and its strange radiance. Everything else, the room, the dresser, the mirror, vanished. As though in a trance, she slowly payed the necklace through her fingers, her attention focused on nothing else. Her heart pounded so loudly it almost hurt her ears. She wanted to cover them with her hands but she couldn't let go of the necklace to do it.

A sensation of terror began to creep over her—intensified by the fact there was no reason for her to feel frightened. Her mouth grew dry and her throat tightened as she trembled, her shaking steadily worsening as she continued holding the necklace.

She wanted to scream—to make *some* kind of sound—but she could not force any air through her throat. All her struggles simply drew her attention back to the necklace, its radiance and her terror: nothing else existed for her.

She started as her fingers encountered an obstruction on the necklace: a steel ring with a gold object, like a charm, attached. If there was a catch holding it together, she couldn't see it.

Puzzled, she looked over the gold object. Although she was holding it a few inches away, she couldn't make out anything definite: it might have been a charm or logo but it could also have been a medallion or ball. There was a vague suggestion of a human figure in its outline but no matter how hard she tried, she could not tell what it was. An occasional brief flash of vision appeared as she examined it but these never lasted long enough for her to understand them.

She gently twisted the necklace and, to her surprise, it opened. Hardly daring to breathe, she brought it closer to see if she could figure out the catch mechanism but the two halves were completely rounded and solid. Puzzled, she put them together and twisted: it locked. She twisted them again: it opened.

The gold object continued to distract her. As she stared at it, still trying to study it, she felt her lips moving soundlessly, as though forming words. What the words might have been—if they *were* words—she could not tell.

She became aware, through the fog in her senses, she had opened the necklace again and was slowly bringing the halves around her neck. Her vision cleared somewhat to reveal her reflection in the mirror but it was distorted and blurry. Her eyes began blinking rapidly, tearing up as though she were standing in the fumes of a campfire. As she felt the necklace encircling her throat, an unbearable feeling of horror overcame her: a cowering, quivering, screaming, fear. The tighter the necklace drew, the greater the feeling grew—but she could not stop herself from fastening it. She felt the halves meet, twist...

"What the fuck are you doing?? Put that down!!! **Drop it!!!"**

She cringed, unexpectedly released from the spell and frantically covered her ears. There was a sound of glass shattering, a roar, a noise she could not describe—possibly a growl—shaking that felt like an earthquake and howling winds. Her eyes cleared; the necklace dropped onto the dresser with a metallic *thunk!* echoing loudly, as though she'd struck a Chinese gong with a sledgehammer.

She whirled around and came face to face with Andy, who was staring at her lividly, her eyes blazing and her lips drawn away to show her teeth.

"I wasn't trying to steal it!" she quavered, frightened at the look distorting Andy's face.

Her full senses returned, her throat swelled, she burst into convulsive sobbing, threw her hands over her eyes and blindly rushed forward. Strong arms wrapped around her arresting her flight, then warmth, softness and the sound of a heartbeat, a comforting sound— the natural lullaby. Her legs stumbled and gave way beneath her.

Her consciousness faded away.

As her mind slowly returned, she realized she was in a warm, tight embrace, gently rocked back and forth like a child in its mother's arms awakening from a nightmare. A voice, a gentle, sweet voice, kept repeating, over and over, "It's okay. It's okay. You're safe."

These words released more tears and she reached out and drew the source of warmth closer to her. There was a gentle kiss on the top of her head. She shivered and lay trembling in the arms of her rescuer.

She finally, painfully, regained her sense of time and place, gradually realizing she was sitting on Andy's lap at the edge of the bed. Raising her head, she looked around the room as though she had no idea where she was while Andy continued holding and comforting her.

Her memory came rushing back. Lisa struggled, broke free of Andy's embrace and stared at her with frightened eyes.

"I wasn't trying to steal it! I *wasn't!*" she wailed.

Andy pulled her back into her arms and held her again. Lisa felt her warm breath in her ear and her voice surrounding her as she spoke, still rocking her gently.

"I *know* you weren't girlfriend. I know. I wasn't mad at you. I know you wouldn't steal."

Lisa closed her eyes and sighed with relief, gratefully snuggling against Andy.

At last, all feeling drained from her, she opened her eyes and looked straight at Andy. Andy quickly turned away but Lisa had seen the tears—with a look that held nothing but concern and worry.

Andy turned back, her eyes clear.

"What happened?" asked Andy, gently.

Lisa shivered but Andy pulled her close again and she relaxed.

"I just wanted to do my face," she faltered into Andy's neck, "And I saw your stuff and just tried things on..."

"Where did you find that last one?"

"Why—on the dresser with the rest of them. Why?"

"It was *out?*"

The alarm in Andy's voice frightened her.

"Y—yes. It was just—lying on the top..." but Andy, gently released her, rose and walked over to the dresser, staring grimly at the surface.

Andy muttered something that sounded to Lisa like, "Leave her alone, she's got nothing to do with *you*—don't mess with my friends," but that made no sense. On the floor lay the shattered remains of a coffee pot, a tray, two cups and some creamers.

Meanwhile, Andy picked up the strange necklace, holding it with a look of disgust on her face. Lisa started as she realized the strange radiance she had noticed earlier was gone, as were the feelings that went with it.

It looked like an ordinary necklace.

Lisa shivered and hid her face in her hands for a moment. When she looked up, Andy was still holding the necklace, her hand covering the gold charm, looking around the dresser, then in the drawers, muttering to herself.

"Ah!" cried Andy with savage triumph, retrieving a box from the floor. Lisa stared at it: without a doubt, *it was made of the same material as the necklace.* She turned her eyes away.

When she looked back, the necklace was nowhere to be seen. Andy locked the box with a key she put on the dresser with her other items. She slipped the box into one of her dresser drawers. She closed this, and—to Lisa's amazement—locked this too. Andy's expression throughout all this was one of angry determination.

Then she swiftly returned to Lisa who reached out to her as she approached. Andy wrapped her arms around her again and they clung together for a few minutes.

"What happened to—" began Lisa, pointing to the wreckage on the floor.

"My fault," said Andy. "Forgot what I was doing."

Lisa shivered and remained quiet for a few minutes.

"Andy?" Lisa asked in a quavering voice.

"Mm?"

"What—what—what *is* that thing?"

Andy hesitated, then said, "It's a key."

"A key? What do you mean?"

Andy did not respond immediately. Then, reluctantly, she said, "It's dangerous."

Lisa shuddered.

"Why?" she barely whispered.

Andy relaxed her hold, leaned back and looked her straight in the eyes with a stern expression.

Lisa braced herself with fearful anticipation—but Andy just sighed and resumed holding her, saying, "It has very bad memories. And very bad dreams. Don't think about it anymore."

Lisa did not ask any more questions about the necklace.

At last, she glanced over at Andy's clock. It was now three in the morning. She shivered with fatigue and fought down a yawn.

Andy, gingerly, carefully freed herself from Lisa and stood up. She vanished through her door into the hallway. Lisa, on the verge of exhaustion, heard a door open, shut, footsteps. Then Andy returned with a broom and dustpan.

"Gotta get this out of the way," she said and methodically attacked the wreckage on the floor. She removed the debris and returned with a couple of towels to wipe up the coffee and cream. Lisa watched all of this in drowsy silence.

"I'd better go home," said Lisa, shivering, after Andy returned from rinsing the towels.

"Are you up to driving?" asked Andy sharply.

Lisa shook her head.

"Mom dropped me off."

"If you think *I'm* driving anywhere at *this* hour you're crazy."

Terrified at the thought of walking home alone, tears in her eyes, Lisa slowly got to her feet, her lips trembling as she stared at Andy.

"Where are you going?" asked Andy.

"Home," quavered Lisa but Andy replied, "No, no, girlfriend. You're not walking home in the dark. You're staying here. You've been through way too much tonight."

Lisa teared up again but nodded her head, wiping her sleeve over her eyes. Andy walked over to the bed and pulled her close again.

"Thank you," choked Lisa.

Andy gently slipped free, walked over to the light switch and turned it off. There was still a faint glow at the window from the streetlight outside but the room remained completely shrouded in darkness.

Lisa remained still for a moment. Some noises caught her attention and she realized Andy was stripping off her clothes. Lisa was too spent by that point to react.

"Where will I sleep?" she asked, stretching and yawning.

"Next to me, of course. I don't think you want to be alone, do you?"

She jumped as Andy touched her arm.

"Okay," she nodded her head.

"I didn't bring any sleeping stuff," she continued but Andy laughed.

"You know you don't need it."

Lisa blushed although it was invisible in the darkness. She heard Andy reach the bed, toss the book aside and climb on to it.

She clumsily slipped out of her clothes; gingerly unhooking her bra with a sigh of relief; and finished stripping down to her panties. She carefully made her way in the darkness to the edge of the bed and put a cautious knee up on the blankets.

"Here you go, girl," came Andy's voice.

Lisa felt Andy's hand grip her arm and gently guide her onto the bed, the blankets already turned down. Shivering uncontrollably, she gratefully slipped underneath them and pulled them up; rearranging her pillow before laying back on it, staring toward the ceiling with blank, empty eyes.

"Come here," came Andy's voice. "Just let me hold you."

Without much conscious effort, Lisa glided into Andy's arms and felt them wrap around her, a comforting warm glow that gradually worked its soothing way deep into her senses. The memory of fear and terror she struggled with melted away. She sighed and fell asleep.

Andy smiled as she heard and felt Lisa's heart slow and her long breaths begin. Gently running her fingers through Lisa's hair, she lay her head down and drifted off into oblivion.

Friday Evening Part Two

Derek stared at the door, astounded.

No doorbell? Sheesh!

That was the least of his worries. The closer he examined his surroundings, the less comfortable he felt. The porch and the door built of spongy, unpainted, weathered wood; the walls, what he could see of them in the fading light, looking even worse; the house itself hiding in the woods at the bottom of a silent valley that cut a steep, narrow slice into the south hill of town. There were no other houses; the only access was a steep, slippery path from the street; the woods and the high walls of the valley blocked any sounds from outside.

That isn't the only thing funny about this place, he thought. The house was dark and silent; no sounds came from inside and no light was visible. If he hadn't known better, he would have thought it abandoned. *They don't even have electrical lines.* He already knew they didn't have a phone or cable. But *no electricity?*

He wasn't afraid of darkness and silence—but something triggered a sense of unease that grew worse the longer he stood there. He kept looking around behind him but there was nothing to see except the last remnant of light fading to darkness.

He glanced around once again, thankful no one was there to witness his nervousness and knocked on the door with a trembling hand. He waited, his ears straining for the slightest sound, trying not to think about the dark woods behind him.

"Hi Derek!"

He nearly jumped out of his clothes. He had no warning the door was opening or that someone was approaching it from inside. He blinked his eyes, straining them.

There was a faint suggestion someone was standing under the lintel. The interior was black without a glimmer of light.

"Derek?"

He blushed, but answered with his usual suavity, "How you doing tonight, Cara?"

She laughed. The sound of it allayed some of the uneasiness he was experiencing. It would have completely vanished if he could have seen anything in the darkness flowing out of the doorway.

"I'm doing great. *You* look sharp tonight," she said, admiringly.

"I do? How can you see me?"

Another laugh.

"I can see you just fine. I guess because I'm used to it."

"I wish I could see you," he responded, without taking notice of the odd wording of her last sentence.

"Eventually you will," she said.

It was an innocuous remark but it sent a chill through him.

"Are you ready?" he asked.

"Yeah. Let's go," and she stepped over the threshold.

He turned to go but stopped when he heard her say, "I'll be out late tonight." He whirled around but the door had shut, cutting off any view of the interior. The silence was starting to bother him.

"You okay?" she asked.

He forced himself to laugh; even to him it sounded unnatural.

"Yeah, I'm fine, babe. Just fine."

He felt her hand grab his and barely suppressed a cry. The warmth and softness of her touch quickly flowed through him and his usual air of calm indifference returned. He turned so he was again facing away from the house and took a few tentative steps forward.

"Not that way," she warned.

He stopped.

All around him was darkness.

"Why don't you lead, then?" he asked, not knowing what else to say.

She giggled and moved to the front, reaching out her hand to him. He gripped it and she moved forward without any hesitation. There was a profound silence—made all the more intense as they passed into the darkness of the trees. The feeling of uneasiness grew steadily worse. His head and shoulders began to bow as though a heavy weight was on his back—a weight that grew harder and harder to carry with each step. At the last possible moment before he collapsed, he felt the grade steepen sharply and looked up. The faint glow of the streetlight was visible, far above.

Why hadn't he seen it earlier?

'Sorry I didn't get to meet your parents," he said. He felt a need to hear his voice in the silence.

"Oh they saw you," she responded.

"How?"

He could have bitten his tongue off.

"They were at the door—and we saw you coming," she explained, matter-of-factly.

He did not want to ask how they could see him in the dark or why he hadn't heard or noticed them at the door.

As the light grew stronger, a fear began to grip him he could not shake off. *He was afraid to look at her face—almost terrified.* The mere vision in his mind of her turning toward him was enough to petrify him. Try as he might, he couldn't explain why he felt that way or what he was afraid he'd see.

They reached the top of the slope and rested for a moment, breathing heavily. She turned around unexpectedly and he stiffened in fright but she pulled him to her before he could see her face clearly and held him for a moment. It took him a few seconds but he circled his arms around her and drew her close.

He felt a kiss on his forehead as she withdrew.

"It's okay," she said, as though reassuring him.

He looked her over in the light and his dark feelings faded away. A different look was in his eye as he took in her voluptuous, full figure, advantageously displayed by her outfit. She smiled at him as he devoured her full breasts, lips, wide, deep-blue eyes, beautiful face and her hair, which cascaded almost to her knees like a golden mantle.

"What are you thinking about?" she asked, slyly.

"You don't want to know," he answered in the same tone.

She gently reached out to him and touched his face.

"I think I can guess."

"You don't mind?"

She smiled.

"I might not."

He looked at her for a moment, puzzled by her last utterance. Then, shrugging off his doubt, he walked to his car, opened the door for her and gently closed it behind her. After a couple of deep, shuddering breaths, he walked over to his side, got in, closed and locked the door and fastened his safety belt. He checked to make sure she had done the same.

"I'm so excited!" she said, eagerly gripping his arm. "I've been waiting for this for *years!*"

'For Prom night?" he asked as the car began to move.

She nodded vigorously.

"That too. It's a very special night tonight."

They reached the main street; there was still enough traffic to require his full attention. He carefully made his way down to the light and up the hill.

He felt her lean into him and kiss him.

Sweet! he thought as the glow spread through his senses.

The dance hall came into view and he slowed, looking for a parking space amid the crush of arriving cars. There were students everywhere, springing out of cars, wearing costumes of fantastic vanity, shouting to each other, slapping palms, giving themselves over to the magic of the night.

Derek smirked as he slid the car into an open space, shut the engine off and put the transmission in Park. He turned, unhooked his seatbelt, and, all at once, he found himself in a tight embrace, his face pulled against hers, her full lips opening invitingly. He did likewise and, for a while, the world did not exist for either of them.

They broke free with a gasp and a smile. She gently squeezed his arm again as he turned to open his door. He walked around, opened her door, helped her out and locked the car. Arm in arm, they walked toward the entrance, both of them radiant with excitement.

"I'm glad you asked me out. I didn't want to miss this," she said, snuggling her head on his shoulder for a moment.

"I'm glad you came," he said.

He was dimly aware of the whispers and gestures following in their wake. He smiled as he saw the shocked faces of his cohorts, disbelief mirrored in their eyes, the pointing fingers and hands held over mouths.

I love being in the spotlight, he thought, grinning as he passed through the entrance.

The music began immediately, the hypnotic thump of the drums resounding through the air and shaking the floor. The lights activated and the dancing exploded all across the hall in a whirling chaos of skirts, dresses, coats, arms, hair and blurred faces.

Some of the students brought in light sabres of different colours, adding a spice of the exotic to the evening as they swung them about. The feeling of release, of freedom after nine months captivity, the heady thrill of an uncharted future, was like a fire burning in the crowd, engulfing all of them with its heat.

The chaperones, familiar with the atmosphere of this event, wisely kept out of the way and let them vent unrestrained. No one had any thoughts of eating, drinking, or anything outside of the narrow bounds their world had shrunk to: the fever and passion of the dance.

At last, Derek and Cara, exhausted and exhilarated, shuffled off the floor and collapsed at one of the tables, trying to recover their breath.

Derek pulled out his cell phone, glanced at the screen and said, "It's almost midnight."

"Mmm," was Cara's throaty response. She leaned over and brushed her softness against his arm. He shuddered with pleasure and put his arm around her.

"How much longer does this go?" she whispered in his ear, her lips lingering.

"'Til two, I think."

Moving even closer to him, she said, "I don't really want to stay. Do you?"

His face soured.

"You have to get home?"

She laughed.

"Who said anything about going home?"

He should have felt his confidence and superiority swell beyond all bounds at this suggestive speech. He did feel something *like* that. But something he could not name put a chill in the heat of his desire.

This isn't like her. This is nothing like her.

It worried him for a moment. With a great effort, he managed to put it out of his mind and smiled as he stood up, she with him.

"I'm ready to go if you are, babe."

She leaned into him again and kissed his cheek. They gathered their coats and quietly slipped out in the middle of another round of frenetic ballet, the music reaching out and engulfing them, trying to pull them back into the whirlpool of the dance.

The cool air outside revived them. They both took deep breaths of it and gazed up at the sky.

"Wow!" he said. "Look at that moon! It's huge!"

She looked up and laughed.

"I told you it was a special night."

They reached his car. He helped her inside, slipped into the driver's seat and locked the door, starting the ignition at the same time.

She placed her hand on his knee.

"Where do you want to go?" he asked.

"You decide," she said, squeezing his knee.

This is getting weird flashed through his mind, even as he put the car in gear, backed out of his spot and drove away from the dance hall.

She moved closer to him as they drove and gently ran her hand up and down his leg. He reached over and put his hand on her leg, savoring the feel of her heat rising through the thin fabric of her dress. He tentatively pulled the material up with his fingers; there was no resistance, so he continued until he contacted the naked flesh of her legs.

They were warm, soft and silky—delightfully challenging his efforts to remain calm and cool. His fingers shook—he could not stop touching her.

"Wow!" he said, almost in awe.

"What?" she asked, shyly.

"Your legs—they feel—they're—*damn* they're *hot!*"

She leaned back in her seat as his grip tightened, his fingers savoring her warm, smooth skin. She took his hand once and kissed it and gently placed it on the swell of her breasts, continuing caressing his fingers as they drove into the wilderness of the mountains surrounding the city. His sanity teetering, he felt her softness with his fingers and tentatively slipped them just under the material but did not go further than the hem. She pressed his hand in closer.

He trembled.

Later—much later—he brought the car to a stop. It was dark and silent once the engine switched off and the feeling of isolation swept over them like a soft, warm blanket. No lights were visible; the sky glittered with stars like diamond shards cast on a black velvet cloth. The moon lit the scene with an eerie, silvery glow. He undid his seatbelt. She did the same. They looked at each other and instantly clung together in a passionate, furious embrace, kissing deeply.

They broke loose for a moment—staring at each other, breathing intensely. She tugged at her top and pulled it down, exposing the top portion of her body, her breasts enclosed in a lacey white bra. She leaned into him and guided his arms around her to the bra clasp. His mouth dry and heart pounding, he tentatively began to undo it.

Without warning, he broke loose, sat up and just looked at her. Surprised and shocked, she did the same. There was a moment of silence.

"Is something wrong?" she asked.

He hesitated.

"Yeah."

"What?"

He took a deep breath.

"What is going on?"

It was her turn to hesitate.

"What do you mean?"

"What do you think?" he burst out, unable to hold back his frustration. "You're sucking face just as hard as I am, you're letting me touch you *all over*—this—this isn't *right!* This isn't *you!*"

For a moment, her eyes hardened. Before he could react, they softened again and she spoke, quietly.

"How do you know it isn't me?"

"Sheesh!" he snarled. "You've been running around with Andy for years and never so much as *looked* at anyone else. They call you the *'school virgin.'* You're supposed to be—I don't know—all cold, like ice. You're not supposed to be interested in sex; or in boys; or in—well, in people like me."

She looked down at the floor, absently stroking his arm.

"Who says that?"

"It's what everyone says!"

"You're right, in a way. I'm not interested in any of those things—but I am interested in *you.*"

He shivered.

She quickly looked up at him.

"What did Andy tell you?"

Why did that question scare me? he thought.

"Nothing. She said nothing about you."

Her grip tightened slightly and her voice changed enough for him to stare at her, his hair rising as she said, "That's not true, Derek. You *know* it isn't."

He swallowed hard.

"She said—she said you wouldn't give it up."

Cara gave a short laugh.

"That's not quite everything, is it?"

Almost unwillingly, he continued, "She said you would only give it up to the person you'd spend the rest of your life with."

She looked at him, steadily.

"You see?" she said, again in that altered tone of voice. "You're wrong about me. I'm not cold like ice and I *do* give it up—under certain conditions."

He tried to move away from her but her grip tightened.

"Y—y—y—yeah," he squeezed out of a rapidly constricting throat.

"Well? I know you want me—and I want you; why torture yourself? Why not *be* that special person?"

"What do you mean?"

"Why not spend the rest of your life with me?"

All the uneasiness and terror he felt when he called at her house to pick her up instantly came rushing back; he shuddered at the impact. *I do want her,* he thought, *why am I afraid?*

"Suppose I say, 'yes'?"

"Then you can do whatever you want with me. Forever."

His terror increased. Sweat began forming on his forehead.

"But—but—what if I change my mind?"

You dipshit! Why did you say that?

"You won't," she said.

She sounds like Andy.

He did not like the reminder.

"What makes you so sure I won't?"

"Because you are going to prove that to me—before we do anything."

His heart was pounding hard enough to burst through his chest and his teeth chattered. Yet he managed to croak out, "What do I have to do to prove that?"

"It's really simple," she replied and looked up at him. The moonlight flooded her face with its cold light; she reached around, unhooked her bra and tossed it aside. At the sight of her vulnerable nakedness spilling free, terror flared up in him so intensely he wanted to vault from the car and run away, screaming into the darkness...

He swallowed hard.

"Okay," he whispered.

She laughed again, even lower in her throat and slowly reached out to him. His fear raged out of control; he wanted to get away; to flee; to break loose somehow. But he was paralyzed—held motionless by her eyes. He could not so much as blink.

He felt her hands touch his neck, circling...

Monday Morning

...oh Gawd! Already?

A shaking arm slowly made its way out from under the blankets, groping clumsily along the edge of the night table. The fingers found the alarm button and punched it savagely. The arm withdrew under the blankets in silence.

I don't want to do this.

She turned over under the blankets defiantly. It only took a minute for her conscience to kick in. She smirked, bitterly.

Okay. Okay. I gotta do it.

With a long sigh, the blankets kicked aside revealing the sleeper beneath. She staggered to her feet and roughed up her hair, then sat on the edge of the bed.

She caught herself just before she fell asleep again.

Come on, girl!

She snarled in response but stood up, stretched and made her way to the bathroom, yawning lustily. Whipping the shower curtain aside, she twisted the taps open and tested the water.

*I don't care what the dermatologist said. I want it **hot.***

Steam began to pour from the tub enclosure. She gingerly stepped over the edge, staggered a bit; then flung the curtain shut and stood under the water for a few minutes.

Then, with another sigh, she reached for the soap, the sponge and began vigorously cleaning. She looked at the shampoo bottle for a moment, tossed her head in contempt and put soap on her hair instead.

Don't need it anyway—nothing like a low-maintenance hairdo.

Finished, she shut the taps, flung the curtain aside and grabbed a towel from the rack. She stepped out of the tub as she dried herself, shivering a little once out of the steam. She hit the switch for the ventilation fan and looked herself over in the mirror.

Makeup today? Nah.

She glanced at the curling iron and hairbrush and sneered.

Glad I don't need those. I need to keep it short—I keep forgetting how much bullshit you have to do with long hair.

Without bothering to wrap the towel around her, she made her way back to her bedroom and began pulling clothing rapidly out of the dresser. She started when the box came into view and froze in position for a moment.

I thought I put that in the locking drawer. What the hell is it doing **here?**

She stood still for a moment, her senses in high pitch, as though expecting to hear something, her eyes closed to aid her concentration. She finally opened them and looked at the box, scowling.

Grabbing the box, she fished up the key, unlocked the drawer, placed the box and made sure she saw it resting inside, then locked the drawer and threw the key on the dresser. She glared at the drawer as though defying it to open itself. But it didn't.

She forced herself to ignore the drawer and continued assembling her outfit. Once she was dressed, she pulled out a pair of running shorts and some extra underthings. Kneeling down on the floor, she spied her gym bag and retrieved it from its place in the closet. She placed the running shorts and other items in the gym bag and zipped it half shut.

She looked at the clock.

I have some time yet.

She instinctively looked around for her backpack but caught herself in time, smiling sheepishly.

Forgot—I don't need that today. It's the last day.

A chill shot through her as she realized it was more than just the last day. It was her last day of high school. Graduation wouldn't be until the weekend but she was officially done at this point. She didn't have to go today if she didn't want to. However, there was no way she could stay home; it was her last opportunity to experience a part of her life that would soon be over forever.

Her eyes teared up for a moment.

Stupid! I guess I've just ignored it until now. Might as well get it over with.

The tears poured out for a few moments and she closed her eyes, leaning against the wall. It was soon over. Her mind purged of emotional poison, she grabbed a tissue, blew her nose and tossed it into the trash as she left, gym bag in hand.

There was a light on in the kitchen.

That's strange. Is she up already?

She peered around the door curiously.

"Come on in, um—*Andy*," came the voice. She smiled and walked in.

"You're up early this morning," said Andy.

Her mother laughed.

"Couldn't sleep any more. Stupid pain pills just aren't working today."

Andy did not respond to this.

"Hey, I already got you a cup right here," her mother called out as Andy made her way toward the cup rack.

Andy stopped, slowly turned around and walked over to the table. She picked up the teacup, took a sip and gave a choking gasp.

"It's kinda hot, girl," remarked her mother, wryly.

"No kidding," replied Andy, blowing on the cup.

"Sit down. You still have time. We need to talk anyway."

Andy reddened and shook her head but sat down at the table without argument. She stared into her cup without looking up.

There was a brief silence.

"I was surprised Lisa stayed here, Friday night," began her mother. "Is she your latest?"

Andy looked up, scowling, her eyes gleaming dangerously.

"Not 'no' but '*hell* no'," she spat out, dropping her gaze back to the cup. She blew on it again.

"Well, why *did* she stay the night?"

"We stayed up late watching the movie and talking. I wasn't going to drive her home at three in the morning and no way was I going to make her walk."

Her mother hesitated for a moment.

"I'm sorry. I shouldn't have asked you that."

Something in her tone made Andy glance up, sharply. To her surprise, her mother's eyes were wet, blinking rapidly.

"Mom?" she asked, jumping up from her seat and running over to her mother. She wrapped her arms around her and held her closely for a moment. Her mother smiled faintly and stroked her arm.

"I'm not mad at you," assured Andy as she released her. "Really. Just not awake yet."

"I guess I have to admit I'm dealing with that empty nest syndrome," her mother laughed through her tears. "I can't believe you're leaving. It's hard. It's been a long time—"

Andy held her tightly for a moment.

She made her way back to her seat as her mother wiped her eyes.

"Anyway," Andy continued, "Lisa just showed up on the doorstep—I had no idea she was coming over. I really didn't want her to stay but she pulled the Bambi-eyes thing on me so I *had* to visit with her. At least the movie was good."

"Why did she just show up like that? She hasn't been over here in a long time."

Andy took a generous drink of her tea.

"She never said. She might have been upset she didn't get a date for Prom. Or maybe she was going to ask me to go with her. But *I* think she came over because she knew Cara and me were through. She's got a terrible crush on me."

Andy took another drink.

"She wants to be Cara's replacement?"

Andy nodded.

"Yup. But I got enough on my plate without adding *that*."

"I didn't know she was gay," said her mother, thoughtfully.

"She's not," stated Andy, firmly.

"But I thought you said—"

"Yeah—I know. But Lisa—Lisa doesn't have a clue *what* she is. I'm not going to play her therapist. That's *one* reason I don't want to get involved with her."

She finished her tea and stood up, cup in hand.

"Time to go?" asked her mother.

Andy nodded, walked over to the sink, rinsed out the cup and put it into the dishwasher. She grabbed her gym bag, opened a cupboard, fished out and stuffed some water bottles into the bag. She zipped it up all the way, ran over, kissed her mother and then, with a sigh of relief, walked out the front door, shutting it behind her.

* * *

It was still early morning but it was already warm enough to be uncomfortable out of the shade. Ignoring the brutal heat, Andy grimly made her way from the locker room to the track and set down her bag with a sigh. She gritted her teeth and began her warm-up stretches.

"Hey, girlfriend!"

Andy was shocked into immobility—turning to disbelief followed by annoyance when she saw Lisa's grinning face. When she noticed what she was wearing she nearly fell over.

"So how many times are we going for?" asked Lisa.

"Lisa—" began Andy but Lisa interrupted, "I know, girl. I know. I just want to run with you this morning—nothing else," she added with a naughty wink.

"Oh, *Gawd,* Lisa!" growled Andy, but she couldn't help grinning.

Lisa grinned back and they both began to do their warm-up stretches.

"I had no idea you ran," remarked Andy, looking over Lisa's outfit. It was similar to Andy's but the colours were a bizarre mix of hot yellow, hot pink and hot-lime-green. She stared at it with shocked amazement.

"What?" asked Lisa, breathing hard as she stretched out her calves.

"It's for sure you aren't going to get lost in *that* costume, girl," replied Andy.

"Yeah. I kinda just threw it together."

"D'uh."

The two friends finally finished their warm-up and walked onto the track.

"So how many times?" asked Lisa again.

"Twelve—minimum," replied Andy. "You up for it?"

Lisa shrugged. "No harm trying."

They broke into a steady rhythm, matching their footfalls and their breathing.

After their fifth lap, Andy glanced over to Lisa in surprise.

"How long have you been doing this?" she panted out as she ran.

"About a year," gasped Lisa.

"I had no idea," said Andy.

Lisa did not reply.

After fourteen laps, both of them inclined off the track and dropped to a fast walk—slowing down gradually. Andy looked at Lisa admiringly.

"Wow. You weren't kidding. You *are* into it."

"Hey, girlfriend, gotta keep up with my role model, ya know."

Andy blushed but ignored the comment.

"Hey! You guys!" shouted a voice. They looked at each other in dismay.

"Oh Gawd, it's Spivey!" muttered Andy.

"Wonder what's happened *this* time?" added Lisa.

"Well—we can't just walk past her. It doesn't work," said Andy with a sigh.

"I know," said Lisa.

Spivey, the sweat glistening on her face in the heat, waved at them frantically. Reluctantly, they returned her wave; she brightened up and headed over toward them.

"Guess we'll have to pause for a few," said Andy, wryly.

When Spivey reached them, they stopped walking and immediately began doing stretches—neither of them wanted their muscles to lock up. Both of their faces flushed a deep red from stopping their cool-down too quickly, struggling not to hyperventilate as they continued stretching.

"Hey you guys! Guess what?" bubbled Spivey.

"What is it now?" asked Lisa, wearily.

Spivey lowered her voice conspiratorially and bent down toward them.

"Cara didn't come to school today."

They both froze and looked at her—Lisa curiously, Andy with a white, drawn face.

"Maybe she's sick," faltered Andy, half-heartedly resuming her stretching.

"Nah uh," said Spivey, positively. "She's on the absent list," and she grinned at them, enjoying herself.

Andy, fighting to keep her voice steady, quavered, "Did Derek show up?"

Spivey snorted with laughter as the other two stared at her in amazement.

"Yeah," she said and she laughed again.

"What's so funny about it?" asked Lisa.

"He—he," Spivey fought to suppress her giggles, "he's dressed like a total dork. I mean a *total* dork!" and she laughed again.

Lisa had no reaction to this news but Andy's concern increased to alarm.

"Spivey!" she barked.

Spivey cut herself off and looked at her wonderingly.

"What's he wearing? A dress or something?"

"No," said Spivey. "He's wearing this—this skin-tight *turtleneck*. Some ugly red colour. With long-sleeves yet. He's already sweating to death in it—but he doesn't want to take it off. He's gonna pass out if he keeps it on."

"A *turtleneck?*" Lisa echoed. "Sheesh. What's the deal—is he trying to hide a hickey?"

Both Spivey and Lisa giggled at this one—but Andy clenched her jaws and fists, her agitation growing.

"Did he—did he—did he *do* Cara?" asked Andy, forcing the words out.

"I dunno," replied Spivey. "She was at Prom with him and they were sucking face pretty hard."

"Are you just saying that or did you really see it?" queried Lisa, severely.

Spivey looked hurt.

"I was there and I did see it. She was wearing this real cute low-cut—"

"Did they leave together?" snapped Andy.

"Yup," Spivey nodded vigorously.

"What time?"

"Just after midnight," replied Spivey. "Why?"

"Oh, Gawd," breathed Andy and she closed her eyes for a moment.

"Girlfriend?" snapped Lisa, noticing her swaying. "You okay?"

Andy nodded and opened her eyes, steadying herself. She stared wildly at Lisa.

"I gotta—we—*Spivey!*" she barked again, suddenly turning toward her.

Spivey jumped.

"Yeah?"

"You got something to write on?"

"Well—I—" she began but Lisa cut in with, "I do. Hold on!" and she sprinted over to her gym bag. Zipping it open, she reached inside, fumbled, then pulled out a small notebook, a pen and rushed back to them.

"Gimme!" said Andy, snatching the items from Lisa, who stared at her in amazed surprise. Andy wrote on the paper furiously, tore out the page and held it out to Spivey. Spivey reached out a trembling hand and clutched the paper, her eyes not leaving Andy the whole time.

"Listen," she said, her voice taut as steel. "You gotta do this for me. You gotta promise you're gonna do it!"

Spivey, frightened at this sudden metamorphosis, quavered, "Y—y—yes, Captain."

"Okay," and Andy pointed imperiously toward the main building. "You get in there and keep an eye on Derek. Follow him wherever he goes. No matter what. If he gets pissed, just stick to him."

"Okay," agreed Spivey, trembling.

Andy grabbed her head, forcing her to look her in the eye.

"That's not all. Make sure he doesn't wind up being alone. If you lose him, if he vanishes or something, you text me. *Like right then!*" she shouted as Spivey cowered.

Andy forced her to look up again.

"*I mean it. Right* away. Can you do that?"

"W—why—do you—" began Spivey, near tears, but Andy pulled her even closer, nose to nose, her voice the envy of a Marine drill instructor.

"Don't ask why. Just *do* it. Okay?"

Spivey nodded. Andy let go of her and she staggered back, still clutching the paper tightly.

"That's my cell," said Andy, pointing to the paper. "Get going. *Now!*" she roared as Spivey, frightened and nearly crying, dashed toward the building as fast as she could go.

Lisa stared at Andy in opened-mouth shock.

"What is going on, Andy?" she asked, quietly.

Andy said nothing.

"I hope she doesn't kill herself," said Lisa, watching Spivey's progress. "I've never seen her go that fast."

"Come on!" snapped Andy, grabbing her gym bag.

"What? Where—?"

"Just come on! Get your stuff!"

Lisa grabbed her bag on the run and caught up to Andy who was already in the parking lot, heading for her car. They collapsed against the sides for a moment, breathing heavily, painfully. Andy roused herself, furiously keyed open the door and reached over to let Lisa in. Lisa barely had time to get in the front seat before Andy shot from the parking lot in a spray of gravel.

"Jeeszas girlfriend, *slow down!*" cried out Lisa.

Andy did not look at her although she did slow to the speed limit. Her knuckles were white as she gripped the steering wheel, her jaw tight and her eyes blazing. Lisa opened her mouth to say something, caught sight of her face and remained quiet.

Andy savagely maneuvered the car around turns, side streets, all the while her face and knuckles growing whiter. Lisa, too scared to even make a sound, tried to piece out where they were going but she didn't recognize any of the streets—although she knew it was *somewhere* on the south hill.

The car jerked to stop, brutally slamming into the curb. Lisa winced but Andy already was out the door and running. Lisa vaulted out in pursuit, noting Andy was heading for what looked like the edge of a cliff. She shrieked as Andy ran up to the edge and vanished from sight—as though she had jumped or fallen over.

"Andy!" cried out Lisa, terrified. She doubled her speed and skidded to a stop at the edge.

To her amazement, there was a narrow path descending steeply into the valley below, vanishing into a thick grove of trees at the bottom. Lisa only hesitated a moment before she stumbled down the slope, fighting to keep her balance on the loose rocks. There was no sign of Andy.

She reached the bottom and plunged into the belt of trees. Ignoring the sudden chill in the air, she continued through the woods, concentrating on nothing but running, running...

"Oh Gawd!" cried out Lisa when she heard the scream. A scream of pure terror—a gut-wrenching, throat-bursting, ear-drum-breaking scream. She stopped and put her hands to her ears, her eyes shut tight.

The scream stopped.

Lisa, breathing hard, cautiously removed her hands from her ears and listened tensely. It was deathly silent. Not even a hint of sound from the outside world echoed in the dark valley. All at once, she became aware, as though physically struck, of the chill, the gloomy sky and the severe stuffiness of the air. Her head and ears pounded as though she was at a high mountain altitude.

Reluctantly, Lisa forced herself to walk along the path, hoping nothing had happened to Andy. The silence bothered her: she was afraid to make a sound and equally frightened of hearing anything. She was shaking uncontrollably when she reached the clearing in the middle of the woods. She stopped again as her ears finally caught a sound: someone was crying their eyes out nearby.

Turning her head, she spied Andy and rushed over to her. Andy was on her knees, her arms outstretched, the tears pouring out of her eyes, her breath gasping and heaving as she sobbed. So intense was her grief that Lisa felt the tears rising in her eyes as well.

"Andy!" announced Lisa, softly.

Andy did not respond.

"Girlfriend! *Oh*—*!*" she cried, rushed up to Andy, gathered her in her arms and held her tightly, as she had been held two nights before. Andy relaxed into her embrace and for a while, there was nothing but the sound of her traumatized emotions in the grim forest.

Lisa, terrified at seeing Andy like this, was totally unnerved. She continued holding her but felt helpless, not knowing what else to do.

Andy finally stopped shaking and her breathing slowed down. She stiffened in Lisa's arms, struggled and stared straight at her. Lisa closed her eyes and shuddered—what she saw in Andy's eyes, she never wanted to see again.

Andy relaxed and clung tightly to Lisa. Lisa, encouraged by this response, opened her eyes, gazing into her face.

That terrible look was gone.

As Andy calmed down, Lisa began to look around the clearing and caught sight of the house for the first time. She was so occupied with Andy she hadn't noticed it earlier—but it had her full attention at this point.

It was an old, dilapidated wood-framed house with gaping holes in the roof, furred with moss, boards missing, broken windows and crumbled walls. The glassless windows revealed an interior clogged with debris to the ceiling. Its age was frightful—it looked to Lisa as though abandoned for hundreds of years. *And that's impossible,* she thought. *No one was here to build houses until about a hundred and forty years ago.*

Its age was not its only disturbing aspect. Malignancy oozed from the structure like a foul scent, poisoning the air around it. It was so intense that Lisa had a hard time convincing herself the house wasn't alive—and eyeing her with menacing hatred. She shuddered as she continued looking at it, unable to turn away.

Andy, calmed and tranquil, looked straight at the house, seemingly unaffected by its aura, her face grieving but resigned. She sighed.

"It's no good," said Andy. "It's too late. They're both lost," and she struggled to her feet, Lisa aiding her.

"Where the hell *are* we?" breathed Lisa, growing more uncomfortable as she surveyed their surroundings, the silent house, the dark trees and the dim light getting more on her nerves the longer she stayed. She kept looking back at the house anxiously.

"She used to live here," was Andy's cryptic response. She turned away and began walking slowly up the path to the car.

"Wait! *Who* used to live here?" asked Lisa, running up to her, but Andy shook her head without answering. The heavy silence fell once again as they passed into the forest and neither of them felt like breaking it.

As they continued, both of them kept glancing behind them, first Lisa and then Andy. There was nothing to see, but a feeling of pursuit kept growing stronger until they almost were afraid to face forward for fear of ambush from behind. Their senses grew painfully intense–the sensation something like electrocution: paralyzing waves flowing through the nerves, heart pounding, frozen in position. An urge to curl up in a ball, fall down and scream with terror was getting harder and harder to resist.

Andy's expression when she looked back puzzled Lisa. She was just as terrified as she was, but there was something else in her expression Lisa couldn't place at first.

There's something wrong.

Lisa gasped fearfully as Andy abruptly stopped and turned around swiftly—staring wide-eyed. It took all of Lisa's strength to turn too, but there was nothing but the silent, dark trees behind them.

"Oh my Gawd," breathed Andy softly. "*That's* why."

"W—w—what do you mean?" quavered Lisa, not daring to move.

"They didn't close the gate..."

Lisa stared at her, mutely.

"Come on!" Andy cried out. She turned, grabbed Lisa's hand and began pulling her along the path, their adrenaline at fever pitch.

"We've got to get out of here!" muttered Andy.

Lisa was too frightened to say anything.

All at once, they broke out of the forest, the sunshine dimly perceivable far above through the thick fog. They began their ascent of the cliff with exclamations of agony—their muscles, tightened from their earlier run, making their climb a painful torture. The light grew stronger as they rose, dispelling their fear and apprehension as it brightened. It took all of their strength to keep going—Lisa continuously fighting off a nightmarish feeling they weren't moving at all.

When they reached the top, they were both hot and sweating profusely, breathing hard with their mouths wide open. With their last ounce of strength, they forced themselves over the rim and stood in the bright sunlight—the heat pouring over them and the sky mercilessly clear. They staggered to the car and leaned against it for a few minutes to regain their wind—and as they did so, a thought struck Lisa. She opened her mouth to say something to Andy, but thought better of it and said nothing.

Why did it look foggy while we climbed the hill?

There was no sign of any fog or clouds in the sky. But when Lisa looked up from the bottom of the valley, the sunshine was muted as if shining through a veil of grey. She puzzled about this for a few minutes and then let it go with a shudder, not wanting to remember any details about what she'd just experienced.

She did not intend to ask what the 'gate being left open' meant.

"Andy?" asked Lisa. "Are you okay?"

"Yes, I am," said Andy.

She tremblingly keyed open the door and collapsed in her seat with hardly enough strength to let Lisa in. They both sat for a few more minutes, trying to clear their heads and hearts.

Andy reached out and grabbed Lisa's hand, squeezed it, then looked at her.

"Thank you for being there," she said, simply.

Lisa glowed and squeezed her hand before letting it go.

Andy started up the car.

"Where are we going now?" asked Lisa in an exhausted voice.

Andy glanced at the dashboard clock.

It was two thirty.

Lisa looked at the same time she did and she gasped.

"Is that clock right?" she asked, quietly.

Andy nodded, put the transmission in gear and entered traffic.

"How long were we *down* there?" wondered Lisa.

"Too long," said Andy.

Monday Lunchtime

"Did you lose something?"

Sue, startled out of her reverie, looked up sharply to see Brett's smiling face.

"Yeah, my mind," she replied with a touch of acid.

"Looked like you had a touch of the last-day blues," he noted, taking the chair on the opposite side of her table.

"I suppose. Partly anyway."

Brett carefully spread his lunch out on the napkin and looked up at her curiously for a few seconds. She deliberately ignored him. He shrugged his shoulders, turned back to his lunch, picked up a sandwich and started eating.

Sue watched him sullenly for a few moments. Then, taking a deep breath, she stood up, walked over to the refrigerator, retrieved her lunch and took it to the table. She went back to draw a cup of coffee, then began attacking her salad.

"Yeah," she added, "I guess it *is* the last-day blues," and she smiled. Brett gave her one in return and they resumed eating.

"You seen Andy today?" asked Sue, stirring her coffee.

"Yeah. She took off around ten. Her and Lisa," he answered, trying not to eat and talk at the same time.

"I don't know why she bothered to show up," remarked Sue, "she didn't have to."

"True," agreed Brett, drinking some of his coffee with a bitter face. He set down the cup and looked at it, sourly.

"Cold," he explained in answer to her questioning look. He stood up, walked over to the counter and drew another cup. Sitting down once again, he took a tentative sip and backed away quickly.

"Hot?" asked Sue with a grin.

He glowered at her in mock anger but his smile broke out despite himself.

All at once, Sue sat up in her chair and looked straight at him.

"Did you say '*Lisa*'?"

Brett laughed.

"Nothing going on *there*," he said. "They've hung out together before."

Sue looked doubtful but resumed drinking her coffee.

"Well, she should have stuck around. She missed a pretty good show."

Brett looked at her, puzzled.

"What are you talking about?"

"Derek," she began, taking another sip. "You know how he always sits at that table in the Commons with his sycophantic acolytes?"

Brett grinned at her choice of words. "His harem, you mean? Yeah."

Sue continued, "Well—today he came in and sat down at the table like usual. And two seconds after that, everyone got up and walked away. All at once."

Brett, his coffee cup half way to his mouth, stared at her, amazed.

"*Seriously?*" he finally choked out.

Sue nodded.

"Hmmm," Brett mused, drumming his fingers for a moment.

"You should have seen what he was wearing," remarked Sue, attacking her salad again.

"And?"

She giggled.

"A *red* turtleneck. *Bright red*. With long sleeves no less," she finished, an amused smile on her face.

"*In this heat?*" he exclaimed.

She nodded again.

"Yeah. He was sweating to death already. He had the damn thing all the way up to his chin. Looked really stupid."

"Wow—that's beyond weird," observed Brett. "The guy who set the fashion for the school goes bizarre—" he swallowed the last of his coffee and set the cup down.

"What did he do when everyone left the table?"

"That's the other weird part," said Sue, "he just stared at them—but never said a word. He just sort of sat there. Dazed."

Brett's eyes darkened.

"Might have something to do with Cara," he muttered.

"What about her?"

"She didn't come to school today."

"So what? She's a senior—she doesn't have to be here today."

"It's hardly likely she'd miss an opportunity to get out of the house before summer," returned Brett.

"Well, so she didn't show up. What's that got to do with him?"

"He took her out to the Prom," said Brett, as if that statement explained everything. Sue, however, still looked blankly at him.

"So?"

Brett made a gesture of impatience.

"*You* know. The great '*Prom Night*' myth?"

Sue flushed, an old memory igniting her temper.

"Oh yeah," she replied bitterly, looking into her cup. "Sure. What was it they said? '*The one night you are guaranteed to—*'" she gave a disgusted snort. "Yup" and she raised her face, her tone more edgy than before, "Why do guys *think* like that?"

Brett gave a snicker but the bitterness in his voice was even stronger than hers.

"Why? Because that's how we're programmed. All the way from birth, we're programmed that way. You're supposed to seduce everyone you can get your hands on—but, of course, once you get them you have to move on to the next one. Something's wrong with you if you go back for seconds. You're taught to believe the only reason females were created was to serve as an outlet for our sexual needs."

The sarcastic tone of his voice and his sudden display of deep emotion shocked her into silence. She stared at him, wide-eyed.

NIGHTMARES THROUGH A DARK WINDOW

"You know what it is like to grow up being a guy?" he asked her. "Yeah—I know we're supposed to have all the power and have it easier than the women. But that isn't all there is to it. That power comes at a price. You have this tight, narrow script you gotta follow—it's social suicide if you don't. You gotta know all the sports, you gotta know all about cars, you're supposed to be tough, you aren't supposed to show feelings..." and he took a deep breath.

"Your whole life is based on a lie—everything you do reeks of it. You never get to be yourself. You're not allowed to fail. You have to get everything in a bra and panties into bed with you—but no *way* are you marrying anyone but a virgin. You're supposed to be the leader in the bedroom; you're supposed to want to do all the wild stuff. But if your wife wants the same, she's a slut and no good for you. *Gawd!*"

His knuckles whitened as he gripped the cup.

"And the ugliness goes both ways. *I* never collected hearts and *I* always treated my girlfriends with respect and all that. You know what *that* did for me? They all thought I was less than a man. They called me a wuss; weak; a loser. One of them told me the reason she left me was because I *'let her walk all over me.'*"

He slammed his fist down on the table. Then he hunched in his whole body, fighting to subdue the fury erupting from some poisonous spring, deep inside his mind. He took several breaths and finally looked up again.

"And I *didn't* go to my Prom," he added, then fell silent for a few minutes.

Sue reached out her hand and squeezed his arm.

He looked up, saw the expression in her face and managed a wry smile.

"Sorry," he said, "I've been carrying that one around for way too long. It's hard to let go of fifty years of your life and start over. I'll do it—somehow. But..." and he sighed, lapsing into silence.

"So—what if Derek *was* successful?" she prompted, quietly.

"I think if he was successful he just broke a major rule—one of those unwritten teen rules. He went too far."

"Well, good grief! It isn't like he hasn't done it *before!* Half of the people who sit with him are his ex—" sputtered Sue.

"They weren't like *her,* though."

"Oh—so the other ones were sluts so it was okay?" she fired off sarcastically.

"No—not that. She was different, she—" he groped to find the words. "She may have been their ideal of perfect innocence—someone who had—I don't know," he laughed without humor. "One of the nicknames they had for her was, '*The Angel.*' The school angel," he smiled.

"*I* heard some of them call her the 'school *virgin,*'" interjected Sue, wryly.

He nodded.

"I heard that, too. But I don't think they meant it as a jibe. I—" he threw his hands up. "I can't explain it. I just feel that, somehow, Derek's crossed a line his peers will not forgive."

He fell silent for a few minutes.

Sue absently stroked her empty cup.

"You know," she said, at last, "I think you're right."

He sighed and looked up at her again.

"There was something else," said Sue, frowning at the memory. "Spivey came and sat down at the table with him."

"*Spivey?*"

Sue laughed.

"Yeah. And you know what he did? He got up and left her sitting there just like his friends did to him."

"Knowing Spivey, I'm not surprised," remarked Brett with a chuckle.

"It didn't faze her. She got up and followed him out of the room."

"Hmmm," muttered Brett. "I wonder what *that's* all about."

"Playing with fire?" offered Sue.

"I don't think she's *that* desperate. Or stupid."

He glanced at the wall clock in the faculty lounge, sighed, stood up and cleared off the remains of his lunch, rinsing his coffee cup out at the sink.

Sue hesitated, then stood up and asked, "You going for your walk?"

"Yup," responded Brett, drying off the sink area.

"Need some company?"

Only a brief tic of his eyebrows registered his surprise.

"Sure," he agreed.

* * *

They made their way through the hallways to the outside exit. Although classes were nominally in session, there were more students than usual wandering aimlessly through the building, some quiet, some agitated and some in earnest conversation with their friends. They fell silent as Brett and Sue approached but quickly resumed their chatter after they passed.

Noticing a puzzled look on one of the student's faces, Brett remarked, "They're expecting us to ask them what they're doing out of class," and he laughed.

"As if we don't know it's the last day," added Sue.

Reaching the outside door, they passed through and began to walk at a steady pace toward the athletic field. They were silent at first. The heat was intense; walking in the shade only made it worse.

"I can't believe Cara went out with Derek," remarked Sue.

"I'm more surprised her parents let her go to the dance in the first place," returned Brett. "They keep that young lady on a seriously tight leash."

"Oh?"

He nodded.

"You should see the file. She can only go straight from home to school and back. Can't go to any off campus field trips unless she is watched constantly; no after school activities," he smirked wryly.

"They never let her out of the house except for school."

Sue was shocked.

"How do you know that?" she asked, her eyebrows raised.

"I'm her counselor, remember? Andy's told me some things too."

"Sounds like some serious controlling, to me," observed Sue, her voice deepening with concern. "What's the deal? Are they religious or—?"

"No," said Brett, firmly. "I don't think it has anything to do with religion. For one thing, there'd be curriculum restrictions and forbidden activities. Besides, most of the students in *that* kind of situation are home-schooled."

"But you told me no field trips—" she began but he broke in.

"Yes—but only the field trips where she wasn't under constant observation. What she did in school and all that was never addressed."

He looked up at her as they continued, reached the running track and turned to follow it.

"She's taken all the sex-ed classes; all the health classes, science, all the stuff that usually gets tabooed by people like that."

"Hmmm," muttered Sue, her eyebrows furrowed.

"What are her parents like?" she asked, after a moment.

"Have no idea," said Brett, with a shrug. "I've never met them in person."

Sue nearly stopped walking at this statement.

"*What?*"

"To be honest, I don't think *anyone* has; except for Andy maybe."

"But—but—surely they show up for conferences?"

"No. I send them a letter with any concerns I have about her progress. They send one back acknowledging they've seen it. She's done pretty good in her class work so they've seldom commented on them."

Sue was growing more and more astounded.

"And they don't have a phone," she recalled, thoughtfully.

"Nope. No cable, no television, no radio. They don't even have electricity."

"No elec—they can't *do* that!"

"Why? The building codes say you have to have the connections to the power grid in place but nothing says they have to be turned on."

"I suppose her father has his own generator?" she mouthed, contemptuously.

"No," said Brett positively. "They just do without."

They walked on in silence for a while.

"Does she *ever* leave the house except to go to school?" asked Sue.

"Not according to Andy," responded Brett. "She said she always had to go over there if she wanted to spend time with her."

"Hmmm," Sue pondered. "Sounds to me," she continued, her tone growing severe, "Like *abuse*—not religion."

"You think that hasn't already occurred to me? Trust me, when they tried to enroll her in school, there were at least three investigations including one with Child Protective Services. And every single one of them came back with: no findings," and he cleared his throat.

"Anyway, she has none of the classic signs: no mysterious bruises, broken bones, heavy makeup, unexplained behavior patterns, mood swings. She isn't withdrawn and is a good learner," and he took a deep breath.

"So the answer is: no. Whatever is going on, it isn't abuse."

"Well, okay, but her social skills—"

"Her social skills haven't suffered at all. She has no problems with anyone at school; people like her..." and he cleared his throat again.

"Her parents are just people who value their privacy and isolation. That's all."

"But that's impossible," sputtered Sue, "You can't isolate yourself in our society! You have to have medical care, buy food—"

"I know," agreed Brett. "You can't keep it out but you can certainly wall yourself in. I think they've done a pretty good job of it—it works for them."

She looked at him for a moment as they walked.

"How can you *do* that?" she asked with more than a tinge of exasperation.

"Do what?" he responded.

"How can you just—*ignore* all that? I mean if it were me, I'd be going crazy trying to figure this out. You just take it all so *calmly,*" she struggled for a moment to find the words.

"It's like you don't *care*," she finally tore out.

He remained impassive.

"I don't. Don't get me wrong," he continued as her eyebrows rose, "I'm just as puzzled as you are about it. On the other hand, the only thing I am responsible for is seeing she's safe and meets the graduation requirements. The rest of it doesn't matter.

"I know it sounds weird," he continued, "but that's the way I deal with stress. It took me a while to figure the system out and stay within the lines, but I'm good at following my rules. Ignoring stuff I have nothing to do with makes things a lot easier for me."

This time she made no effort to mask her disgust.

"Where did you get *that* from? Are you into Zen or something?"

"No. It's just something I've figured out on my own," he replied.

"*Gawd!*" she exploded, her voice loud with frustration.

He looked at her in surprise.

"What?"

"*You!* You—you just—you think you know it all! Nothing shocks you. You don't need to ask questions because you *know* the answers. You don't get curious because you *understand* everything!" she flung out.

There was a brief silence.

"Tell me something," he began, quietly. "Do you value my friendship?"

"What do you think?" she flung back, still angry.

"Do you?" he repeated.

"Of course I do!" she retorted, not detecting the subtle change in his voice.

Without warning, Brett stopped, grabbed her by the shoulder and spun her around to face him directly. She staggered to keep her balance, flushing with anger as she looked up at him.

Then she was ice cold with shock.

His eyes were blazing; his fists clenched; muscles taut and his pulse visible in his neck. He spoke tersely, gritting his teeth hard enough to grind them to powder:

"Don't you *ever* accuse me of that again!" he ground out. "The next time you do will be the *last* time you and I have anything but a professional conversation," and he leaned back slightly, crossing his arms over his chest, glaring at her.

"I—I..." she faltered but he broke in again.

"'*Understand*' everything! I *never* said that. I *never* use that disgusting word. What would you do if you were a rape victim fresh from the crime scene, bruised, in pain, the foul sperm still dripping from your vagina and flavoring your breath and I said to you, '*I understand how you feel*'?"

She bowed her head.

"You'd probably say something like, '*Listen asshole—you don't understand a fucking thing about what I'm going through!*'" and he snorted derisively.

"I grew up in the 70s. I was in school during the '*there are no wrong answers*' and feel-good psychobabble bullshit era. It totally fucked up our educational system—we're *still* recovering from the damage. It was almost funny to be sitting in the office still bruised up from a kid kicking my ass and hear that soothing, '*Yes, yes, Brett. I understand where you're coming from. But you need to look at it from his point of view. You need to work on communicating so both of you understand each other...*'"

He viciously spat at the ground.

"Yeah—I used to be like that too. I used to say that shit all the time. I still said it when I started doing counseling. I thought I really meant it. I wonder how many lives I wrecked? I can't stand to think about it," his voice rose.

"Fifty years I spread that bullshit gospel. *Fifty fucking years!* And all the time I thought I was such a great role model; such a great advocate for kids; such a great advisor.

"If someone hadn't finally set me straight and punctured my ego, I probably never would have figured it out. I was supposed to be an advocate for women but used sexist language. I was supposed to be the benevolent mentor when I didn't have a clue how condescending I was. I always said I *understood* everything and I didn't have a fucking clue.

"I don't want to be that person any more. I want to be what I always thought myself to be. I'm still not perfect: but I'm a hell of a lot better than I was three years ago. And I'm *definitely* walking the talk now. I don't try understanding *anything*—I just *accept* it. Cara and Andy fall in love with each other—so be it. Cara decides she wants to go out with Derek—so be it. Do I understand why she's doing this? No—and I'm not going to try."

He glared at her, enraged.

"Have you ignored everything I've said since we've known each other? The reason I never act surprised at what people do isn't because I understand them. I don't *want* to. I'm not interested in justifying their actions for them.

"The only thing I know—that I *do* understand—is I will *never* understand *anything*. My role is to watch and pay attention to the important stuff. The rest of it is none of my fucking business."

He turned on his heel and strode away without looking back.

Sue, shaking, clamped her jaws together to keep her teeth from chattering. She stayed where she was for only a few minutes. Then she ran and caught up with him.

He did not acknowledge her but he did not try to leave her either. They simply walked in silence, off the track and back toward the main building.

"Brett?" she asked softly, not looking at him.

"Yes?" he replied without turning his head either.

She swallowed.

"Who was the person who '*set you straight*' on your—opinions?"

"You," he replied tersely.

She reached out, gripped his arm and brought him to a stop. They looked at each other wordlessly; then flung themselves into each other's arms in a tight, fierce hug.

"I'm sorry," she said.

"Don't apologize for being you," he responded.

"Can we still be friends?" she asked as they both released each other.

"Of course. We've been through worse than this."

He smiled and she glowed.

An anguished scream broke the silence, shocking them back into awareness of their situation.

"Did someone see us or something?" she asked as they sprang apart.

"No," said Brett. "It came from over there," and he half-ran, half-walked in the direction of the sound, Sue right with him.

"What the devil?" exclaimed Sue.

Derek stood at the door like a wild animal brought to bay, his face inflamed with anger. He wasn't alone. Spivey, struggling, was trying to raise herself up from the sidewalk where she'd fallen.

"Great," muttered Brett as they rushed forward.

Sue grabbed Spivey and assisted her to her feet. Derek, his face sullen, stuffed his hands in his pockets and leaned against the door.

"What's going on, Derek?" asked Brett, calmly.

"That *bitch* won't fucking—" Derek spouted but Brett broke in, his voice crisp.

"Derek," he warned, looking him in the eye.

"I'm sorry, Mr. Kell," he said, in a lower voice.

Brett nodded.

"What is she doing that's torking you off?"

"She keeps *following* me!" he said, almost wailing. "She won't go away. I can't shake her off. I don't want her bugging me!"

"Did you hit her?"

Derek looked away and flushed.

"Naw," he finally mouthed. "I pushed her away and she fell down."

He looked at Derek for a moment, then back at Spivey. She had calmed down and stood on her feet, one arm supported by Sue. Her heavy, wheezing, breathing complimented her flushed skin and the sweat pouring off her face.

Brett turned to Derek. *He's not doing much better,* he observed, noting the turtleneck clinging to Derek's frame and the telltale dark stains under the arms and elsewhere. His face was dripping.

"Kinda hot for that, isn't it?" Brett remarked, pointing at the turtleneck.

Derek wrapped his arms around himself as though afraid Brett was about to pull the turtleneck off.

"I'm fine," he said.

If you want me to believe that you have to be a hell of a lot more convincing, ran through Brett's head but he said nothing.

He walked over to Spivey.

"Did he hit you?"

She shook her head positively.

"No, Mr. Kell. He just pushed me and I lost my balance."

"Why are you following him?"

"I have to," wailed Spivey, trembling.

"Why?"

Derek, straightened himself up, then opened the door and walked into the building, forcibly shutting the door behind him. Brett looked back, made as though to stop him—then let it go and returned to Spivey.

"Why?" he asked again.

"I—I've got to go *with* him," she blurted, struggling to break loose of Sue's arm.

"Why?" asked Brett for the third time.

"He—He—He's *with* him! I can't let him get away!" she struggled again and then burst into tears, all resistance gone. She sank limply against Sue.

Brett looked at Sue.

She shrugged her shoulders.

"She's going to kill me! She's going to kill me!" sobbed Spivey.

"Who is?" asked Brett, sternly.

Spivey looked up at him, tears dripping down her trembling face.

"A—Andy," she quavered and burst into tears again.

"What did she say to you?" asked Sue.

"She—she said if I didn't do what she said she'd kill me. Her and Lisa..."

Spivey broke down and sobbed without restraint.

"What did she ask you to do?" asked Brett.

"F—f—follow Derek," but she could no longer speak and cried heavily into Sue's shoulder.

"Spivey," broke in Sue, raising her head, "don't exaggerate. You know Andy and Lisa didn't really mean that."

"She—she's," and again Spivey broke down in tears.

"What did she do to you?" asked Sue.

Spivey struggled to find her voice.

"She grabbed me—she grabbed my head—made me look right at her—she scared me…" and she began crying again, this time without stopping.

Sue looked at Brett, dumbfounded.

He took a deep breath.

"Call her mother," said Brett, "Have her come pick her up."

Sue nodded.

"Where are you going?" asked Sue as Brett turned away.

His face was grim.

"I'm going to have a chat with a couple of students I'm very disappointed in. About intimidation and bullying."

He turned and walked rapidly toward the parking lot, Sue staring after him with dismay.

"Come on Spivey," she said, "Let's go inside."

"Derek—!" she cried out but Sue firmly steered her toward the door.

"Derek can take care of himself," she said, opening the door.

* * *

Brett made his way to the parking lot and looked around. He spied a burly individual wearing a security uniform standing in one of the rows and waved his hand. The man waved back and began walking toward him. They met in the middle of the lot.

"Munson?" asked Brett, in greeting.

"Yeah?" replied Munson, his muscles rippling beneath his uniform.

Brett gave him a grim smile.

"You on parking lot duty today?"

"Yup," he affirmed.

"Have Lisa and Andy been back?"

"No," responded Munson. "Not since they left around ten. You looking for them?"

Brett hesitated.

"Yeah. I need to see them."

"Treat them rough?" asked Munson, noting Brett's dark expression.

"No," said Brett. "Just make sure they come straight to my office without any side-trips."

Munson nodded and resumed walking through the parking lot, his eyes darting left and right. Brett turned and headed toward the main building.

* * *

Sue was waiting for him in his office.

She looked apprehensive.

"Her mom come to get her?" asked Brett as he reached his desk.

"Yeah and she won't leave. She's furious. She wants to talk to you."

Brett let out a sigh.

"Send her in."

Sue left and returned shortly with Spivey, still crying and a slim, fierce looking woman enclosed in an outfit that would have done credit to a high fashion magazine.

"Mr. Kell," she began, furiously, "I *demand* to know why those two girls did this to my daughter! I demand to know why you let it happen—"

"M'am," spoke Brett, keeping his eyes directly on hers. "I was in my office when the incident happened. You can rest assured if I *had* been there I would've put a stop to it."

"She's been teased and tormented and made fun of for the entire time she's been at this rotten school and nothing's been done about it! I'm seeing my lawyer about this! This is the *last straw!*" she snarled.

"M'am," said Brett, very politely, "Your right to consult an attorney is not ours to take away from you."

This response threw the woman off her stride; she relaxed a hair.

"Well they had no business threatening to kill her," she snapped.

"That's not what happened!" cried out Spivey.

"Don't stick up for them!" admonished her mother.

"But it's—" and Spivey broke down again.

Her mother looked at Brett in triumph as though she had confirmed something he doubted.

"You see?" she said.

"I see," replied Brett, evenly.

"I expect something to be done about this! I want those two girls punished!"

"You have my word I will see to that."

"See that you do!" she spat, turning toward her daughter.

"Come on, honey, let me take you home," she said as if addressing a much younger child.

Spivey tried to say something but her sobs broke loose again. She bent forward and pressed her hands over her eyes.

"Come on, baby," said her mother, gently lifting her to her feet and urging her toward the door.

With a last glare at Brett, the woman shepherded Spivey through the door and slammed it heavily behind her. The sound of her litany and her daughter's sobbing echoed in the hallway—gradually fading to silence.

Brett let out his breath.

Sue looked at him, her face troubled.

"I'm sorry. She insisted she had to see you."

He smiled coldly.

"Had to be done," he said and sat down at his desk.

"Do you think she's going to sue?"

Brett grimaced.

"She usually talks a good game," he admitted. "But I think she's serious this time. I haven't seen her *that* torked in a long time."

He fell silent, defeated.

Sue looked at him for a few minutes.

"Brett? Do you need me to tell—?"

"No—I'll take care of that. You can go if you want to," he responded, wearily, leaning back in his chair.

"Can you drop by for dinner?" she asked.

He nodded absently.

"I'll be there."

She started to leave but paused at the door.

"Brett?"

"Yes?"

"What was Spivey talking about? You know, when she said '*he's with him.*' What's *that* supposed to mean?"

Brett frowned.

"I don't know," and he shrugged. "It sounds like a typical Spivyism," he finished.

She gave him one last glance and left him in his office.

* * *

Derek, free of the shadow dogging his footsteps, raced aimlessly along the hallway, not paying attention to where he was going. His only concern was to keep moving—to not stay in one place long enough to think about what was going on.

"Hey there stud! Whassup?" came a shout.

Startled, Derek raised his head and collided with a stranger who slapped Derek on the shoulder, hugged him tightly and shook his hand. Derek, taken by surprise, allowed all this to occur without any resistance or reaction. As his thoughts began to settle, he gave his companion a sharper glance and pushed him away.

"Do I know you?" he asked.

The stranger laughed.

"Forgotten already? I played you three rounds at the tournament back in March!"

"March?" he repeated, absently.

"Yeah—*you* know. The *Cribbage* meet," said the stranger effusively.

"Y—yeah. I think I remember you," said Derek uncertainly.

"Got that short attention span thing going, man?" the stranger laughed. "You might as well get to know me anyway—*I'm* gonna win it next year."

Derek stared at him.

"So whatcha up to? Can ya hang out for a few?"

"I guess," responded Derek with a shrug.

"You *still* don't remember me?" asked the stranger.

"What's your name?"

"Nemo," was the reply.

Derek nodded.

"Come on," urged Nemo, taking him by the shoulder, "Let's go chat someplace out of the way."

"Where at?" asked Derek, suddenly filled with suspicion.

"It's a sunny day outside," came the reply.

Derek stopped where he was, flinging off Nemo's arm.

"No," he said firmly.

"Well, then *you* pick a place," said Nemo, his eyes dancing.

"Library?"

"You can't *talk* in the library!" laughed Nemo.

"Not in the library. The game rooms," Derek clarified.

His companion nodded.

"Sounds kewl. You lead the way."

Derek, still suspicious, walked toward the library, Nemo at his side, obviously fighting off a laughing jag. Derek gave him an annoyed glance but this only made it worse. Nemo was still desperately trying to keep cool as Derek opened the door, let him pass through and slipped quietly inside behind him. He looked to his left and spied a man with horn-rimmed glasses in a stark grey outfit standing behind the checkout counter, looking straight at him.

Derek nodded. The man stared back at him without responding until the door clicked shut. A puzzled expression came across his face. Then he went back into his office, shaking his head.

Didn't he see me? thought Derek.

"Who's that?" asked Nemo.

"Mr. Chambers. The librarian," replied Derek.

Nemo grinned.

Derek's face grew more and more troubled as he looked at Nemo. Nemo caught the look and asked, "Something wrong?"

"What's so funny?"

Nemo nearly laughed out loud.

"Nothing. I'm just in a good mood. Is that what's bugging you?"

"I don't know," replied Derek. "I can't help thinking I've seen you somewhere before."

"I told you already."

"No, someplace *else*. Not the tournament."

"It's possible," laughed Nemo without explaining the remark.

They passed through the main part of the library and continued to the back. There were some rooms along the rear wall, each of them with a windowed door and an interior window allowing a full view of the room from without. To the far left was an outside window; to the right an alarmed fire exit. All of the rooms contained a table, four chairs and a shelf along the back bristling with cards, board games and other such items.

"Hey—*here* we go!" exclaimed Nemo, opening one of the rooms and walking through the door.

Derek followed reluctantly and took in the scene: the usual table, chairs and a deck of cards with a cribbage board in the middle of the table.

"What's wrong *now?*" asked Nemo, noting Derek's confused look.

"It isn't like Mr. Chambers to let people leave games out on the table," he explained.

He had taken a seat at the table before he realized what he was doing; he recalled himself and glanced around, his suspicions heightened for some reason. He looked back at his companion but Nemo was at the shelf, turning over the game boards with an admiring grin.

"Wow," said Nemo.

"What?" asked Derek.

"You guys got a lot better stuff here than where I come from," he responded. "You even have a copy of Stadium Checkers. I didn't know they made that anymore!"

Derek nodded absently.

Nemo stepped back from the shelf, shut the door and looked at Derek.

"So, you really think you're going to win again next year?"

"No reason I can't," replied Derek.

Nemo laughed, throwing his head back.

It was a little louder than it should have been, even with the door closed. Derek looked around anxiously but Mr. Chambers did not make an appearance to chase them out. He relaxed a shade.

"There is no *way* you'll win next year," said Nemo.

"Whatever," said Derek, apathetically.

"You seriously think you can play better than me?"

Derek looked at him, puzzled.

"I did before, didn't I?"

Nemo grinned.

"Yeah—but that was *before*."

Derek picked up his ears. There was something odd about the way Nemo stressed *'before'*—it sounded off-key, as if he really meant something else.

"Why should it be different now?"

Nemo grinned again.

"Shall we see for ourselves?" and he pointed to the board and cards on the table.

Derek reached for the cards, Nemo taking the seat opposite. Derek shuffled and placed the deck on the table. Nemo cut. They drew two cards.

"Four," said Nemo.

"King," said Derek.

He gathered the cards and reshuffled. Nemo cut the deck again and Derek dealt out six cards to each. Derek glanced through his, discarded two and put them on the table. Nemo did the same. Nemo turned up the top card in the deck: a jack of spades.

"Heels," announced Nemo, putting a peg in the second space of his slot on the board.

Derek glanced at his hand and frowned. *No jacks.*

He pulled out a queen and placed it on the table.

"Ten," he announced.

"Twenty for two," responded Nemo, putting down a queen of his own.

"Thirty for six," grinned Derek, putting down a third queen.

"Thirty-one for two," announced Nemo as he played an ace. Derek scowled.

"One," announced Derek, playing the next card.

Nemo raised his eyebrows, but put down a card.

"Nine."

Derek grinned and put down a six.

"Fifteen for two."

"Twenty-one for four," said Nemo triumphantly as he laid down another six. Derek's face fell.

They reclaimed their cards and began the count.

"Fifteen-two, two" and Nemo moved his peg four spaces.

"Two," and Derek moved his peg two spaces. He picked up the discarded hand.

"Fifteen-two, six," and moved eight spaces.

Nemo gathered the cards and repeated the process of cutting and dealing.

"One," announced Derek.

"Two," said Nemo.

"Ten."

"Fifteen-two."

Derek scowled.

"Twenty-four."

"Thirty-one for two."

Nemo moved his peg.

"Eight."

"Fifteen-two."

Nemo moved his peg again. Derek doubtfully gathered his hand.

"Run for three," he said.

"Twenty-nine," announced Nemo with a flourish.

Derek stared at his hand, not believing what he saw.

He swallowed.

Nemo played his crib.

"Eight," he announced, cheerfully moving his peg.

Derek gathered the cards and shuffled.

"Good thing we're not playing for money," he remarked, his lagging score graphically illustrated by the pegs on the board.

"You're right. What we're playing for is much more important than money," remarked Nemo idly as he arranged his hand, his eyes on his cards.

Derek looked up.

"What do you mean *'what we're playing for'*? What *are* we playing for?" he demanded.

Nemo was still arranging his hand.

"Honour," he said.

"Honour?" repeated Derek, not sure he had heard correctly.

"Well, yeah," said Nemo looking up from his cards.

Derek started to say something, then swallowed and began rearranging his hand. He grinned mentally: he had four fives, a six and a four.

Excellent, he thought.

He discarded two of the fives. Nemo turned over the starter card.

It was a five.

It took a few seconds for the significance of this to sink through Derek's head. He stared at the five and snapped up his head, his eyes glaring.

"What the *fuck?*" he asked, rising to his feet, violently pushing back the chair.

Nemo looked up with a grin.

"Something wrong?"

"Yeah!" he exploded. "I got four fives. What's *that* five doing there?" he slammed his hand on the table.

Nemo's grinned widened.

"You sure about that?"

Derek spread his hand on the table, then spread the crib.

One look was enough.

His face turned white, his eyes bulging.

There was only one five in the crib.

His knees gave way and he fell back into his chair, breathing hard.

"What—what—what the fuck is going on?" he half whispered. "I *know* I put two fives in there!"

Nemo nodded.

"You did."

Derek looked up at him, his mouth open.

Nemo laughed. The sound of it triggered a feeling of apprehension in Derek that intensified the more he stared at him.

"You *do* have short-term memory loss," said Nemo. "You forgotten about Friday night already?"

Derek sat bolt upright, staring at Nemo, horrified. He jumped to his feet and stood back from the table.

"*That's* where I saw you before," he almost whispered, his face white, "My Gawd. It's *you!*"

Nemo laughed again. This time the sinister overtones were plainly audible to Derek. He cringed as though in pain and covered his ears.

"You should pay more attention to what you read," continued Nemo, "or you'd remember I'm allowed to add something unexpected to each round of the game. Makes it more interesting that way."

Derek went cold, shivered and took another step back.

"I'm not playing with you," he uttered with soundless horror.

Nemo's smile hardened.

"Why not?"

"I'm not playing with your rules. There's no way I can win. I won't do it."

"You should have thought of that before you put *that* on," and Nemo pointed to Derek's neck. Derek's hand flew to his throat protectively. He cowered against the wall.

He fumbled at the turtleneck, frantically pulling it down.

"What are you doing?" asked Nemo.

"Taking *this* damn thing off!" spat Derek, clawing at his throat.

"You can't," said Nemo, resuming arranging his cards.

Derek continued to claw at his neck. He stiffened, his eyes bulged, his face turned red and grew darker. He clutched at his throat, struggled to draw breath and turned to Nemo in desperation.

"Make it let go!" he whispered.

His normal stance returned, he gasped and caught his breath, pressing his hand on his heart. He looked back at Nemo; the mocking expression on his face flared his anger again and he straightened up, walking away from the table.

"I'm getting the fuck out of here!" flung Derek as he reached for the doorknob.

"Try it," remarked Nemo, without looking up from his hand.

Derek touched the doorknob and froze. He struggled, his muscles straining and veins bulging, but he could not open the door or force the knob to turn so much as an inch.

"Go ahead and scream if you want to," continued Nemo, keeping his eyes on his cards, "It's useless."

Derek, unable to stifle his fear any longer, broke out in anguished screams of terror tearing through the room, pounding violently on the door and clawing at the window, the blood from his knuckles smearing the glass and wood.

There was no response.

He finally ran out of strength and his arms slowly lowered to his side. Painfully bruised, his voice gone, he leaned against the window and sobbed.

At last, he slowly turned around and shuddered as he met Nemo's cold, pitiless glance.

"Shall we continue?" asked Nemo, pointing to the cards.

"Why are you doing this to me?" asked Derek, his voice small and weak.

"You brought it on yourself," was the cold reply.

"I didn't know it was for real! I thought it was a dream or something!"

Nemo's eyes glittered evilly.

"No you didn't. You *knew* it was real. Don't play the innocent victim with *me*. You had plenty of warning you were in danger but you chose to ignore it."

"I didn't!" wailed Derek.

"'*Don't make promises you can't keep*,'" quoted Nemo in a cruelly deliberate voice.

"She tried to save you. Even though she had nothing but cause to hate you, she tried to save you. But you blew her off. Instead of taking her advice, you ran to her coach, got her in trouble. You even put Spivey up to confirming it. The coach chewed her out the next afternoon. Really disgusting of you," said Nemo, shaking his head.

"I'm *not* going to play," stated Derek, although he was trembling violently.

"You know what happens if you don't," warned Nemo.

"I'm going to lose *anyway!*" cried out Derek.

Nemo shrugged.

"Perhaps. But if you break *this* promise you will *never* be free of the consequences."

Derek, his will completely shattered, staggered back to his seat and collapsed, staring at Nemo listlessly as he gathered the cards and shuffled for the next round.

Monday Afternoon

"Oh *great*," moaned Andy.

Lisa echoed her as she, too, watched the departing school buses and the plethora of cars crowding for space as their fellow students left school for the last time that year. Both of them gritted their teeth while Andy carefully picked her way through the mob, nearly screaming with frustration as the obstacles grew more frequent.

The cloudless sky darkened—turning a deeper shade of blue. The ground trembled and everyone in sight froze where they stood, their heads turned in fright toward the main building. The air throbbed as though shock waves of intense sound were booming. There was a blinding flash that would have been attributed to lightning had there been any clouds in the sky.

Andy and Lisa looked at each other, wordlessly, then cringed as a blast of hurricane-force wind twisted the trees. A thunderous roar screamed out, shaking the ground violently, its echoes reluctantly fading to silence.

It was over in a few seconds. The sky returned to normal; the wind stopped; and the people—who had remained petrified throughout this incident—relaxed and resumed their lives.

Andy took a deep breath; Lisa did the same.

"What was *that?*" breathed Lisa, frightened.

Andy looked grim.

"That sound," said Lisa, the panic in her voice rising, "I heard it before. When that thing—" Andy swiftly grabbed her hand and held it to her breast. Lisa stopped and remained silent, Andy watching her face carefully.

A raucous honk shook them out of their trance.

"Give it up, jerk," muttered Andy as she released Lisa's hand, put the car in gear and continued forward, the crowd rapidly thinning out.

At last, Andy reached the parking lot, turned in and scouted for a spot, the lot deserted except for a car or two. She pulled into a space, shut the engine off, drew a deep sigh of relief and then quickly vaulted from her seat, Lisa right behind her.

She had just clicked the lock button on her key fob when an unexpected voice boomed out, her already overwrought nerves screaming. She heard Lisa gasp; she echoed it as she raised her head and beheld the figure of Mr. Munson approaching.

"Mr. Kell wants to see you," announced Munson, his face grim.

They looked at each other. There was no reason to be afraid. And yet...

"Why?" asked Andy.

Munson did not answer.

"Come on," he ordered, waving them ahead of him.

They glanced at each other again and walked toward the main building. They entered the doorway and turned to the left, their footsteps echoing oddly in the deserted hallways. Most of the faculty had left; they were the only students remaining.

Reaching Brett's office, a cold, "Get in here, you two," burst from an unsmiling face they had never seen on him before. Their apprehension rose as he strode past them and shut the door.

They stood in front of his desk as he made his way back from the door to his chair. He sat down heavily and stared at them for a few minutes.

It felt like hours.

"What have you got against Spivey?" he asked.

Baffled, Andy replied, "Nothing. Why?"

"*Nothing?*" echoed Brett, the sarcasm in his tone grating harshly in their ears.

"No," affirmed Andy.

"She's a *friend* of yours?"

Andy was growing more and more puzzled by this conversation.

"She's not my friend but she's not my enemy either."

Brett looked skeptical.

"Why did you threaten to kill her?"

This shocked them both into stunned silence. Andy felt herself going numb as she stared into Brett's unsmiling expression, realizing something had critically gone wrong.

"I didn't threaten to kill her!" she breathed.

"That's not what *she* says," he responded.

"Mr. Kell," Andy began, "I didn't do anyth—" but he broke in, standing up from his chair.

"I suppose you're going to tell me you didn't grab her by the back of the head and force her to look at you either?"

Andy was stunned into silence.

"I am really disappointed in you, Andy. And you, too, Lisa. I thought better of you both than this."

The two friends looked at each other open mouthed, their mutual terror igniting in their eyes.

"Derek takes out your girlfriend and scores a point on you. Instead of letting it go and letting him have the last word, you had to take a swipe at him before you left. That's bad enough. But dragging Spivey into it? I didn't think either of you could sink that low."

Lisa's lip trembled and she burst into tears.

Andy, growing more frightened and confused, stammered out,

"What are you talking about Mr. Kell? I didn't do *anything* to Spivey *or* Derek!"

"Come on, Andy!" exploded Brett. "Get off that routine. You know how serious this is? You both are over eighteen. If you get charged with bullying and intimidation, you'll be charged as *adults*—not in juvy. Spivey about cried her eyes out in my office and her mom is out for your blood!"

Andy, shaking her head and trying to control the numbness flooding through her, opened her eyes and stared at Brett wildly.

"Oh my *Gawd!*" she exclaimed and began fumbling in her purse.

"Put that cell phone away if you don't want me to take it from you," warned Brett, moving away from his chair.

Andy paid no attention. She stared at her phone, pressed some keys and gave a cry of horror. Lisa looked up at her through her tears in surprise.

"Derek! They're closing—!" cried out Andy. Seizing Lisa's hand, the two of them turned and fled from the office, ignoring Brett's rising shouts to come back. They heard his phone ring; heard his voice as he picked it up; and then they were too far away to hear anything more.

"The library!" gasped Andy.

The two of them turned the corner and shouted out, "Mr. Chambers! Wait!"

Mr. Chambers removed his key from the library door and looked up in surprise at the two young women rushing up to him. They nearly knocked him over when they reached him and he pushed them away, angrily, brushing at his clothes as if soiled from their contact.

"Please open up the door, Mr. Chambers!" cried out Andy.

"The library is closed for the day," responded Mr. Chambers in a stiff voice.

"You've got to open up! We've got to get in there—" begged Andy but Mr. Chambers glared angrily.

"You had all day to come in and retrieve your things," he admonished them. "It's too late. I've locked up and I'm going home. You'll have to come back tomorrow," and he turned away from the door.

"Open that door or I'll break it down!" barked Andy, her pleading tone gone.

Mr. Chambers stopped in surprise; stood still for a moment; and then slowly turned around, his whole demeanor swelling up in offended rage.

"You will do *no* such thing, young lady. You and your friend need to leave this hallway. Who do you think you are, making threats and giving orders?" he lectured, sternly.

Andy, breathing hard, her eyes wide and nostrils flaring, moved closer to him. He backed up against the wall despite himself.

"I'm *telling* you right now," she uttered, her voice cold and hard, "open that fucking door or I'll break the trophy case and throw one through the window to get in!"

"How *dare* you use such language!" gasped the shocked Mr. Chambers. "You leave here at once! I'm ordering you!" he shouted, pointing his finger to the exit.

"What is going on?" a sharp voice interrupted that caused all three of them to turn.

A woman in executive dress with silver streaked hair and steel blue eyes glared at them, angrily.

"What's going on?" she asked again.

"These two girls—" began Mr. Chambers but Andy interrupted him with, "There's someone locked in the library and he won't open the door!"

"That is absolutely untrue!" shouted Mr. Chambers, his self-control gone.

"How do you know?" asked the woman.

"I personally checked all the rooms and stacks before I locked that door! There is *no one* in there!" he screamed, outraged beyond bearing.

"Ms. Lentmik," began Andy but the woman thus addressed held up her hand to silence her. She turned to Mr. Chambers.

"Unlock the door," she commanded.

"But Ms. Lentmik, I assure you—" but she wearily cut him off.

"Unlock the door, Mr. Chambers."

He stared at her, trembling with rage.

"Are you saying you don't believe—" but she interrupted him again with a touch of asperity.

"I'm not saying I believe or disbelieve you or anyone in this hallway. The only issue at stake right now is whether someone is in the library or not. It's simple to resolve: unlock the door."

Pale and shaking, Mr. Chambers fumbled with his keys, pushed one into the lock and turned. Andy and Lisa flew past him into the library as he pulled the door open and began running up and down the aisles between the stacks.

"Turn on the lights and check your office area," said Ms. Lentmik, "I'll check the storeroom."

Mr. Chambers gave a gasp of impatience but he did as she asked. The lights flashed on and he went behind the counter and looked into his office. Ms. Lentmik opened the storeroom and looked through it carefully.

A few minutes later, all four of them gathered in the main area.

"Find anything?" asked Ms. Lentmik.

"No," admitted Andy, despondently.

"You see?" cried out Mr. Chambers triumphantly.

Ms. Lentmik looked thoughtful and glanced around the room.

"You went all the way to the back?" she asked.

"Yes, m'am," responded Lisa.

"Did you look in the game rooms?"

Lisa and Andy looked at each other and dashed toward the back of the library.

"Gloria," sputtered Mr. Chambers, "I *personally* checked the rooms before I left. There was—" he broke off with a horrified gasp as the screams burst forth.

Gloria, startled into immobility by that terrible sound, snapped out of her trance as Lisa came running toward them, her eyes wide with horror.

"What's wrong? What is it?" barked Gloria.

"Oh Gawd! Oh my Gawd! It's—it's *Derek!*"

Lisa collapsed to her knees, dragged herself over to a waste can and vomited into it.

Mr. Chambers and Gloria turned away.

"Rutherford," she fired off, "call 911. Keep an eye on Lisa," and she immediately ran toward the back as another scream broke. Lisa, hearing it, succumbed to another bout of nausea, crouching even closer over the waste can.

Gloria's ears began to catch some snatches of words mingled with a sobbing lamentation ahead of her. She reached the back of the library and checked both directions. Her eyes narrowed at the sight of an open door.

"Oh my Gawd! He's gone. He's gone. I didn't hate him like *that*. I didn't want this to happen. I *tried* to save him. I tried *so* hard. Why did you have to *do* this to him? I never asked you for—" and the words faded into sobbing.

Gloria gingerly approached the room with the open door, noted the bloodstains, peered through the window and nearly fainted at the sight before her eyes. She had to take several deep breaths before she could look again and make her way through the door into the room.

Andy, hunched over the remains of what had once been Derek, rocked back and forth with her arms tightly wrapped around her knees, tears streaming down her face. It was hard to say which was more frightening: the mangled corpse on the floor or the sight of Andy, Andy the stoic, the imperturbable, the ever stable, completely broken down emotionally.

Gloria leaned down and touched Andy gently on the head. Andy shuddered but did not relax.

"Andy?" asked Gloria in a gentle voice.

No response.

"Andy? Can you hear me?"

A brief nod.

"Andy? You need to come away with me. You need to go somewhere safe. There's nothing we can do for him. He's gone."

Andy trembled.

"I didn't want this to happen," she wept.

It was a strange remark but Gloria had no time to waste.

"You did your best Andy," she said, soothingly. "It's not your fault. But you need to come with me, now. Okay? Can you stand up?"

Gloria reached out and laid her hand on Andy's arm; Andy shivered but did not pull away. Slowly, trying hard not to look at what was left of Derek, she gradually persuaded Andy to rise.

Getting Andy to her feet, out of the room of death and back to the lobby was a dreadful ordeal. Forced to uphold a slow, gentle pace while holding Andy upright on her useless shaking legs, Gloria feared they'd never get there. When they finally reached the lobby, Gloria, drained emotionally and physically, was near collapse herself.

Andy spied Lisa, sitting on the floor, bent double and holding tightly to her stomach. She easily slipped free of Gloria and quickly joined Lisa, wrapping her arms around her and holding her.

Gloria, leaning against the counter and catching her breath, watched this scene sadly, then turned away as Rutherford came up to her.

"They're on their way," he told her.

Gloria nodded.

"Thank you, Rutherford."

"Gloria?" he asked.

She looked up.

"Is—" he swallowed hard, "Is Derek—?"

She shook her head.

"He's dead, Rutherford."

Rutherford turned pale.

"I swear to you, Gloria, I didn't see *anything*—" but Gloria stopped him before he could grow hysterical.

"Rutherford," she said, firmly, "I believe you. We'll figure all this out later. Do me a favor," she continued, "run out front to meet the police so they don't waste time looking for us. Would you do that?"

"Yes, Gloria," said Rutherford.

"You may leave after that if you wish. I'll lock up for you. If they have anything to ask you they can talk to you later."

"Thank you," stammered Rutherford. He turned and rapidly left the library. She sighed and looked back at Lisa and Andy, still clinging to each other, finding comfort in their mutual embrace. Gloria took a deep breath, a step toward them—then decided to remain silent and leaned on the checkout counter again, trying to recover her strength.

The sound of a radio transmitting and crackling behind her caused her to turn around. A uniformed police officer was striding through the door as Rutherford held it open for him. As soon as the officer was fully in the library, Rutherford shut the door and left.

"Where is it?" asked the officer.

"In the game rooms," said Gloria, motioning him to follow. They quickly made their way to the back; Gloria pointed to the open door and the officer walked over and looked inside.

He grabbed his microphone, his face neutral.

"Dispatch—Kemp," he stated.

"Go ahead," the radio crackled.

"Eighty-six the medics and get the coroner out here: we have a homicide victim."

"Ten-four. Are you seeking CSI support?"

"Affirmative."

"Ten-four and out."

He replaced the microphone in its holster and turned away from the door.

"Any idea what happened or when it happened?" he asked.

"No."

"Who discovered the body?"

"The two students out by the counter," she answered.

"You recognize the body?"

"Yes," she nodded. "It's Derek Wenlok. He's—he *was* a student here."

The officer looked around and began to frown.

"Has anyone been back here since the body was found?"

"No."

"When was it found?"

"About ten minutes ago."

"Who was with them?"

"I was."

"And no one has been back here since?"

"No, officer."

He looked around again with obvious doubt.

"Is something wrong?" she asked.

"Are there any other exits from the library, aside from the main entrance?" he asked, ignoring her question.

"There is a fire door at that end—but it's alarmed and needs to be reset if it's opened. No one's touched it."

Officer Kemp walked over to the door and examined it briefly.

"What about that window at the other end?" he asked.

"It's sealed. It doesn't open," replied Gloria.

"Well, let's go back out front and talk," and he led the way back to the checkout counter.

By this time, Lisa and Andy had regained their feet and were sitting opposite each other, at one of the round tables, their faces buried in their hands. Kemp gave them a brief glance and turned back to Gloria.

"Tell me exactly what happened," he demanded, pulling out a voice-recorder. He placed it on the counter and activated the device.

"I heard some loud voices in my office from the hallway," she began.

"What time?"

"About three or shortly afterward," she replied.

He nodded.

"I got up to investigate and found these two students at the door of the library along with the librarian, Mr. Chambers."

"Were they arguing? Shouting?"

"Yes," she nodded. "They were asking him to unlock the door and he'd already locked up for the day."

The officer frowned again.

"Why did they want him to unlock it?"

She took a deep breath.

"They said a fellow student of theirs was still inside."

"What were they arguing about?"

"Mr. Chambers, he's the librarian, he didn't want to unlock the door because he'd already checked the library before he locked it and didn't see anyone. He was on his way home. He's kind of a fuss-budget when it comes to things like that and doesn't like to break his routine," she added.

"So he refused to unlock it for them?"

"Yes. I came up and asked him to unlock it and he did."

"And the two girls went inside and found the body?"

Gloria's eyes flashed briefly but she kept her tone calm.

"The two *women*," she emphasized, "searched the stacks while Mr. Chambers and I looked through *this* part of the room."

"And they found the body?"

"No. They came back to the front just as we'd finished looking and said they couldn't find him."

"*Him?* So they knew who it was before they came in here?"

"They never mentioned his name."

"Then why did you say they couldn't find *him?*"

"Because I know who it was, now," responded Gloria sharply, "As I said, *they* never mentioned a name."

Kemp tapped his fingers on the counter for a moment.

"So," he continued, "you all gathered again. Then what?"

"I asked them if they'd looked inside of the game rooms—"

"Those rooms at the back?" interrupted Kemp.

"Yes. They went back there—"

"By themselves?"

Her eyes flashed again but she continued, "Yes. We heard a scream and Lisa, the dark-haired one," she pointed at Lisa, "ran back here and said Derek was there."

"And then?"

"I had Mr. Chambers call 911 and keep an eye on Lisa while I went back to find Andy. She was in the room next to—to the body."

"What was she doing?"

This time her tone sharpened.

"She was on her knees, crying."

"What did you do then?"

"I got her to come with me and brought her out here. She went and sat down with Lisa and they've both been here since."

Kemp nodded.

"Did either of them know this boy? Derek?"

Gloria took a deep breath but answered politely, "Yes, they both knew him."

"They were friends?" Kemp insisted.

"No. They just knew each other."

"Then why were they in such a rush to find him?"

Gloria's eyes hardened.

"I don't know."

"I can't see why they were so concerned. If he *had* been '*trapped in the library*' he could have let himself out, couldn't he? That door doesn't lock from *this* side, does it?" and he pointed to the entry door.

"No," she replied, thoughtfully.

"How did they know he was there in the first place?"

Her voice tightened.

"I have no idea. He might have sent them a text message or something. Or else they realized he was missing when everyone left. There weren't *that* many students here today."

Kemp did not waver.

"There's no sign of a cell phone anywhere in that room. Has there ever been trouble between them?"

Gloria hesitated.

"Well?" he prodded.

"There *was* trouble but it was a long time ago."

"When?"

"About five years ago."

"What was this '*trouble*'?"

Gloria straightened up and stared at him defiantly, her arms crossing over her chest.

"Andy punched him in the face," she stated.

"I see," said Kemp, coldly. "Why did she do that?"

"Because Derek called her and her friends a '*bunch of fat slutty dykes*' at the lunch table. He'd been picking on her for two years prior and she'd had enough of it."

She tightened her muscles.

"And they've left each other alone since?" asked Kemp, dubiously.

Gloria flushed.

"No. They had a brief confrontation last Thursday."

"I *see*."

"It wasn't anything more than a shouting match," she added, irritably.

"What about?"

She took a deep breath.

"Derek was taking her ex— her friend to the Prom and she was concerned he would take advantage of her. He had that reputation."

"He was taking out her ex?"

"Her ex-girlfriend," said Gloria through clenched teeth.

Kemp raised his eyebrows.

"Sounds like jealousy to me."

Gloria's eyes hardened and her face flushed.

"It might have been," she ground out, "but I doubt it. I think Andy was only concerned about her friend being raped. Nothing else."

Kemp was unmoved.

"And nothing else happened between them?"

"She had no contact with him today."

"That you know of," he added.

Gloria kept her poise although her tone was as sharp as steel.

"If there had been any problems I would have been told about it."

Kemp was not convinced. He shut off the recorder, picked it up and walked over to the table where Lisa and Andy sat. They looked up as he approached and paled; their eyes fixed on his every movement.

"I'm afraid I'm going to have to ask you two some questions," he began. The two friends looked at each other and back at the officer, panic flaring in their eyes.

"I'm sorry if you aren't up to this right now. But I need to find out some things about what's going on here before I can let you leave. Both of you come with me into the office," and he waved toward Mr. Chamber's glassed-in sanctum behind the counter.

They looked at each other again in desperation and stood up, trembling.

"Negative," snapped a voice. "These students are going home."

They whirled around.

"Mr. Kell!" two of them gasped.

Brett's face was firm and resolute as he faced Kemp; his mouth set as steel and his eyes glittering. Although his tone was polite, it was clear he was not going to let the officer intimidate him.

Kemp looked at him for a few minutes, astonished. Then, his face flushing, he began, "I'm sorry to have to break this to you, but—"

"I'm sorry, too, Officer," Brett broke in. "And I deeply apologize for appearing to make light of your authority in front of these students. I mean that. But the fact is, they are going home. You will have to talk to them another time."

Kemp straightened up.

"Listen, mister, you—" began Kemp but Brett cut him off once again.

"My name," he said tersely, "is Mr. Kell."

Kemp nodded coldly.

"And, I reiterate, these folks are going home. They were at school before class started; they are still here nearly an hour after dismissal. They have just been through a horrific, traumatic experience: finding the corpse of a classmate. They are tired. They are exhausted. They are at the end of their endurance. They need to go home and be with their families. In any case," he added, "you cannot question them without their parent's consent and I assure you *that* will not be forthcoming."

"That's not true, Mr. Kell," said Kemp icily. "I have the authority to question them without their parents consent in cases like this."

"You'll have to make that argument in court, Officer. The county prosecutor does not agree with you. The district has had three lawsuits filed in the last five years over this issue. All three times, we allowed questioning to take place without permission—we lost our case every time. It doesn't matter if verbal consent is given over the phone—the parents have to be physically present. Our counsel has given us pretty clear instructions. There will be *no* fourth lawsuit on my watch."

Kemp glowered but said nothing.

"As I said before, I sincerely apologize for having to present myself in this way to you; especially for having to do it in front of impressionable young adults. I respect your authority and am fully aware of the gravity of your responsibilities. I swear to you," he said, handing his card to the Officer, "by the virtue of my position as Dean of Students and as a citizen and taxpayer of the State of Washington, you will be able to contact these students at the proper time and they will appear in court when summoned. *My* responsibilities are to my students—and I am taking them home to their parents."

Before Kemp could react, Gloria spoke up.

"He's right, officer. Please come with me," and she led Kemp to the door of the library, pointing down the hall toward the main entrance.

"My office is right there. I will wait there until you have finished your investigation. Any time you have the opportunity, please step over and I will give you all the contact and identity information you may need."

"Thank you, m'am," said Kemp.

Gloria nodded her head and walked back to her office.

Kemp took a deep breath and turned back to Brett.

"I'm sorry," he began but Brett waved his apology aside.

"Please do not apologize, sir. I was out of line and I am fully aware of that. The circumstances drove me to use that approach but I am very sorry I was forced to do so."

The two men shook hands.

Brett turned back to the two women. They were, as he stated, near the end of their endurance, pale and trembling with frightened eyes.

He smiled at them.

"Let's go, you two."

They mechanically followed him as he made his way back to his office. He stopped them at the door, stepped inside, returned with two thick envelopes and continued walking toward the outside door.

Reaching his car, he opened the doors and they both slid into the back seat from opposite sides, sinking gratefully into the cushions. Brett made sure they were secure, then got into the front seat and started the car. Carefully, he made his way through the now deserted parking lot to the main road.

"Mr. Kell?" asked Lisa in a very small voice.

"Yes?"

"Are you taking us to jail?"

Brett smiled, sadly.

"No, Lisa. I'm taking you to your homes."

Something in his expression struck them both—they had seen him furious, they had seen him concerned and they had seen him friendly. But they had never seen him grieved. It shocked them but there was no mistaking that look: it mirrored in their eyes as they watched him.

"Mr. Kell?" began Andy, quavering. "I didn't do anything to Spivey. I can explain—" but Brett interrupted her with an upraised hand.

"It's okay, Andy. Spivey's mom called just after you left my office and told me everything. Spivey finally told her what *really* happened once she calmed down. Her mom apologized for accusing you both of something you didn't do."

"But," pleaded Andy, "there's more to it than that. I want to explain—" but Brett interrupted her once again.

"Andy," he warned. "You don't need to tell me. And I don't want to know. Don't get me wrong," he continued as Andy stared at him unbelievingly. "I am aware these waters are a lot deeper than they look. I think I can guess why he was wearing that turtleneck. And that thunderbolt out of a clear sky—but I don't need to know whether I'm right or not. For your sake and mine, it's better you *don't* explain anything to me. No," he said, with a sigh, "the two things I *do* know are enough."

Andy couldn't reply.

"First, I know neither you nor Lisa had anything to do with Derek's death. You left the campus at about ten; you didn't come back until after three. I saw Derek shortly after lunch. I think I can guess what time he died. You two weren't anywhere near the campus when that happened. Whatever occurred, you had nothing to do with it.

"The other thing," and he hesitated as though his throat bothered him, "the other thing is I betrayed the trust you had in me. I had no right to do that. I had no reason to. Throughout the twelve years we've known each other, I never doubted your word. I always believed you. Today, I doubted your word. I was wrong. I have no excuse and I am really, really sorry I did that. I'm never going to forgive myself. Please believe that."

Andy, her throat burning, said, "It's okay, Mr. Kell, I know—"

"It's not okay, Andy," he responded. "That was a terrible thing for me to do. I accused you without giving you a chance to tell your side of the story. You did nothing to deserve that treatment. And neither did you, Lisa," he added. "The hardest part is I'll never have an opportunity to make it up to you."

Two pairs of hands gently touched him on the shoulders and squeezed reassuringly. He blinked his eyes rapidly but said nothing.

"Mr. Kell?" asked Lisa. "Can I please go to Andy's house? I don't want—I don't want to be away from her right now."

Andy reached out and held her.

"Lisa," said Brett, "I have to take you to your mom. It's for sure Gloria already called both your parents. Your mom is worried to death about you. She isn't going to be reassured by a simple phone call from you—she wants to see you, to hear you, to hold you. That's the only thing that will convince her you're really and truly safe."

Tears appeared in her eyes.

"I promise," continued Brett, "I will ask her if I can take you to Andy's when we get there."

Andy gently wiped away Lisa's tears.

As they pulled into Lisa's driveway, her mother, who had been standing outside watching the street anxiously, dashed over and yanked open the door before Brett had completely stopped. She half pulled, half lifted Lisa out and clung to her, tears streaming down her face.

"Mom, I'm okay. I'm really okay," said Lisa as though embarrassed; but her tears flowed freely too.

"I was so worried about you! I couldn't think straight after I got the phone call," and she kissed her daughter several times.

Brett and Andy turned discreetly away while this was going on. After a few minutes, Brett opened his door, stepped out and approached the two women still clutching each other tightly.

"Oh!" gasped Lisa's mother, "Mr. Kell! Oh thank you for bringing her home!" and she threw her arms around him. Brett gently disengaged her and stood back, looking very flustered.

"No problem, Ms. Kothman," he said, finally. "Lisa wanted me to ask if it was okay if I took her over to Andy's."

Ms. Kothman turned white and mutely shook her head.

"I think it might be better for her," he continued, quietly. "They both have been through a terrible shock. It would help them both if they could grieve together."

Ms. Kothman turned to Lisa.

"Do you really want to leave me here by myself?" she asked, tearfully.

"Please, Mom," pleaded Lisa, "I need to be with Andy."

"Why don't you come along with us?" suggested Brett. "I'm sure Ms. Kasly won't mind."

Ms. Kothman nodded her head and got into the front seat; Lisa resumed her place next to Andy. Brett looked back, carefully reversed out of the driveway and continued to Andy's house.

Andy's mother was just getting out of her car when Brett pulled into the driveway. She looked up, startled, then anxious as she made out their faces. Walking quickly toward the car, she asked, "Is something wrong?"

Andy staggered out of the back seat and collapsed against her mother, shaking. Ms. Kasly instinctively tightened her grip while looking at Brett curiously over Andy's shoulders.

"Did you just get home?" he asked.

"Yes. Why?"

Brett sucked in his breath and continued.

"You didn't get a phone call?"

"No. I've been out most of the day. What's wrong?"

He hesitated.

"Derek Wenlok died at school today. Andy and Lisa found his body."

"Oh—my—Gawd," breathed Andy's mother, pulling Andy closer to her. She turned her face away but not before Brett caught sight of an expression in her eyes that startled him deeply. It was something beyond grief—far too intense for the situation.

"Lisa wanted to stay with Andy and her mother didn't want to be by herself so I brought her along. I hope you don't mind," he added.

Ms. Kasly straightened herself up and smiled.

"Of course not," and she turned toward Ms. Kothman.

"Why don't both of you come inside so we can collapse together?"

Ms. Kothman laughed through her tears and they led their daughters inside the house, leaving the door ajar. Brett remained outside for a few minutes; then, recalling something, returned to his car. Emerging with the two envelopes he'd taken from his office, he approached the front door and stepped through, shutting it behind him.

At first, he had no idea where to look for them. He peered into the kitchen but it was deserted. He caught the sound of a sob, followed the source and found all four of them sitting together on a couch, clinging to each other for comfort. They looked up and fell silent as he entered the room. He smiled, a little sadly and handed the two envelopes to Lisa and Andy.

"Present for you," he explained.

They looked at each other.

"Go ahead—open it," he urged.

They broke the seal on the envelopes and stared at the paper inside; tears gathering rapidly in their eyes.

"Your diplomas," he said. "I thought you might not want to attend graduation in person so I figured I'd give these to you now. This way you have the option of showing up or staying home. Congratulations."

He turned to leave.

"Mr. Kell—wait!" came a cry behind him.

He turned around.

"Thank you," said Andy. Lisa echoed her.

"No," said Brett firmly, "this isn't something you thank *me* for. *You* are responsible for this. You worked hard for twelve years to get these. This is your victory—not mine."

"But without you we'd never have made it!" said Lisa.

"No," he said again.

"All I did was give you the tools you needed for the job. It was up to you to learn how to use them and use them correctly. These are *your* trophies. Congratulations and welcome to the adult world," and he turned away quickly, walking rapidly to the door.

He was only able to make it as far as his car before the tears broke loose. He swayed and leaned against the frame of the vehicle for a few minutes, defeated.

He nearly died of fright when he felt the tap on his shoulder.

Andy's mother was there, the expression that disturbed him earlier flooding her face.

"Mr. Kell," she began, tentatively.

She took a deep breath and continued.

"Did Cara come to school today?"

He stared at her for a moment.

"No. She did not."

Tears came into her eyes and she bowed her head.

"It isn't your fault," he added. "There is nothing you could have done. They've closed the gate."

She looked up at him sharply but he placed a warning finger against his lips.

"I see," she said, finally. "Thank you, Mr. Kell."

She turned and went into her house without looking back.

*** ***

Andy's mother roused herself from sleep and looked around the room. The sun was low in the sky and the light was nearly gone. She glanced over at the other couch and saw Ms. Kothman's sleeping form, her breathing regular and quiet.

She smiled.

Then she carefully got up and walked quietly up the stairs. Turning the corner, she approached Andy's bedroom door and gently turned the knob, pushing the door open just enough to look inside.

Andy and Lisa were lying together on the bed, their arms wrapped around each other. They were both sound asleep.

I hope they don't dream, she thought.

She carefully closed the door and withdrew.

Andy and Lisa lay together at peace; temporarily released from the torment of the vision burned forever in their eyes: *the sight of Derek's naked body, his severed head placed on his chest, the necklace still knotted tightly around his throat—the necklace Andy had seen so often clasped around Cara's sweet, white neck—the cord pulled tight enough to slice through his skin and snap his spinal cord...*

Afterwords

For those who are curious, here are some extra details (and a few clarifications) about the stories in this book.

First—the legal stuff: All the works within this book are fiction. They are not based or drawn from any real incident, past present or future. Some real locations and real buildings are used to provide verisimilitude where needed, but this does not imply the events took place there.

The characters in the stories are not based or drawn or intended to be seen as based on real people, past, present, or future. Any resemblance to any person, living, imaginary or dead, is a regrettable coincidence. The names used are not derived or intended to resemble any real person, living or dead. Any resemblance to any person, imaginary, living or dead, is a regrettable coincidence.

Next, a warning. If you are the sort of person that needs explanations of what is going on and why, you are going to find my writing frustrating. I deliberately *avoid* providing explanations. Why? Because I am trying to create a realistic atmosphere and in real-life we are *never* provided explanations.

Since Dracula, a compulsory character for all horror novels is an enlightened scientist who steps in and explains what's going on to the frightened protagonists. In Dracula, Van Helsing explains what Dracula is, what he does and how he can be vanquished. The action conveniently pauses while he does this.

And for reasons that baffle my understanding, everyone seems to expect that character to appear in any horror story written since.

If you think about it, that's ridiculous. The truth is, if we faced an unknown danger, the *last* thing we would do is seek out a scientist or sit quietly waiting for an explanation. We would be either fighting for our lives or terrified out of our skulls. We wouldn't understand what was going on. In fact, we'd probably never find out. To me, that is the essence of true terror—to let the imagination and our fears run loose. It's as realistic as it gets.

Elegy for a Dryad

The idea behind this story concerns our lack of knowledge about the era of the Greek myths. Most people are familiar with them, but there are often multiple versions of the same story, which sometimes conflict with one another. There is no way to identify which of them is the *'correct'* version—if you think about it, there is no way to ensure we know the *whole* story either. Considering how long ago those stories were created, it's more than likely some details are forgotten. And those missing details might be critical.

The two lovers in the Elegy make the mistake of calling on the ancient powers for help. It turns out, unfortunately, that those powers demand a price for their aid and sometimes play cruel practical jokes. We will never know why things went amiss—but it is a safe bet to assume the lovers got the invocations wrong and offended the powers by doing so. And if that happened...

Note on the 'Greek' invocations: The landowner and Dmitri are correct—the invocations are rendered into Greek using an automated translation program. (I deliberately created them that way). The originals used by the hapless lovers must have been in English—or some other language. The landowner's mockery is right on target. No doubt, this factor only made things worse.

Season's Greetings

This was the result of a writing prompt challenging the authors to write a Christmas story involving Santa Claus with a horror slant. It took first prize in the contest.

The Sabre-Toothed Rabbit

First, this story is *not* based on the killer-rabbit scene from a well-known movie. I first became acquainted with this bizarre creation back in the late 1960s, long before they scripted the movie. The sabre-toothed rabbit was part of the infamous Aurora® plastic snap-together model kit depicting the laboratory of Dr. Deadly (a mad scientist). The creature struck me as hilarious rather than frightening—and much of the tone of this story *is* humorous, if a bit on the dark side.

Second, I *was* at Mather Air Force Base during the period the story takes place. The atmosphere was as described. There *were* (and are) herds of jackrabbits wherever you looked. Admittedly, they weren't frightening but they did *not* look friendly up close. They struck me as being wild and cruel—*not* something you would have as a pet. And, come to think of it, there *were* several people who went missing…

Boirac's Coil

Boirac refers to Émile Boirac: the first person to use the phrase *'déjà vu'* (literally: seen before). The nightmare that claims our protagonists is definitely a déjà vu experience. The terms *'Apogee'* and *'Perigee'* are the two points in the elliptical orbit of a satellite caught in our gravitational field: the point furthest away from the earth is the *'Apogee'* of the orbit, the point closest is the *'Perigee.'* The theory says as the orbits (spirals) continue, they will get smaller and faster as gravity pulls in the satellite. Eventually it either hits the ground or explodes in the atmosphere. This is the reasoning behind the chapter names.

The phantom identified as 'Her' is a personification of the powers of darkness. She is based on the Celtic *'Morrigan'* who is infamous for foretelling doom and disaster. Jerrod joins forces with Her because he needs Her help to create his snare. Dirk obviously had previous experience with Her and deliberately purged Her out of his life. *That's* why he is so concerned when She appears.

The use of 'adult' language by the protagonists is, unfortunately, a correct picture. Anyone who does not agree with this has likely never spent much time with those who only live to survive. Refinement is for the leisured. Dirk and Raye are simply acting out of their own experiences—terrible as they might be.

Diana's Pact

This story began as a stereotypical *'love-triangle'* drama. Since that type of story is overused and retold too often, I made a conscious decision to defy convention on several points.

First, the love triangle is a woman and a man competing for a *woman*. Second, the story involves a same-gender relationship—without graphic sexual content. I think this second aspect is what makes this unique.

It seems when a story involves same-gender relationships, much of the writing concerns graphic sexual encounters or dialogue about graphic sexual encounters. Sometimes this is all we wind up knowing about those characters! That isn't a problem. The problem is if that same story used so-called conventional characters, there would be little or no emphasis on sexual encounters.

People who prefer the same-gender are *not* defined by their sexual technique. It doesn't overpower and rule every aspect of their lives. They are defined by their actions, words, motives, likes and dislikes— *just like anyone else*. As obvious as this may be, it's hard to find in fiction.

(Some people have argued the scenes in Andy's room *are* sexual encounters. They are not. Intimate, yes, but *not* sexual. Comforting a friend by holding them is not unusual. The presence of concern and care is there, but not *lust*).

One thing about Andy most people don't notice: she is monogamous. That is another major break with conventional fiction. The accepted stereotype is: people who prefer the same gender are incapable of monogamy, cannot form permanent relationships and always have a stable of partners available. I deliberately broke away from this view in creating the characters. To be frank, I seriously doubt Andy and Cara *ever* engaged in any sexual activity during their relationship.

In the end, Andy alone defines Andy. She is the Captain of the basketball team, the hardened realist, the determined student, the ambitious lawyer. She is *a real person*. No more—no less. If nothing else, I wanted to create a positive role model. Others will have to decide if I succeeded.

What is the *'pact'* the title refers to? It obviously has something to do with the necklace and the background behind it (which remains unclear). If one keeps in mind Cara's obsession with virginity and the fact Diana is the avatar of the virgins, it starts to make sense.

Alas for Derek. Truly, he has no self-awareness. When Cara mentions she's 'looked forward to that night for a long time', Derek assumes she means Prom Night. She doesn't deny this *but she doesn't confirm it either*. Her response is the enigmatic, 'That too.' The fact Cara draws attention to the moon is also significant: the moon is an icon for Diana.

About 'Nemo' (who is *not* based on the Jules Verne or animated character)—remember in the original Latin, 'Nemo' means 'No Name' (or 'Without a Name'). When Derek asks who he is, he assumes the response, 'Nemo,' is his name. 'Nemo' hasn't really answered his question—all he said was, 'I have no name.' Derek does not catch this.

(One reader of the proof edition suggested Nemo is actually Cara—which would explain the intensity Derek's reaction when he says, "It's you!" I like the idea—who knows? It might be right.)

As far as who (or what) Cara is, her parents, the mysteries of the necklace, the only person who knows those things is Andy. But she will not tell.

Note on the cribbage game: This is *not* an orthodox game. Several liberties were taken with the rules and scoring. This is no error—it is yet another warning Derek doesn't catch. Poor guy.

About the Author:

Brian S. Monroe (1959—) lurks somewhere in the Pacific Northwest amid its dark mountains and grim waters. He suffers from the delusion he is an author and carries this to the point of publishing his 'books.' They make great campfire starters or to lay a trail behind if escorted into the woods by a wicked stepparent. There are occasional impressive flashes of excellence within the pages, but for most, the best part of the story is the ending.

His first efforts saw the light of day in the late 1960s. Despite a movement to place his works on the Index and jail him for criminal boredom, he thwarted all attempts to restrain or convict and thus continues his destruction of Western literature unabated. So blame them.

At home in several styles, his major focus is the style of H.P. Lovecraft—-horror/science fiction if you will. His stories push (and sometimes break) the accepted boundaries of reality leaving the reader in confusion about where imagination begins and reality leaves off— sometimes by design. He writes in other styles such as erotica, nonfiction, technical manuals and wry humor.

If you should meet him on the street, be sure not to approach too closely unless you have a good stock of hot fudge sauce or whipped cream. These can distract him while you run to safety. Should he capture you, prepare to be bored out your mind while he inflicts you with his latest verbal creation, much as the Ancient Mariner in Coleridge's poem. Those who survive are never quite the same.

We hope he'll drift away from literature to something else—but he'll likely run *that* into the ground too. Like most disturbing intruders, he has developed immunity to his repellent, leaving us to suffer as he continues to serve up creations of the written word.

www.ingramcontent.com/pod-product-compliance
Lightning Source LLC
Chambersburg PA
CBHW020406150626
46554CB00012B/327